One Night With You

DON'T MISS THESE OTHER NOVELS BY
BESTSELLING AUTHOR
FRANCIS RAY

The Falcon Novels

Break Every Rule

Heart of the Falcon

The Taggart Brothers

Only Hers

Forever Yours

The Graysons of New Mexico Series

Only You

Irresistible You

Dreaming of You

You and No Other

Until There Was You

The Grayson Friends Series

All of My Love (e-original)

All That I Desire

All That I Need

All I Ever Wanted

A Dangerous Kiss

With Just One Kiss

A Seductive Kiss

It Had to Be You

Nobody But You

The Way You Love Me

A Family Affair Series

After the Dawn

When Morning Comes

I Know Who Holds Tomorrow

Against the Odds Series

Trouble Don't Last Always

Somebody's Knocking at My Door

Invincible Women Series

If You Were My Man

And Mistress Makes Three

Not Even If You Begged

In Another Man's Bed

Any Rich Man Will Do

Like the First Time

Standalones

Someone to Love Me

The Turning Point

Anthologies

Twice the Temptation

Let's Get It On

Going to the Chapel

Welcome to Leo's

Della's House of Style

One Night With You

Francis Ray

St. Martin's Griffin
New York

This is a work of fiction. All of the characters, organizations, and events portrayed in this novel are either products of the author's imagination or are used fictitiously.

Published in the United States by St. Martin's Griffin, an imprint of St. Martin's Publishing Group

www.stmartins.com

ISBN 978-0-312-36506-6 (mass market paperback)
ISBN 978-1-250-08253-4 (trade paperback)
ISBN 978-1-4299-8273-3 (ebook)
ISBN 978-1-250-62404-8 (trade paperback)

Our books may be purchased in bulk for promotional, educational, or business use. Please contact your local bookseller or the Macmillan Corporate and Premium Sales Department at 1-800-221-7945, extension 5442, or by email at MacmillanSpecialMarkets@macmillan.com.

First St. Martin's Griffin Edition: April 2020

10 9 8 7 6 5 4 3 2 1

Carolyn Michelle Ray, my fantastic research assistant. You never give up until you find the answer.

Acknowledgments and Thanks

Patti Berg, romance writer and rancher, who is fortunate enough to live in Montana. Her expertise on the animal and wildlife in the Billings area was invaluable. She also directed me to several resources including *The Cowboy Way: Seasons of a Montana Ranch* by David McCumber, which was simply fantastic.

Jenna Black, romance writer who studied physical anthropology, who answered my desperate e-mail for assistance on the time frame of a dig. She was kind enough to send me pictures of her on a dig—which were wonderful.

Jason M. LaBelle, Ph.D., Assistant Professor, Department of Anthropology, Colorado State University, who helped me with rancher/archaeologist concerns. You were great.

Information was also gathered from: Museum of the Rockies, The Getty Institute, Pictograph State

Park, Montana Fish and Wildlife, and the Chauvet Cave.

It was a pleasure and a challenge to write about a rancher's life in Montana and how to authenticate pictographs/cave drawings. Any mistakes are my own.

The McBride Family Tree

Paul & Stella McBride
(divorced)

Duncan McBride (3a)	Cameron McBride (2a) m. Caitlin Lawrence	Faith McBride m. Brandon Grayson (3)

The Graysons of New Mexico Series

1. *Until There Was You*
2. *You and No Other*
3. *Dreaming of You*
4. *Irresistible You*
5. *Only You*

The Grayson Friends Series

1a. *The Way You Love Me*
2a. *Nobody But You*
3a. *One Night with You*

One Night With You

Prologue

Love sometimes needed a helping hand, Ruth Grayson thought as she studied the wedding pictures of her five children on the mantle in her living room. Ruth had taken great pride in seeing that each child found the one person for them to love and be loved by in return.

First, there was Luke, the protector and the oldest. For him, Ruth had chosen Catherine Stewart, a noted child psychologist. Catherine possessed a quiet spirit except when it came to championing abused children or her husband. For Morgan, the defender and Ruth's second born, the ideal match for him had been Phoenix Bannister, a renowned sculptress, who might appear quiet but burned with an inner fire.

Ruth's gaze moved to the third photo, of her middle child, Brandon, the nurturer. The perfect woman for him was Faith McBride. Faith possessed the same warm, caring spirit as the man she adored. Pierce, the thinker and Ruth's fourth son, learned there were no rules in love when he fell in love with Sabra Raineau, a Broadway star.

A smile curved Ruth's mouth upward as she stared at the last photo. Sierra, her youngest child and only daughter, still believed she had chosen her life partner, Blade Navarone, without her mother's help. It didn't matter. The important thing was that Sierra, gifted with a knack of discernment, had captured the heart and soul of Blade Navarone, the only man whose passion matched hers.

As Ruth's fingers touched the smiling faces of Blade and Sierra, she thanked God and the Master of Breath for keeping them from harm when Sierra was kidnapped. Ruth would forever be grateful to Shane and Rio, the two men in charge of Blade's security at the time, for their expertise and help in bringing everyone home safely.

Ruth's gaze moved to the picture of Shane Elliott and his smiling bride, Paige, on the coffee table. After receiving Shane and Rio's help, Ruth had begun to think that they deserved the same blissful happiness that her children had found. It had only taken Paige's mother, Joann Albright, asking Ruth for assistance in keeping Paige from becoming engaged to an unscrupulous man for Ruth to set the wheels in motion to bring Paige and Shane together.

Ruth sighed and thought of Rio—silent, watchful. He would require more in-depth thought and study, but there wasn't a shred of doubt in Ruth's mind that the woman for Rio was out there, waiting. Ruth and her sister-in-law, Felicia, wouldn't rest until they'd brought the two together.

In the meantime, Ruth had another opportunity to possibly give love a helping hand.

She picked up the picture next to Shane and Paige's, a wedding photo of Cameron McBride and Caitlin Lawrence. The picture included the couple's cute and precious son, Joshua; the groom's brother, Duncan, and sister, Faith, and Brandon; and the groom's divorced parents, Paul and Stella McBride, who stood as far away from each other as possible.

Ruth's heart went out to Stella. She'd learned too late that the grass wasn't always greener on the other side. A tough lesson to learn at any age, but particularly daunting for a woman past sixty. Divorcing Paul, as Stella readily admitted to Ruth more than once and again during her unexpected phone call an hour ago, was the worst mistake of her life.

Stella lived with regret each moment of every day. Loneliness, not the man she loved, was her companion. She didn't want the same hopeless existence for her older son, Duncan. While Duncan wouldn't take his ex-wife back on a platinum platter, his unhappy marriage had hardened his heart toward women in general and love in particular. The McBride family curse—successful in business and unhappy in love—probably wasn't helping him move forward.

Duncan's brother and sister might have beaten the odds, but Ruth could understand that as the oldest, he probably thought, looking at his unhappy parents, that the family curse couldn't be escaped.

Ruth believed otherwise. It wouldn't be easy to make him see the possibilities instead of the pitfalls. It would take a special woman to stand up to a strong, commanding man such as Duncan McBride on his Montana ranch.

The opportunity to do just that had just presented itself. Ruth replaced the photo and moved to the telephone in the kitchen and dialed Raven La Blanc's number. Brilliant, perceptive, and as independent as they came, Raven was a friend and a fellow professor at St. John's College in Santa Fe. She had once told Ruth that she wanted stability and permanence more than anything in the world.

Raven needed to learn that security wasn't always a place.

"Hello."

Ruth straightened. Time would tell if she was able to help another mother's plea to aid her child. "Raven, it's Ruth. A once-in-a-lifetime opportunity just presented itself and I immediately thought of you."

Chapter 1

Duncan McBride knew trouble when he saw it and he was looking at it in spades.

He could handle sudden snowstorms, droughts, brush fires, and ornery or sick livestock with grit and determination. He planned to leave his mark on the land, and for that he knew he had to work hard.

However, no matter how he wished otherwise, there were times he'd come out on the losing end. He didn't like it, but he accepted the harsh truth and worked harder so that the next time he'd walk away the winner.

Standing on the front porch of his ranch house east of Billings, Montana, on a beautiful summer morning, Duncan dispassionately watched a woman emerge from the driver's side of a dusty black Jeep that had seen better days. Before her booted foot hit the paved driveway, he knew trouble had come again to the Double D Ranch.

Long-legged, elegantly shaped, with generous breasts, she had a small waist and come-hither hips that gently flared in body-hugging jeans. Those features alone would have been enough to bring any man to his knees, but added to that stunning combination was a breathtakingly sculptured face with high cheekbones and a generous mouth painted berry-colored. The explosive package sent a punch straight to Duncan's gut.

He didn't have to watch his foreman, Ramon, a renowned ladies' man, and his newest hand, Billy, almost trip over themselves rushing to meet her to know he was right. Unmoved, Duncan folded his arms and leaned against a stone post on the porch. Whoever she was, she would be leaving in a hurry.

He'd learned the hard way that beautiful women didn't like isolated ranch life and they weren't happy unless a man was fawning over them, catering to their every whim. Duncan didn't have the time or the inclination to do either. He had a ranch to run.

"I'm Ramon Vasquez, and this is Billy Hunt; welcome to the Double D," Ramon greeted her, tipping his black Stetson, his white teeth flashing in his olive-colored face.

"Good morning, Ramon, Billy. Raven La Blanc," she returned, extending her small hand, a smile curving her sensual lips.

It took Ramon's elbow in Billy's side to get him to stop staring with openmouthed fascination and remember to speak. "G-good morning, Ms. La Blanc. Welcome."

"Thank you," Raven said, gently disengaging her hand when Billy continued to hold it. "Could one of you please direct me to Duncan McBride?"

Ramon and Billy turned to Duncan, their twin expressions openly envious. The woman stared at him as well. With her face of a man's most erotic and forbidden fantasy, Duncan found he wasn't immune to her obvious allure any more than his two ranch hands. However, he controlled his body, not the other way around.

He easily dismissed the stirring of his lower body. He wasn't dead, just selective. And it was just his bad luck for his body to remember he hadn't been with a woman in two years.

"I'm Duncan McBride."

The smile that slowly spread over her golden-hued face caused his gut to tighten for an entirely different reason. Her slender hand swept the thick mass of long black hair out of her face. For one traitorous moment Duncan could imagine too well him doing the same thing for her, his mouth following.

She was definitely leaving, he thought as she started toward him. The admiring gaze of his two ranch hands followed.

As Duncan straightened, his eyes narrowed in anger. His men were staring at her butt. Several feet away, she paused, her head tilting to one side, studying him. She surprised him by not running back to her Jeep. His men had certainly taken off. He could almost admire her for standing her ground.

Almost.

"What can I do for you, miss?" he prompted, wanting to get rid of her as soon as possible so he could get to work. There never seemed to be enough time to complete the endless jobs needed on a ranch the size of his. Today, they were bringing in the calves to start branding. One of his prize mares was taking her own sweet time about foaling, and the Angus cows he'd purchased were due to arrive soon. He didn't have time for a woman.

Raven La Blanc did her best not to stare at the gorgeous man on the porch. He was broad shouldered, with smooth, creamed-coffee-colored skin, a tempting mouth, and piercing onyx eyes beneath a worn black Stetson.

She'd seen handsome men before, dismissed them without a moment's hesitation, but something about the unsmiling man intrigued her. From the way he was staring at her in his defensive stance, he clearly didn't share her interest. He wanted her gone, but she hadn't driven over a thousand miles to turn around and go back to Santa Fe.

Being a woman with a mixed heritage of Native American and French, Raven was used to challenges. Her smile widened as she closed the distance between them, stopping at the foot of the steps to stare at up at his unwelcoming face. "Good morning, Mr. McBride. I'm Raven La Blanc, the archeologist Ruth Grayson spoke to you about. I'm here to authenticate the ca—"

"What?" Unfolding his arms, he quickly descended the steps. Raven had to back up to keep him from plowing into her. "You can't be the one I'm expecting."

Raven had heard it before. People tended to look at her face and quickly decide there was nothing but air in her head. She'd fought the battle repeatedly in her collegiate days and throughout her academic career. She'd fight again if needed. This was too important.

She needed an edge to put her on the fast track to tenure at St. John's College. The goal of obtaining one had brought her to the Double D.

"I assure you, Mr. McBride, I am. I am very interested in—"

"Mrs. Grayson said the woman she was sending had experience," he said, cutting her off once again.

Patience, Raven reminded herself. *This is your chance*. "I might be young, since I earned my Ph.D. at twenty-two, but I've been a professor at St. John's with Ruth Grayson for the past year. Before I accepted the position there I was on several digs in America and Europe."

"Doing grunt work no doubt," he hurled. "I wanted someone capable of getting the job done."

Raven's blunt-tipped nails dug into the palms of her hands. Condescending men irritated the hell out of her. "My credentials speak for themselves. I don't plan to stand here and argue with you. According to Mrs. Grayson, you were pleased to learn that someone of my experience was free and willing to come here. You wanted the authentication done quietly and secretly."

Black eyes narrowed on her face. "That was then."

Raven's chin jutted. "Think what you will about me, but you've given your word that I could study and authenticate the find, and that's exactly what I plan to do. If you don't want me staying at your ranch as planned, that is your right. I'll get a room in town and be back at eight in the morning to start. Good-bye."

Spinning on her booted heels, Raven stalked back to her Jeep. With an irritated flick of her wrist, the motor ignited. Shifting the vehicle into gear, she spun around in the wide driveway, lamenting she wasn't on dirt so the tires could spit dust in Duncan's condescending face.

He'd just thrown a monkey wrench into her plans. She'd counted on staying at the ranch to conserve time and money. That was out of the question now, but she had no intention of leaving Elks Ridge. If the drawings were authentic, and they certainly looked that way from the sketch he'd sent to Ruth, it was important that they be preserved and studied.

The fly in the ointment was that she needed the owner's permission to study them. The government jurisdiction didn't extend to private property unless there were human remains.

Raven's hands tightened on the steering wheel. She refused to think he might be a big enough jerk not to show her the cave. Ruth had spoken highly of him. Just goes to show that a man could fool even the most intelligent woman. That was one lesson Raven had learned the hard way and didn't need a refresher course.

The Jeep had barely straightened before Duncan whirled to stalk back up the steps and into the house. He didn't stop until he was in his office, the phone gripped in his calloused hand, dialing the home of Ruth Grayson. He had always trusted Mrs. Grayson's judgment, but not this time.

He'd accidentally discovered the drawings a couple

of months ago and wanted them authenticated, but not at the expense of disrupting the ranch's routine. Last year vandals had destroyed another find in the area. His mother had called shortly after he'd returned to the ranch the evening he'd found the drawings and he'd mentioned it to her.

She called the next day and recommended Mrs. Grayson, a longtime friend of the family and the mother-in-law of his sister, Faith. Mrs. Grayson was a woman he respected and admired, so he called her. She in turn recommended a "renowned archeologist" who was on the faculty at St. John's with her. At the time, he'd been busy with calving and hadn't paid much attention to a name.

"Hello."

"Mrs. Grayson, this is Duncan McBride."

"Duncan, what a coincidence! I planned to call this morning and thank you for allowing Raven to authenticate the cave drawings you discovered. She has literally been counting the days for the semester to end so she could drive up to your place. So much so that she turned down a position to teach this summer and is doing this at her own expense." Light laughter floated though the phone.

"I don't have to tell you that the salary of a teacher at a small college isn't much. Offering her a room at your ranch was a godsend. Then, too, I won't have to worry about Raven being alone and unprotected, since she is with you."

Duncan plopped into his chair behind his desk. Trapped. He couldn't see how to ask for a replacement after Mrs. Grayson had painted him in such a good light. What reason could he give? Raven made him hot and horny?

Groaning, Duncan swiped his hand across his face.

"Duncan, are you all right?"

No, but he'd get there. "Yes, ma'am."

"Forgive me for running on and not letting you speak," Ruth apologized. "I'm almost as excited as Raven. It's important that the history of The People be preserved, but you know that or you wouldn't have contacted me."

"Yes, ma'am."

"There I go again not letting you tell me why you called."

Stuck, Duncan hesitated.

"Everything is all right, isn't it?"

"Yes, ma'am. I just wanted to let you know that Raven arrived this morning."

"Wonderful. She promised to call, but I guess she's just excited. She told me her Jeep would make the trip, but I was still worried," Ruth said. "Can you please ask her to come to the phone?"

"She's busy," Duncan said, wincing at another lie. He normally prided himself on his honesty.

"Of course. Just ask her to call me later when she gets a chance."

"I will." As soon as he found her. "Good-bye, Mrs. Grayson."

"Good-bye, Duncan."

Hanging up the phone, Duncan headed for the kitchen and grabbed the keys to his truck. Slamming the truck's door, he spun off. Just as he'd suspected,

Raven hadn't been on the ranch five minutes and she'd managed to disrupt his routine. Instead of bringing in calves for branding, he was wasting precious time going after a woman he didn't want on the Double D in the first place to talk her into coming back.

Trouble with a capital *T*.

Raven needed to clearly map out her plans, but first she needed to get something to eat. She thought better on a full stomach. There wasn't much in the small town of Elks Ridge to choose from, so she pulled into the first restaurant she saw.

Grabbing her shoulder bag, she got out of the Jeep. The bell over the door of Duke's Place jingled as she entered. The sign on the podium read: *Please wait to be seated.*

"Be with you in a minute," called a dark-haired woman in a pink waitress uniform. In her hands were two plates with tall pancake stacks.

"Thank you," Raven said, sliding the strap of the satchel bag back over her shoulder. She didn't like changing bags, so she had one that was large enough to carry everything from a notebook to bottles of water.

Smiling, the woman approached. "Sorry about the wait. Nell is out sick today." She grabbed a menu encased in plastic. "One?"

"Yes," Raven replied, and followed the woman to a booth near the back of the restaurant that had no more than twelve tables. Sliding in, Raven heard the bell ring again.

"Oh my," the woman sighed, thrusting the menu

at Raven. She barely missed poking her in the eye. "I'll be back."

Sweeping her hand over her hair, the waitress took off at a fast pace. Raven shook her head. Knowing there must be a man involved, Raven opened the menu. Men weren't high on her list; gaining tenure at St. John's College was.

And her one big chance to do that was tied into authenticating the cave drawings on McBride's ranch. If the pictographs were as old as she believed and she was the one to authenticate them, it would up her value and prestige at the college.

At the end of three years, her department head would inform Raven whether she was on-track or he thought she should start looking for another job. The position she presently held was due to a teacher being fired. Raven had no intention of letting that happen to her. She had moved for the last time. When the day came for that meeting, she wanted no doubt that she would remain.

The interim president had let it be known in more than one faculty meeting that he wanted a staff that brought recognition to the school. If Raven succeeded in her quest, she'd be secure at last and have a place where she was wanted, a position that couldn't be taken away from her.

Most of her life she'd yearned to achieve permanence and failed. Finally, it was within her grasp, and that was more important than any man. An annoying voice whispered that if that man was Duncan she might change her mind.

"Not bloody likely," she muttered, her hands tightening on the elongated menu.

"Mind if I sit down?"

The low, rumbling voice washed over her like a hot summer breeze. Her head snapped up, well aware that she'd see Duncan. To her annoyance, he was even more handsome than the first time she'd seen him. The unsmiling face added to the appeal rather than detracted. It was a direct challenge to a woman to put a huge grin on his handsome face.

Standing next to him, the waitress clutched the menu to her chest, a mixture of pique and fascination on her thin face as her gaze bounced from Duncan to Raven. Another woman at a table across from them wore the same rapt expression.

They can have him.

"We have nothing to talk about until in the morning." Raven lifted the menu higher to blot Duncan out. To her increased annoyance, she heard him slide into the booth across from her. He probably wanted to tell her not to bother coming the next day. His expression certainly didn't bode well for her.

"I talked with Mrs. Grayson. She was worried about you."

The menu came down. A huge mistake. Duncan stared across the table at her with the most intense eyes she'd ever seen. It was almost as if he were trying to see her thoughts. She felt a faint stirring of response in her body and ignored it.

Men were off her list, had been for years, and especially this one. She had a hunch that getting over a man like Duncan McBride would be next to impossible, and she had already traveled that road once in her life. It wasn't something she wanted to experience again.

"I apologize for this morning. You caught me off-guard," he confessed.

"That makes two of us," Raven replied.

His Stetson dipped slightly. "I respect Mrs. Grayson. She's family. I'd hate to disappoint her, or make her feel that I can't keep my word. As agreed, we can tell people you're here to do research for a book."

"Then you still plan to let me study the cave?" she asked, watching him closely.

"I do. No one else knows of its existence." His expression hardened. "As you said, I want to keep it that way. I don't want a lot of people tramping over my ranch, disrupting my routine, especially during one of the busiest times of the year."

She wanted to ask about staying at the ranch, but considering her body's reaction to him, she wasn't sure that was a good idea. However, she probably didn't have enough money to stay at a hotel while she was there.

His black eyes narrowed at her continued silence. "You've changed your mind?"

She fought to keep from squirming under his penetrating stare. "Not exactly."

"You—," he began just as his cell phone beeped. "Excuse me." He jerked the phone from his belt loop. "McBride." He listened, then muttered under his breath, "Saddle Black Jack. I'm on my way." He closed the phone and stood. "The offer is open if you want. Your choice. I have work to do."

Without another word, he tipped his hat and hurried toward the door, his long-legged stride quickly carrying him out of the restaurant. For a big man, he moved with elegant grace. Raven leaned back against the booth, noticing she wasn't the only one watching Duncan. And he hadn't paid attention to any of them.

At least she wouldn't have to worry about him walking in his sleep . . . if she decided to stay at the ranch. Being ticked at Duncan was one thing; being foolish was another. He wouldn't ask again. She could accept the olive branch he offered or be stubborn and find a place in town to stay and use up what little money she had.

"Are you ready to order?"

"I'm sorry. I've changed my mind." Digging in her bag for a couple of dollars, she laid them on the Formica-topped table and stood. It looked like she had some grocery shopping to do.

Two hours later, Raven pulled up in front of Duncan's ranch house. It was as restful and as beautiful as the first time she'd seen it. Two stories with a stone and wood façade, it would last for generations.

It was exactly the kind of house she wished she could live in, instead of the cramped quarters she'd grown up in as her father moved his family from one place to another for his job with the Army Corps of Engineers.

Not once in all those years growing up had she

ever heard her mother or her sister or brother complain. Their nomad existence was exciting to them. Raven hated it but kept her thoughts to herself. She loved her father, but she craved stability. She wanted to know where she'd lay her head each night. Instead, she was afraid to make friends because what was the use? She'd soon move again anyway.

Today her sister was an international flight attendant and her brother, who had followed their father into the army, was currently stationed in Germany. Raven wanted to keep her feet on terra firma in the US of A.

Getting out of the Jeep, she slung the wide strap of her handbag over her shoulder and grabbed a bag of groceries. Giving her a place to stay was generous of Duncan, but that didn't mean he had to feed her as well.

Going up the steps, she knocked on the door that was at least eight feet tall. In fact, while shopping she'd come to the conclusion that the less she and Duncan saw of each other, the better. She seemed to rub him the wrong way. And as annoying as it was, he excited her as no other man ever had.

A bad combination.

Shifting, she knocked again on the solid door, then considered going back and honking her horn when the door swung open. Standing there was a stern-faced man about five-feet-five—two inches shorter than she was—with a frown on his gray-bearded face. "You were in a dang hurry for me to answer the door, so spit it out."

Seemed she was batting even so far with the men on the Double D. Two wanted to flirt; two wanted her gone. "Good morning; I'm Raven La Blanc. Is Mr. McBride in?"

"You don't see him, do you?"

Her eyebrow lifted. "No, but that doesn't mean he isn't in."

"At ten in the morning, it ain't likely. The boss ain't the kind of man to let others do his work," the man said, still standing in the doorway.

"I don't suppose he mentioned that he had a houseguest coming?" she asked.

"Sure, but you ain't her," he said, looking her over.

Raven recalled Duncan's surprise on seeing her. "I'm afraid I am." Shifting the bags, she extended her hand. "Professor Raven La Blanc."

Black eyes narrowed under bushy eyebrows. He peered at her a long moment before he whistled, finally taking her hand. "You're sure you're her?"

The man certainly didn't take things at face value. Just like his boss. "According to my birth certificate, driver's license, and multiple degrees, the one and only that I know of."

"I'll be. Come on in." He reached for the bag of groceries. "Phenias Higgins, but everyone calls me Rooster. I take care of the house for the boss."

Raven stepped inside and found the house as inviting as the outside, with a mixture of leather and overstuffed furniture in warm earth tones of brown and green. "Thank you, Rooster."

"Pardon me, Miss Raven, but I thought you were one of them women trying to pester the boss." He shook his graying head. "They try every trick, but the boss is too smart for 'em."

Since Raven had seen the attention Duncan attracted, she could well imagine. "I have some other groceries and my luggage. If you have time to show me to my room, I'll let you get back to work."

He waved her words aside, continued down a hall, and entered a spacious kitchen—where the smell of burnt food permeated the air. There was an open window over the sink. He placed the bag on the cluttered counter.

"I got time. Don't have to start supper until later. Boss makes up his bed and keeps his room clean."

She couldn't help but ask. "You do the housekeeping and cook?"

"Yep," he said proudly. "When Effie Faye left two weeks ago to go stay with her daughter in Billings and keep her first grandbaby, I took over to help out. I can tell you the boss hated to lose me as one of his top hands, but somebody had to do it." He leaned closer. "The boss tried to talk me out of it, but I know he needed someone to help out."

Raven just bet he had. Apparently, Duncan had his good points. "I'm sure he values you. If you'll tell me where my room is, I'll get my things.

"Upstairs, the last room on the left. Boss's on the right." Rooster's eyes narrowed. "You married?"

"No."

"Engaged?"

She had a good idea why the questions. "No, but I have no intention of bothering your boss. I'm here to do research on a book I'm writing," she said, using the cover story they'd come up with.

Rooster rubbed his whiskered chin. "I have my

own little house. I'll ask the boss if he thinks he needs me to move in to temporarily chaperone."

Raven stuck her tongue in the side of her mouth to keep from laughing. "That's very thoughtful of you, but since we're on opposite sides of the house, we'll be all right."

"I reckon," he said, but he didn't look convinced.

"I'll go look at the room, then finish unloading the Jeep." Smiling, Raven headed for the stairs. She wondered if Rooster was trying to protect her reputation or Duncan's. He didn't have to worry about her. She was here to do a job.

Her hand on the banister, she ran up the stairs. At the top, she looked at the fine layer of dirt on her palm and shook her head. Duncan didn't appear the slovenly type.

The yards were well maintained, the area around the house and barn well kept; the furnishings appeared to have been cared for. His shirt and jeans had been pressed and clean, and according to Rooster, Duncan kept his room clean. He'd want a clean house as well. With Rooster, it wasn't happening. From the way Rooster kept squinting, she wondered if perhaps his eyesight wasn't the best. Not her problem.

Opening the door to her bedroom, Raven was pleased to see a small desk and a phone jack for her computer. Since she'd slept on the ground on other digs, she was happy to see a full bed with a nightstand and double dresser.

Crossing the pine floor, she opened the door to what she hoped was a bathroom. She grinned on seeing the claw-foot tub.

At the basin, she turned on the water to wash her hands. The soap smelled like a mixture of spring flowers. If she didn't miss her guess, this was probably the room Duncan's sister, Faith, used when she visited.

She had mentioned to Raven that she would probably stay in her room. According to Faith, there were enough bedrooms for his brother and new wife and his parents—although since they were divorced they never visited at the same time.

Raven went back downstairs to the Jeep and saw Rooster trying to wrestle the largest and heaviest piece of her luggage out of the back. "That one stays," she said quickly, joining him. "If you'll get the rest of the groceries, I'll get my laptop."

Looking a bit relieved, he picked up two bags of groceries. "You bought a lot of food. You're planning to eat with the boss, aren't you?"

Not if I can help it. "I don't want to impose."

"You won't be. How would it look if we didn't take care of you? You're a friend of his in-law, ain't you?"

"Yes."

Rooster gave a quick nod of his head. "Then you eat with the boss." Turning as if the matter was settled, he started for the stone steps. "Beef stew tonight with my special corn bread."

"I can hardly wait," she mumbled, and followed him into the house.

Chapter 2

Duncan was bone tired, dirty, and hungry. He wanted a hot shower, a good meal, and no problems to come up while he worked on the ranch accounts that were a month behind. Coming out of the barn and seeing Raven's Jeep, he accepted he was fated to get only the first one.

He'd tried to put her out of his mind as he herded stubborn strays back onto his property for most of the day, then repaired the downed wire fence, but it had proven impossible. She kept appearing in his mind, beckoning, her smile promising the fulfillment of every fantasy he tried so hard to keep at bay.

He'd tried to convince himself he wanted her to stay because he hadn't wanted Mrs. Grayson to think badly of him. Not only was she an in-law; she also was the mother of his brother Cameron's best friend, Brandon, and lately she seemed to be developing a close friendship with his mother.

At Cameron's wedding in November Duncan had caught the women with their heads together more than once. Oddly, a couple of times they had been looking at him. With the tense situation between his mother and father, Duncan's mother needed friends.

His mother had surprised everyone by divorcing his father and remarrying in less than a year. Then she surprised them all again when she divorced that man as well. Neither Duncan, Cameron, nor Faith had suspected the reason until Cameron figured out their mother still loved their father and wanted another chance.

Although Duncan's father still loved her, he wanted no part of reconciliation. Trying to keep from being hurt again, he acted as if he didn't want his ex-wife around. At Cameron's wedding his father had been polite to her but distant. Duncan was afraid that only a miracle would get them back together. The McBride curse was at it again.

For eight generations, the McBride men had been able to make money but not make a relationship work. That seemed to have changed with Faith's birth—the first girl in generations. She had beaten the curse, as did Cameron. Both were happily married. Duncan and his father weren't as fortunate.

Opening the back door off the kitchen, Duncan stopped short at seeing Raven setting the table. Normally, place mats and a complete set of flatware weren't used unless his mother or Faith was there.

With the overhead light shining on Raven and her long black hair hanging free over her slim shoulder, she looked exotically beautiful in a simple white blouse and somehow right, a gift to a man after a hard day—a hot meal and a hotter body.

Despite Duncan's best attempt, his unruly body's swift reaction annoyed the hell out of him. The fit of his jeans became tighter. He was too tired for this sort of nonsense.

She glanced up, pausing, gazing at him, her head tilting to one side again as if she was trying to figure out how to soften him up. She was wasting her time. His ex-wife had taught him a lesson he'd never forget. She'd used her body and her face to get what she wanted from men. A wedding ring hadn't stopped her. No woman would ever make a fool of him again.

"Good evening," he greeted Raven. There was no sense in being rude.

She straightened, shoving the heavy, lustrous mass of straight hair behind her ear and over her shoulder. "Duncan." Her gaze ran lightly over him. "Busy day?"

"Yeah." He was dirty from the tips of his boots to the top of his Stetson. If she was that fastidious, she should have stayed in Santa Fe. He turned away from her to see Rooster looking from him to Raven, a frown on his bearded face. "I'm going up and take a shower."

"Well, don't take too long. I was just about to finish with this last batch of hot-water corn bread." Using the metal spatula, Roster flipped a lumpy shape in a black iron skillet. They were almost the same color.

Duncan inwardly groaned. The corn bread on a plate on the counter looked about as palatable as the skillet that it was cooked in. Rooster didn't seem to notice the burnt food. Duncan thought it was probably due to all the years Rooster had eaten on the range.

"Well, hurry up. You don't want to keep your guest waiting." Rooster scooped up the last corn bread and placed it on the plate.

Duncan's gaze snapped to Raven, who wore a pained expression on her face as Rooster took the top off a pot and stirred. "You don't have to wait on me."

Her head snapped around. "No. Wouldn't dream of not waiting."

She wasn't any more anxious to eat Rooster's cooking than Duncan was. He didn't want to hurt the man who'd been on the ranch when Duncan had bought it ten years ago, a man he respected and who had taught him so much, but he wondered about Raven's reason. "I'll be back as soon as I can."

"Take your time," Raven murmured, slowly sinking down onto one of the ladder-back chairs at the long table.

Duncan continued through the kitchen. He was two steps into the great room when he smelled lemon. His steps slowed, he sniffed. He hadn't smelled the scent of wax since his housekeeper left two weeks ago to help her daughter and son-in-law with their new baby. Duncan had feared he'd never smell it again.

Walking over to a table by the stairs, he ran one finger over the round mahogany surface. Not even a speck of dust came away. He looked back toward the kitchen. While it remained in its usual shambles since Rooster had decided to "save" Duncan, the great room was clean. There was only one explanation. Raven. But why would she clean his house when they had gotten off to such a bad start?

He wasn't going to try to figure it out now; he had too many other important things to contend with. Like what had caused the cattle to spook and break through the fence. He just hoped it wasn't a wolf or a mountain lion. Both would play havoc with his livestock. Last year he'd lost several calves to predators.

And his hands were tied. Gray wolves were protected as an endangered species and the mountain lion was out of season for hunting unless it was an imminent threat to humans. Although several ranchers in the area didn't agree with him, Duncan had never liked killing for killing's sake. The animals were on the land long before man.

He took the stairs two at a time and was unintentionally caught by the gleam of polished wood where that morning had been dust. Perhaps Raven had a thing about being clean.

In his room, he sat on the wooden bench at the foot of his bed and removed his boots. If Raven hadn't been there, he would have taken his clothes off in the mudroom and showered in the half bath he'd installed shortly after he'd gotten married.

One boot hit the floor with a loud plop. At least one good thing had come out of the worst fiasco of his life.

Shelley had been beautiful and fun, at least until they'd arrived back on the Double D after their honeymoon. Nothing seemed to please her, least of all his leaving so early in the morning to work and then coming home late in the evening, sweaty and dirty. He fully expected her to grow to love the land as much as he did. It hadn't happened. He'd tried to please her and failed miserably.

After their honeymoon, their first outing in Elks Ridge as a couple has been to a birthday party for a neighbor's wife. Shelley had hit it off with the men but hadn't had very much to say to the women. She'd commented on their way home that women were often jealous of her looks and money.

Duncan had pointed out that he knew many of the women there and they weren't like that. She'd laughed and said men never noticed that type of thing.

Wherever they went, even at church, she drew men, but the women would speak and keep moving. It wasn't long before he began to notice that while men asked about her whenever she wasn't with him, women never did.

She didn't cook, had no interest in learning. She'd provocatively pointed out that he hadn't married her for her talents in the kitchen. Since she had been a Houston socialite and grown up with servants, he'd tried to see things from her perspective and made excuses to his family, especially to his mother and Faith, who were annoyed that Shelley didn't take any interest in her and Duncan's home or the ranch. They hadn't included him on the list, but he'd sensed he was at the top.

Naked, he stepped into the shower and turned the jets on full blast. He had been so gullible, so trusting, and it had come back to haunt him.

Citing boredom, the need to shop, or the need to get her hair and nails done, Shelley began going to

Houston a couple of times a month, then weekly. He actually felt relieved when she found a salon in Billings she liked . . . until she began coming home later and later on her Saturday jaunts. One Saturday night when she wasn't home by midnight, he went to look for her and found her in an upscale nightclub cuddled up to a man.

Duncan's fist clenched in the shower as it did that night. It had taken all of his willpower not to plant his fist in the man's smug face. Instead, Duncan had grasped Shelley's arm to take her home, but she had jerked away.

She was tired of the ranch, tired of the dreary, monotonous life he lived, tired of him trying to force her to live his way. She deserved better. His choice, her or the ranch.

He hadn't even had to think. "I'll send your things to your father's house."

She'd gasped. Shock radiated across her face; then she coldly stared at him. "Your loss."

He'd turned and made his way through the crowd that had gathered to watch the scene and recognized a couple from Elks Ridge. His humiliation would be all over town. Head high, he kept walking.

He'd never looked back or regretted his decision.

But to his remorse, he had wallowed in self-pity for a couple of months. Her cheating had taken a swipe at his pride, his manhood. He should have been able to satisfy his wife. He'd never failed at anything in his life . . . until Shelley.

At the time he'd been foolish and young enough to think the McBride curse wouldn't affect him. He'd been wrong. At least his brother, Cameron, and sister, Faith, had escaped. If he had to bear the burden, so be it.

Shutting off the water, he stepped out of the enclosure and reached for a towel just as there came a knock on the door.

"Come in," he called, knowing he'd see Rooster or one of his hands. He had a feeling that Raven planned to stay out of his way as much as he planned to stay out of hers. A sensible decision on both of their parts.

Rooster quickly entered, closing the door behind him. "I think we got a problem."

"Livestock?" Duncan questioned, his body alert, all tiredness leaving him. His ranch, his responsibility.

"No. No." Rooster stepped farther into the room. "It's about you and that woman sleeping up here together."

A ball of heat zipped through Duncan, tightening his muscles, pooling blood in his groin. Thankfully, Rooster was looking at his face. "We're on opposite sides of the stairs."

"Still close." Rooster rubbed his bearded chin. "Might be a good idea if I bunked in until she leaves."

"No," Duncan said, a bit sharper than he intended. If there was anything worse than Rooster's cooking, it was his snoring. A freight train had nothing on the cowhand, another reason he had a little house all to himself. It was that or have hands bleary-eyed in the morning from lack of sleep. Duncan would be hungry *and* exhausted. Then a thought hit. "Did she say she felt uncomfortable being here with me?"

"No. I can tell she's one of them bra-burning women," Rooster commented with a snort. "Said she had no interest in you."

Good, Duncan thought. "Then I don't see a problem. I'll get dressed and be down shortly."

"All right, but if you change your mind, you know where to find me."

Duncan released the towel as the door swung shut behind Rooster. He'd have to be desperate to have Rooster stay. He and Raven weren't interested in each other. He wasn't dead, but he controlled his emotions.

Shelley had taught him a lesson about beautiful, deceitful women he wasn't likely to forget. He'd have no difficulty remembering that Raven wasn't for him.

Raven had just picked up her glass of sweetened iced tea when Duncan reentered the kitchen. Breath fluttered over her slightly parted lips. The man certainly had the "it" factor in spades.

Not even being dirty and tired had negated the impact he had on her. She'd managed to lock her knees again and appear curious instead of just short of being aroused.

"About time," Rooster groused. "I already took the boys their stew. Ms. Raven must be hungry after all she's done today."

Midnight black eyes glanced to her and stayed. "I noticed. Thank you."

Raven took a sip of tea to ease the dryness in her throat before answering. "You're welcome. I had time."

Rooster set a bowl of stew in front of her. "I would have gotten to it, but I was making this stew."

Raven caught Duncan's gaze as another bowl hit the table in front of him. Rooster took his seat and bowed his head. "Lord, thank you for the food we're about to eat and bless those less fortunate. Amen."

"Amen," she and Duncan murmured in unison, both lifting their heads, both hesitant to pick up their spoon.

Rooster spooned in the stew and took a sizeable bite of the hot-water corn bread. "You two not eating?"

Wordlessly Duncan picked up his spoon and began to eat. Slowly his spoon descended again. Raven saw no escape. She picked up her spoon and dipped it into the watery stew that had jagged chunks of carrots, potatoes, and meat. She had expected it to taste bad, but it was probably the worst-tasting food she'd ever put in her mouth. And considering her travels to primitive areas, that was saying a lot.

"Good, huh?" Rooster said, a gap-toothed smile on his face. "Good food like this will stick to your ribs."

"And throat," Raven murmured, and saw Duncan's eyes widen, the corners of his sensual mouth curve upward. Imagine, the man had a sense of humor. Perhaps there was hope they could at least be cordial. "When you came in, you looked as if you had a busy day."

"Sorry if my earlier appearance offended you," Duncan said, his voice as devoid of warmth as the eyes that drilled into her.

Raven frowned, more concerned with what he had said than his tone. Puzzled, she took the opportunity to stop eating and place her spoon on the plate beneath her bowl. "Why would you think I was offended?"

Lines raced across his forehead. "You said . . . Sorry if I misunderstood."

Raven placed her hands on the edge of the table. "Dirt doesn't offend me, Mr. McBride. As I said, I've been on numerous digs throughout the United States and in Europe. Nothing gets done without getting dirty."

"Sounds like ranching life." Rooster finished off his food and reached for another burnt lump of corn bread. "Are you some kind of gardener or something?"

Raven realized her slip. "Or something."

"Ms. La Blanc is here to gather material for a book she wants to write," Duncan put in.

"You won't find a prettier place in the world than here on the Double D. I've been here most of my life. I plan to stay here until the good Lord calls me home." Taking the empty bowl, Rooster went to the sink. "What kind of book?"

"History," Raven answered.

"You've come to the right place." He retook his seat. "This place is full of it. Everywhere you look. Eat up, and I'll wash the dishes."

"I can do them," Duncan offered. "You can take off."

Rooster straightened. "No, sir. You know when I sign up for a job I stick until it's done." He got up and went to the pot of stew. "Seconds?"

"No thanks," Raven quickly said, taking another tentative bite.

"Boss, you're not eating enough." Rooster frowned, his eyes narrowing on the half-full bowl.

"Guess I'm tired from chasing cows all over the place." Duncan took another bite.

Sadness touched the older man's face. "Nothing like being in the saddle on the range." His hands clenched. "I should be out there helping you."

"You *are* helping me," Duncan said, staring at Rooster. "Taking care of this house is one less worry. You know how hard it was to get Mrs. Owens to hire on. As it was, she hated the times the weather kept her from going home and she had to stay over. Women don't like the isolation of the ranch."

"But your ranch isn't isolated," Raven said, and found herself the subject of two pairs of eyes filled with disbelief. "In my travels," she began carefully, "this could be considered crowded. Billings is an hour away; town is thirty minutes. Some cultures actually prefer not to interact with others."

Rooster frowned. "You learn all that doing research for that book you're going to write?"

"Yes." Raven noticed Duncan hadn't said anything. She picked up her bowl and stood. "Thank you for dinner, Rooster. I think I'll go to bed."

He took the bowl, his frown deepening. "You didn't eat much. Weren't too spicy, was it? Know it weren't the beef. Double D has the best in the state."

Raven easily saw the concern on the older man's face. She smiled to reassure him. "It can't be too spicy for me. Guess I'm just tired from the drive." She turned to Duncan. "What time in the morning should I be ready to leave?"

"I'll return at eight."

She shook her head. "You don't have to come back unless you planned to. I can be ready whenever you say."

"We'll be working at the corral branding, so eight is fine," he answered.

"That was information I could do without."

He stared at her. "It's the law and necessary."

"But I don't have to like it. I'll see you at eight. Night," she said, then left the room.

Rooster stared after her. "She's different from most women."

"Don't I know it. I'll be in my study." He headed through the door. In the great room, his gaze unerringly went to Raven as she climbed the stairs, her back straight and her hips swinging just the tiniest bit.

Temptation and trouble in one delectable package. And not for him!

Duncan continued to his study, wondering how long it would take her to do her research. The quicker she left, the better for all concerned, especially his unruly body. Seems he didn't have the control he thought he had.

Scowling, he pulled out a chair behind the desk loaded with bills, magazines, and correspondence. He didn't have time to think about a woman.

But that didn't seem to stop him.

An hour later, Duncan rubbed his growling stomach with his left hand and made notations in the thick ranch ledger with his right. His accountant sent an assistant out once a month to put the notations in the computer, but Duncan liked to be able to see things at a glance. It had worked out well for all concerned.

For a man who usually made good decisions, he wasn't doing so well lately. If the fiasco with Rooster weren't enough, now Duncan had to deal with Raven. He was honest enough to admit that if she'd been bucktoothed, horse faced, and hitting sixty as he'd imagined, he wouldn't give her another thought.

Instead, she had exotic looks and a heart-stopping figure, and he couldn't seem to keep his thoughts on anything else. He just had to remember that she was off-limits. He—

His head came up. He sniffed. Bacon. For a moment, he thought he might be hallucinating; then he heard the faint sound of a woman humming. Raven. She was cooking in his kitchen, while he hadn't had a good meal since last week when he'd gone into town to take Black Jack to the vet and stopped by Duke's Place.

Another thought struck. Just because she was cooking didn't mean she *could* cook. She could be worse than Rooster. Duncan made a face. Nobody could be that bad. Tossing his pen on the desk, he headed for the kitchen to find out. This was his house; he could go where he pleased.

The aromas grew stronger, his salivary glands happier with each step. He entered the kitchen and went still. Raven, a spatula in her hand, stood in front of the stove wiggling her jean-encased butt as she hummed "If I Were Your Woman" by Gladys Knight.

The sensual combination of hips and the lyrics was too much. If Raven were his woman, he knew what would happen.

He could easily imagine those long legs wrapped around him, her hips reaching to meet his, keeping rhythm with his. He forgot all about food. His appetite for something entirely different coursed though him.

Raven snapped one finger, then spun around, obviously oblivious to him, and stopped in mid-spin. She flushed, her beautiful eyes widened. "Duncan."

"You're cooking," he said, the only words he could get out.

"Oh." She spun back to the stove. "I-I hope you don't mind."

He walked over, the mouthwatering aroma as much as the woman drawing him. "Depends."

She threw a quick look over her shoulder before turning her attention back to arranging the mixture of eggs, bacon, and vegetables on tortillas. "On what?"

"If you plan to share."

She smiled. He felt the impact in his gut. "There's more than enough. I planned to keep leftovers for breakfast."

Duncan's mood took a nosedive. "Rooster is cooking breakfast."

"Then we better enjoy this." Taking another plate from the cabinet, she placed two tortillas overflowing with the egg mixture on each plate. "Have a seat. I'll get the hot chocolate."

"Hot chocolate?"

She laughed, a surprisingly husky sound that vibrated along his nerve endings. "One of my vices."

"Do you have many?" he asked, unsure if he'd meant the words as teasing or serious.

"Nope," she said, pouring the dark chocolate into two cups. Steam wafted up.

"You don't have to share," he felt obligated to say.

"I don't mind," she said, and took a seat across from him. "I'm the oldest of three. You learn to share."

Duncan nodded in understanding, then bowed his head as she blessed the food. "Same here."

"I've met Faith and, of course, Brandon." Raven picked up her tortilla and took a healthy bite. She closed her eyes, softly moaned. The sound vibrated down every one of Duncan's already-on-high-alert nerve endings. Opening her eyes, she stared at him. "Aren't you going to taste it?"

What he wanted to taste was her. That wasn't going to happen. He picked up his food and took a tentative bite. Delicious. He took a bigger bite and heard her laugh. He could easily get used to that sound if things were different. "Thank you."

"Forget it. I'm the one who is thankful for you letting me stay here." She took a sip of chocolate. "The least I can do is share a meal."

"I meant Rooster." He took another bite. "You cook like this, yet you ate his food and never complained," he said, trying to understand.

Her shoulders stiffened. "You think I'm the kind of person who would needlessly hurt a man's feelings when he's obviously only concerned and trying to help. Who would do that?"

Duncan didn't have to think long. Shelley, his ex, would have in a heartbeat. She and Rooster hadn't gotten along, but then again she hadn't liked any of the ranch hands. She'd completely fooled Duncan. "Sorry." He picked up his tortilla.

"Is it me you have a problem with or women in general?" Raven asked, her head tilted to one side as if trying to analyze him again.

He hadn't expected her to be so intuitive or him to be so obvious. "Why would you say that?"

She rolled her eyes. "Come on, Duncan. You made yourself very clear this morning, but I had hoped we'd gotten past that. You don't trust my credentials or think very highly of me as a person."

"I didn't say that," he felt compelled to say.

Her chin jutted out. "You could have fooled me."

He bit into his food. "Perhaps you're being overly sensitive."

"You wouldn't tell another man that." She shoved her plate aside. "I can take it. Tell me exactly how you feel about me."

The erotic, highly sexual words that sprang to his mind, but thankfully didn't go any further, stunned him. His eyes narrowed as he leaned away from her, away from her sensual assault.

"On the ranch you're my concern. My responsibility. You'll be at the cave by yourself. I can't spare any of the ranch hands to watch you."

"I don't recall asking you to."

"You'll be totally isolated," he continued. "We aren't working that part of the range."

"All the better." She finished her chocolate. "We won't have to make up stories as to why I'm going to the same place every day."

"You ever work on authenticating cave drawings by yourself?" he asked, watching her eyelashes flicker and waiting for the lie.

"No," she said, and continued at his start of surprise. "I've helped authenticate other finds, and studied cave drawings extensively. I've been interested in them since my early days as an undergraduate. I've also spoken with several area authorities. I want to do this on my own, but I won't hesitate to seek assistance if I feel I'm in over my head."

He had to give her points for honesty. "When will you know?"

"Once I see the drawings in person." Her eyes glowed. "From what you described and the drawings you sent Ruth, I believe they're authentic. It's not unreasonable, since Pictograph Cave State Park is outside of Billings."

"I understand the attendance is growing each year. They just finished a visitor's center." Duncan frowned. "A couple of years back, a hand on a nearby ranch discovered some drawings and before you knew it, there were TV cameras, scientists, and gawkers all over the place. The drawings were defaced. People were coming from everywhere, trying to be the ones to discover other drawings. It was a mess. The rancher spent more time getting people off his property than ranching. I don't want that to happen on the Double D."

"I understand your need for privacy, but it will take time to study the site," she said. "Besides tracing the drawings, if I have time I want to excavate the area to see if there might be any artifacts."

"You figure on taking your Jeep?"

"Have to with all the equipment." She reached for his empty plate and mug. "You indicated to Ruth that it was rough terrain, but that a Jeep could make it."

He cocked a brow. No one on the Double D questioned him. "Depends on the Jeep."

"Buddy has been with me since I was an undergrad. He'll make it." She turned on the faucet over the sink. "I'll be ready at eight."

He came slowly to his feet. "Can you ride?"

"Yes."

"We'll take the horses."

"Why not the Jeep?" she questioned, shutting off the water to face him.

His eyes narrowed. "It's quicker." And he wanted to check the area again. Shortly after he'd discovered the cave he'd spotted a black bear with two cubs a couple of miles away. Since then he hadn't seen the bears or any tracks.

"Of course. Thank you again, Duncan. I won't let you down."

He went to the doorway and turned. "I'll be in my study if you need anything."

"I won't," she said.

Duncan stared at her a few seconds longer—beautiful, defiant, and trouble to his peace of mind—and headed toward his study. He hoped she was right about being able to take care of herself. The less they were around each other, the better.

Chapter 3

Raven couldn't sleep. She couldn't determine if it was excitement over finally seeing the pictographs or the aggravating but alluring owner of the Double D. Before going downstairs, she purposely waited until she saw from her bedroom window Duncan heading to the barn.

In the kitchen she wrinkled her nose at the mess Rooster had made cooking breakfast. Raven didn't even want to think about what it might have been. Rooster had popped into the kitchen to see what she was doing, then said he was going to straighten up Duncan's office—if she didn't want him to cook her breakfast.

She'd quickly reassured him she just wanted a bowl of cereal and sent him on his way. After eating, she prepared chicken parmigiana in her trusty slow cooker.

The slow cooker had been a gift from her mother after Raven had graduated from college. Raven had put it in a cabinet and forgotten about it until two years later when she'd come home tired, hungry from teaching at a junior college, and stared in the refrigerator, then the freezer, trying to figure out what to cook. She'd been interrupted by a phone call from her mother.

During the course of the conversation Raven had complained about being tired of coming home after work and having to cook. Her mother had reminded Raven that if she used her slow cooker, her dinner would be waiting on her when she arrived home.

After a supper of cold cereal, Raven had pulled out the slow-cooker cookbook and made a grocery list. Now, pouring the sauce over the chicken, she had never been more thankful. At least tonight she wouldn't have to sit through another tense dinner with Duncan.

One conclusion she had come up with as she tossed and turned most of the night was to continue as planned to cook her own meals and use the evenings to record and research what she'd discovered that day.

A knock on the door came just as she set the timer. Opening the back kitchen door, she smiled on seeing the ranch hand she'd met the day before. "Good morning, Billy."

"Ms. La Blanc, the boss wants you to meet him at the corral," the young cowhand told her, his hat crushed to his chest.

"Thank you," Raven said. "I'll get my things." She'd seen the same rapt but harmless look on male students in the past. Slipping the string of her wide-brimmed straw hat over her head, she picked up her field bag.

Today would only allow her to take a few notes; tomorrow—if her hunch was right—she would begin the painstaking process of cataloging her findings. "Rooster, I'm leaving."

The older man came into the kitchen, a dust cloth tucked in his belt. "You sure you don't want to take some coffee with you?"

She didn't even want to imagine how bad it might taste. "No thanks. I have water in my bag."

"All right. You better go. The boss doesn't like to be kept waiting."

Raven kept the smile on her face. The boss didn't like a lot of things, mainly her being there. "You don't have to worry about the Crock-Pot on the counter. It has a timer and will take care of itself."

He looked around the kitchen, then walked over to the cooking pot, leaned down to within a foot of the glass lid. "You're sure?"

"I'm sure." She smiled. Rooster might appear grouchy, but he was good at heart—unlike his boss. "Good-bye."

The young hand held open the door. "He's right about the boss. We better hurry."

"I gather all of you like to keep Duncan happy?" she said as they went down the back steps.

He threw her a quick, easy grin. "It makes life easier," he said, then hastened to add, "Don't get me wrong; the boss is fair. There's not a job on the ranch that he hasn't done or won't do again. He'll work beside you from sunup until sundown if need be. He's a man you can count on."

Raven paused on hearing the loud bellows of calves. "What's going on?"

"Branding time," Billy answered. "We got a late start because we had to round most of them up again."

"The poor things," Raven murmured. "I'd run, too."

Billy laughed. "You're something."

"Billy, you're needed to relieve Pete," Duncan said.

Raven looked up to see Duncan walking toward them leading two horses. He looked strong, commanding, in his element. She had no doubt the proud-stepping black stallion he led belonged to him. They would look magnificent together.

The young man jerked around at the sound of Duncan's voice. "Yes, sir." He tipped his hat to Raven. "Bye."

"Good-bye, Billy," Raven called as he scrambled over the fence into the corral where all the activity seemed to be going on. Watching him leave gave her time to compose herself against the impact Duncan seemed to have on her.

"If you're ready, we can get going."

Raven finally turned to him. He wore the same forbidding expression he had yesterday. She almost sighed in regret. For once she'd like to see him animated or excited or just pleased to be around her. She hadn't given a thought to what a man felt since the debacle with Paul in grad school. She'd do well to remember the reason. "I'm ready."

Duncan gave her the reins to a pretty white-faced

roan mare. "She's even tempered and easy to handle. Plus she knows the way home."

Raven's hand automatically closed around the reins. "You're leaving me there?"

"It's not my intention, but I never know when a problem might come up that needs my attention," he told her. "If it happens, I might have to leave and you might not be ready."

"Like yesterday?"

"Yes."

"Then, I'm doubly thankful that you're taking time to show me the cave this morning." She winced at the protesting bellow of another calf. "And I will be happy to be away for a while."

"As I said last night, it's the law. And it makes it easier to identify them."

"Still I feel for them." She swung up easily into the saddle, then looked at him still staring at her. "What?"

"Nothing." His foot in the stirrup, Duncan swung up on Black Jack. The stallion sidestepped, but he was easily controlled.

"He's beautiful," she said, staring at the horse. "But not shy about testing who is in control."

"That's all right. I admire him for trying. Having a docile animal doesn't appeal to me."

She wondered what would appeal to him but wisely kept her mouth shut. "Somehow I figured that out. Ready when you are."

Duncan stared at Raven a few moments longer, then lightly touched his heels to the stallion's flanks, leaving her to follow.

* * *

Duncan loved everything about the country—the vastness, the endless skies overhead, and the towering mountains in the distance. He might have been born in Santa Fe, but Montana had long since become his adopted home. He'd live and die here. He couldn't imagine living anyplace else—even with the present problems.

He glanced over to find Raven had once again lagged behind. It wasn't her riding skills. He'd been concerned about that. But she handled the horse as easily as he might have. Yet she kept falling behind. "Is there a problem?"

Guiltily she jerked her head toward him. "Sorry. It's just so beautiful here that I'm having a difficult time paying attention to landmarks to find the cave myself in the morning."

Her statement caught him off-guard. His ex-wife had thought the countryside too isolated, too stark. In the low country, there were more scrubs than trees. His housekeeper thought the same thing. Neither saw the beauty.

"You're blessed to live here," Raven said, finally catching up.

He gazed at her face, startlingly beautiful and free of makeup except for cherry-colored lip gloss. Her unbound long black hair whipped in the wind. He saw the truth of her words in her shining eyes. She wasn't trying to con him.

"I know." He nodded toward a rocky hillside a hundred yards away. A small ledge overhead would make it easy to locate again. "We're almost there."

"I'm getting goose bumps." Excitement rang in her voice.

Like Rooster said, she was different. What woman relished the idea of spending times alone in a cave or digging in dirt? Duncan's ex always wanted every hair in place, her makeup on, before she came downstairs. "How did you get into this?" he asked before he could help himself.

Raven brought her horse beside his before answering. "My father is with the Army Corps of Engineers. So we traveled all over the world. While I didn't like moving, I enjoyed learning about different people's cultures and history, became fascinated by their lives and history."

"How did you end up in Santa Fe?" he asked as he dismounted.

"One of those fated events." She dismounted. "I'd seen a travel documentary on television and thought I'd like to settle there. I always wanted to teach at a small college with a good academic reputation. Luckily there was a position open at St. John's."

"And Ms. Grayson?" He tied his reins to a stunted shrub.

"On the welcoming committee. She's become a good friend. Sierra helped me find a house." Raven followed suit, then glanced around. "Are we near the site?"

"You're looking at it." Duncan began pulling brush away from what appeared to be the side of the mountain.

Raven rushed to help when she saw a narrow opening. "A hidden cave!"

"I was out riding the range looking for strays when I was caught in a sudden thunderstorm. I saw a jackrabbit, then a second one run into the brush at a dead run. I investigated and found—"

"The cave," Raven finished, staring at the opening in the side of the mountain that spanned five feet across. "I'll get my flashlight."

"No need." Stooping, Duncan entered, then stopped three feet inside the cave to pick up a high-beamed lantern. "I brought this out here a week later to explore the cave and decided to leave it. That way if I happened to be in the area and had time, I could check it out."

"A week later?" She eagerly reached for the lantern, moving ahead as the cave widened to span several feet across. "You certainly have more restraint than I do."

"The ranch is my main priority."

She glanced over her shoulder at him. "Yet you recognized the importance of the cave paintings. You didn't dismiss them."

"There's been a lot in the newspaper about the Pictograph Caves in Billings and I visited them with Faith. It's important to safeguard the history of any people," he told Raven.

He understood the importance of preserving the past. He might not be too keen on her, but he was keen on recording earlier periods, and for now that was enough. Holding the lantern high, casting light on the wall, she went deeper into the cave.

Fifty feet farther, she saw the markings on the

wall and went still. The hair on the back of her neck stood straight up. With trembling fingers she stopped an inch away from the walls. A chill raced down her spine. "There were left by the Ancient Ones. My ancestors. My People."

"You think they're real?"

"And thousands of years old," she said, her voice hushed.

Duncan took the lantern, once again studying what some might consider children's markings of stick figures. He hadn't because he'd visited Pictograph Cave State Park with Faith and knew of the area's history. "How can you be so sure?"

Raven's hands continued to reverently hover over the drawings. "Because I feel their presence. I don't need to use radiometry." She gripped his arms and stepped closer as her excitement grew. "How far does it go?"

"I don't know," he answered.

She jerked around toward him, disbelief on her face. She reached for the lantern. He held it out of reach. "You can give me yours, or I'm going to get my flashlight out of my pack. I'm not leaving here until I see how far the drawings go."

"I don't like threats."

She blew out an impatient breath. "Duncan, we may be standing on one of the greatest scientific discoveries in this area since the Pictograph Caves were found before World War Two. You own this land. Without your consent I couldn't be here, as we both well know. I'd be a fool to make threats."

He looked at her a long time, then started deeper into the cave. "Stay behind me. An animal might have made a den in here," he said, and continued.

She quickly caught up with him, stepping beside him. He stopped and glared at her. She was glad the poor lighting blunted his disapproval. "You're a big man. I can see better this way."

"You also can get hurt."

"So could you," she told him. "We're wasting time. If you're called away, I'm not sure about my horse's ability to find her way back."

He didn't move. "When I give an order, I expect it to be carried out."

Patience, she reminded herself. Duncan held the key to her future. "Believe me, the last thing I want to do is be injured and have to leave. I'll be careful, but as I said, I can't see walking behind. I could just as easily stumble and fall."

He watched her a few moments longer. She couldn't tell in the dim light whether the thought of her leaving appealed to him or not. Her consolation, if there was one, was that he took his responsibility as owner of the Double D seriously; that meant keeping her safe. Without a word, he started walking again.

Ten steps farther, the cave widened. Light pierced the darkness for the first time in perhaps thousands of years. Raven's breath caught. Excitement flooded through her veins.

"Oh, my goodness!" Her hand clutched his arm. "Look! That's a picture of a bison that has been extinct for thousands of years. The Ancient People moved though this area, following the water and food sources. The series of rims in this area run to Yellowstone Park."

She urged him forward. "Oh my, let's see what else there is. Hurry, Duncan."

"You're holding my arm," he said, his voice rough.

"Oh," she said, quickly removing her hand. "I'm sorry. I guess I got carried away. I wish Ruth could be here."

"So do I," Duncan mumbled, and began walking.

Raven dismissed his comment. This was too important to let personal feelings get in the way. She—Her thoughts stumbled to a halt when she saw the red markings. Two, four, and then dozens.

"I'll be," Duncan said, his voice hushed.

Raven couldn't speak. They stood in a chamber about twelve feet tall and everywhere light touched there were colored drawings, iconography, depicting animals, a basic theme, beside human representations and other signs found in caves.

She was looking at a major find. As far as she knew, in the Billings pictograph caves all were simplistic drawings, with no colorization.

"Do you realize what this means? How important this could be? Nothing like this has been seen in this area."

Duncan heard the words, but it was the woman who drew him. He gazed at her upturned face, felt the irresistible pull of her body. Desire arched between them. He saw it in the widening of her eyes, the delicate flare of her nostrils. Her hand flexed on his arm. He needed to step back, away from temptation.

"Duncan." His name was a ragged whisper of sound on lips that he'd give his last breath to taste.

Muttering a curse, Duncan pulled her into the shelter of his body, holding her against him as his mouth greedily took hers. She opened for him without a moment's hesitation. His tongue thrust inside hers, tasted the fire, the passion.

She pressed against him, kissing him back, her soft breasts flattening against his hard chest, her lower body pressing against his growing need. He wanted more, had to have it.

The thump of the lantern falling from his hand and hitting the ground snapped him out of his passionate daze. He peered down at her, her face in half shadows, but he could hear her heavy breathing, feel her soft, trembling body against his.

He staggered back, appalled by the lack of the control he'd always prided himself on, dazed by the stunning impact of the kiss that affected him as nothing else ever had.

Without a word he spun and walked toward the mouth of the cave, his eyes adjusting more and more to the dark with each angry step. Lord, what had he almost done?

Her body trembling so badly she could hardly stand, Raven watched Duncan leave the cave until darkness swallowed him. She hadn't known a kiss could be so powerful, could take you under so fast.

Unsteady fingers touched her moist lips. She had reveled in the strength of Duncan's arms, her heightened senses, and the hum of her body.

Obviously, Duncan didn't share her thoughts. While she wasn't pleased with the attraction, she didn't understand why it angered him so much.

Picking up the lantern, she started back the way they'd come. If Duncan left, she wasn't sure she could find her way back. As she had told him, the thought of relying on her horse's sense of direction wasn't reassuring.

Stepping outside, she immediately saw Duncan standing with a shrub in his gloved fist. His expression was closed, his body stiff and unbending.

Putting out the light, she placed the lantern back inside the cave and returned to grab a shrub to help him hide the mouth of the cave. As soon as they finished, Duncan mounted his horse.

"You'll be able to bring your Jeep within fifty feet of here with your supplies. I'll help you unload them in the morning, but as I told you, I don't have a man to spare to watch over you."

Raven got on her horse before replying. For some odd reason she felt at a distinct disadvantage looking up at him from the ground. "As I said, I'm self-sufficient. I appreciate the help with the supplies, but working alone won't be a problem." At his continued implacable stare, she felt compelled to add, "I don't want or need a man."

Duncan's gaze heated and settled on her mouth that remembered too well the taste of his. Heat exploded in her body. She felt the response deep in her womb, and there was nothing she could do about it.

His gaze slowly lifted to hers. The confident look on his face said he could prove her wrong if he wanted.

Wheeling his horse, Duncan left her to follow. Raven felt like dismounting to find a rock to throw at his arrogant back. Because, God help her, he was right.

This time, on the way back to the ranch, Raven looked for landmarks. It was past time for her to remember why she was there. She was used to overcoming obstacles, beating the odds. She had no intention of letting an unwanted sexual attraction get in the way of her goal.

She'd been a fool once over a man and it had almost ruined her career. Paul Dunbar, well dressed, articulate, and gorgeous, had been in her master's program. Most of the women in their class were after him. She'd been secretly thrilled when he'd asked her to be his study partner.

It wasn't long before they became romantically involved, but unlike the few men she'd dated in the past, he accepted her decision not to have sex so soon in the relationship. He told her he was willing to wait.

Raven snorted and followed Duncan up a hill. Paul had been willing to wait all right—wait until she finished her thesis so he could steal it. He'd been so apologetic, so remorseful, when he'd accidentally knocked over her laptop, damaging it beyond repair, the night before her paper was due. She'd been frantic. She'd immediately called her professor. He hadn't wanted to hear excuses. He wanted her thesis on his desk by one the next day.

The moment the library opened the next morning

she went straight to a computer, well aware that there was no way what she wrote would be as good as what she'd lost. At one she turned in her paper, hoping, praying.

Later that evening she'd received a call from her professor to come to his office. She'd gone expecting the worst and found Paul there. The professor wanted an explanation as to why the papers were so similar. Paul immediately accused her of stealing his work. She'd been stunned, hurt, and then angry. She could defend what she'd written. She challenged him to do the same.

He hadn't been able to answer one question the professor asked him. Trapped, he'd confessed that while she was in the kitchen he'd copied her file before destroying her laptop. He'd been expelled; she earned her master's degree, but it could have ended much differently.

She'd promised herself never to let a man interfere with her career. Up until now, she had had no difficulty keeping that promise.

Duncan pulled up short just as Raven heard a bleating sound. "You have sheep?"

The incredulous look Duncan shot her bounced off. "Then what is it?" she asked.

"A fawn and it's in trouble. Stay here." Wheeling his stallion, Duncan rode off, disappearing over a hill.

"Not likely," Raven mumbled, and followed. She topped the rise to see Duncan bent over what looked like a fawn. Not sure if her mare would stay if the reins were simply left on the ground like Duncan's stallion had, Raven quickly dismounted, then tied them to a stunted sage bush and rushed over. Seeing the fawn tangled in the barbed wire, she instinctively reached to help.

"Don't," Duncan snapped. The still fawn bleated again and began to struggle. "Just stay back and for once do as you're told."

Raven straightened and moved back. On the other side of the fence stood the watchful, helpless mother.

Eventually Duncan stood with the fawn in his arms and put him on the other side of the fence. "Go to your mother."

The young deer quickly joined his mother, who touched her nose to his, then bounded off, the fawn following. They disappeared over another hill and Duncan turned to Raven. "When I give an order, I expect it to be followed. I don't intend to have this conversation again. Instead of a wire fence, it could have been a mountain lion."

The thought of the fawn at the mercy of a predator took the anger from her. Her hand clutched at her throat. Then another thought occurred. "You didn't have a gun."

"I couldn't have used it anyway," he told her. "It's off-season for hunting mountain lions."

She stared at him, strong, unbending, and courageous. "What would you have done?"

"Taken care of it." He went to his horse, his gait graceful, his back erect. She didn't have a doubt he would have.

Mounting his horse, he waited until she was on

hers. "Barbed wire is nasty. It can slice the skin or tear a chunk out of it."

"I didn't think—"

"You better if you want to stay here. I don't have time to babysit." Wheeling his stallion, Duncan rode off.

Raven stuck her tongue out at him. It was childish but satisfying. She'd show Duncan McBride she didn't need him or any other man. She was a woman to be reckoned with.

Arriving back at the ranch, Raven followed Duncan to the barn. Dismounting, he reached for the reins of her horse, his face as closed as it was forty minutes ago when they'd left the cave. It was as if the heated kiss that filled her with need and hunger had never happened.

Good.

Both of them were going to be sensible adults and forget the kiss ever happened. It certainly wouldn't happen again. She had been caught up in the moment. He probably thought she had thrown herself at him.

Very bad.

"Thank you again," she said, her voice as cool as his expression.

"You're welcome." Turning away, he entered the barn.

Her gaze narrowed at his unbending back, then fell to his prime rear. Telling herself she was glad he was able to dismiss her so easily was one thing, making herself believe it quite another. She might ignore men, but they didn't ignore her—at least not until she met Duncan.

Head high, she went to the house and immediately up to her room to clean up. Finished, she pulled her cell phone from her handbag and dialed. While waiting, she sat on the padded bench at the foot of the bed. The call was answered on the third ring.

"Hello."

A smile curved Raven's lips on hearing Ruth Grayson's warm voice. Raven pushed Duncan from her mind. "They're authentic and in good condition. We might be looking at an amazing find." She explained to Ruth what they'd discovered.

"Raven, that's incredible news! I wish I could be there to see them," Ruth said, her voice animated.

"Me, too." Raven pulled one long leg under her hip. "They're absolutely amazing and well preserved from what I was able to see. What's really needed is a multidisciplinary team, but I'm glad he made the call to you."

"Duncan must be excited as well," Ruth went on to say. "It must have been wonderful sharing the experience together."

Raven squirmed, recalling that wasn't all they had shared. "Yes, it was."

"Can I do anything to help on this end?"

"You've already done enough," Raven said, meaning it. "If you hadn't found a sponsor, I wouldn't have been able to come." And she wouldn't have met Duncan, a man who made her body burn.

"Blade was glad to do it," Mrs. Grayson told her.

"He feels just as strongly as I do about the preservation of our culture."

"It helped that you're his mother-in-law," Raven teased.

"Blade makes his own decisions," Ruth said mildly.

And Blade was crazy in love with Ruth's youngest child and only daughter, Sierra. Sierra, like her four older brothers, adored their mother, and whatever she wanted they made certain she got.

"I'm glad he made this one." Raven stood. "I'm going back this afternoon to deliver supplies so I can start immediately when I get there in the morning."

"I won't keep you then. Thanks for letting me know how things are going. I'm sorry I missed your call last night," Ruth said. "Catherine had all of us over for dinner at their house."

Raven knew "us" meant Ruth's four other children and their spouses. Ruth had been instrumental in marrying off each of them. She'd even enlisted Raven's help to give her youngest son, Pierce, a shove toward the woman he eventually married. "That must have been fun."

"It was. Having your children happy with a life partner is a blessing," Ruth said. "Perhaps one day—never mind. Please thank Duncan again."

"I will." *But I won't like it*, Raven thought. "Talk to you soon."

"Bye, Raven, and I'm proud of you. "

"Thank you," Raven said, hanging up the phone, the euphoria of earlier returning. In the grand scheme of things, Duncan didn't matter. The most important thing at the present was cataloging and authenticating the cave drawings. First, she needed to see how deep the cave was, how far the drawings went.

She wrinkled her nose. If she hadn't grabbed Duncan—if he hadn't kissed her silly—she might know. Annoyed with herself, she stood and began to pack the supplies she hadn't wanted to leave in the Jeep.

Her Jeep was usually reliable, but rain in Arizona had let her know that there was a small hole in the canvas top. Luckily, it had been only a light shower and no serious damage had been done, but she hadn't wanted to take that chance with the paper she'd need to trace the drawings, paper to use in her laser printer, her notebooks.

Crossing the room, she picked up the canvas bag she'd stored her tools in and headed for the Jeep. She didn't need Duncan's help.

On the second trip from the Jeep into the house, she met Rooster on the front porch. He didn't look happy. "The boss wants to know what you're doing," he said.

Her first thought was to tell him to tell the boss it was none of his business, but since it *was* his business, she left the words unsaid. Then another thought struck.

She looked at the corral. It was at least fifty yards away and a beehive of activity. She couldn't see Duncan, but she knew he was there. He wasn't a man to remain idle while others worked. If he were, the Double D wouldn't be as prosperous as it obviously was.

From the sudden bellow of a calf, they were still

branding. She couldn't imagine Duncan had the time or the inclination to pay attention to the house or her. "He's busy. How does he know I'm doing anything?"

The look Rooster gave her was so condescending she was tempted to take back her thoughts of sharing her supper with him. Instead, she briefly closed her eyes.

Usually, she was even tempered, easygoing—unless crossed. She didn't have to think long of the reason for her crankiness. She was in a snit because the kiss apparently hadn't meant anything to Duncan and it had tilted her sensible, well-ordered world. Her problem, and one that she didn't intend to let interfere with the job she was there to do.

She'd had the legs knocked out from beneath her before by a man and survived. She would survive this time as well.

"You can tell the boss I'm getting the Jeep ready for a little excursion," she said sweetly, then walked past Rooster into the house.

In her room, she grabbed her heavy jacket in case it got as cold in the evening as it had the night before. Mapping out her plans for when she arrived back at the cave, she hurried back down the stairs and headed for the front door and ran straight into Duncan. He didn't look happy.

Chapter 4

She had thought she wanted him to show emotions, but looking at his face she wasn't so sure anymore. The man was angry and he was staring straight at her.

"Mrs. Grayson said you were sensible. I'm beginning to wonder."

"I know exactly how you feel. She said the same thing about you." Raven braced her hands on her hips. "First you question my credentials, now my judgment. She and Faith couldn't say enough wonderful things about you."

"You're going to explore the cave alone, aren't you?"

Raven blushed on remembering the heated kiss, the reason they hadn't finished. "It has to be done."

A thumb kicked the brim of his black Stetson back on his head. "You know nothing about this area. You'll be twenty miles from the ranch in a secluded location without reliable communication. Snakes and wild animals don't care about your noble intention."

He cut a glance at her feet. "You could slip and fall in there and no one would be the wiser. You can't tell me that in the digs you were on you worked entirely by yourself. That others weren't around."

He was right. Rule number one: you never went off on your own.

He must have taken her silence as confirmation. "We're setting some ground rules here. Follow them or I'm calling Mrs. Grayson to let her know that I can't be responsible for your safety if you won't follow my orders and ask her to send someone else who will listen."

The ball was firmly in Raven's court. Duncan didn't appear to be the type of man to bluff or talk just to hear the sound of his own voice. He'd make the call and it would make her appear immature and uncooperative at the very least.

"What ground rules?"

"You don't go any farther in the cave than where we went until I can check it out tomorrow."

"I—," she started, saw his eyes narrow, and nodded abruptly in agreement. "Go on," she said, knowing that wouldn't be his only request, make that demand.

"You always tell Rooster when you're leaving. You make sure your cell phone is fully charged, take a radio for backup, and you check in with him at least every two hours. You're back each day by five o'clock," Duncan said. "The days are getting longer with more sunshine, but night comes quickly."

Sensible suggestions and each of them for her safety. "I often become involved while I'm working. I can't guarantee that I'll remember to call."

"I can understand that," Duncan said. "Mrs. Owens left her alarm clock. You can use it."

"Can I have it now?" she asked, still determined to start today. The quicker she finished, the quicker she could leave the ranch. "I'd like to return."

"Ask Rooster. He'll find it for you." Duncan peered down at her from his superior height as if trying to make certain she would follow his dictates. "With your credentials and intelligence, I hope we don't have to revisit this conversation."

The man sure knew how to drive a point home and make a person feel a bit foolish. "We won't."

"Check the gas gauge before you go. If necessary, feel free to fill up," he told her. "We have fuel pumps for the equipment and trucks. Rooster can show you where they're located."

"I'd be happy to pay."

"No need. It's easier this way than having to come rescue you when you run out of gas. This is a busy time of year for us."

Raven had to grit her teeth to hold back a snide complaint. "I assure you that won't be necessary."

"We'll see." He turned and started toward the barn.

Silently seething, Raven walked out on the porch to watch Duncan head back to the corral. How could one man annoy you one moment, infuriate you the next, make you feel childish seconds later, cherished in the blink of an eye, and ticked off before you drew another breath?

Duncan McBride had the knack and was certainly like no other man she had ever met. She'd been so horribly wrong to compare him to Paul Dunbar, who had tried to use her for his own selfish gain. Paul, on the one hand, was easily forgotten; Duncan, on the other hand, was proving to be a problem.

Duncan was used to dividing his attention among multiple tasks. With a ranch the size of the Double D he had to if he wanted to be successful. In the past he'd never had any difficulty in evaluating a problem, coming up with a plan, and seeing it through. That was before Raven.

Straightening from branding another calf, Duncan took off his hat to brush the sweat from his forehead, his gaze going to the front yard of the ranch house as it had every free moment since Raven left two hours ago.

Behind him he heard another calf run into the chute specially made for branding. The area was just wide enough for the calf to pass, and once it was inside, the back gate shut behind the calf, effectively trapping the animal.

"Are you all right, boss?"

"Yeah," Duncan answered, replacing the branding iron he'd just used in the small fire and picking up another one. The cell phone in his pocket went off just as the hot iron touched the calf hip. One ring, then silence. Rooster's signal that Raven had checked in. She was all right.

But after the kiss, Duncan had to wonder if he was.

It shouldn't have happened, but he was honest enough to admit that the idea of kissing her had taken root in his mind almost from the instant he'd first seen her, beautiful, elegant, alluring. He might have ignored the need clamoring though him when she'd grabbed him in her excitement at the cave—if she hadn't said his name.

He could still recall the husky whisper filled with desire, the warmth of her body softening against his. He hadn't been able to resist the siren's call or the elegant body. The chute opened in front to let the calf out. Seconds later the back chute opened. Billy had settled into a nice rhythm. They were getting the calves done in good time.

Things on the ranch were going well. Now, if he could just forget Raven—beautiful and tempting—he'd be fine.

Duncan spit out an oath on seeing the white Cadillac Escalade pull up in front of his house. Just what he didn't need, another problem.

"Looks like Crane doesn't understand 'no,'" Ramon said, coming to stand beside Duncan.

"He will." Duncan jabbed the branding iron back into the fire. After he easily scaled the corral fence, his booted feet hit the hard-packed ground with a resounding thump.

Never breaking his stride, he snatched off his gloves, stuck them in the back of his pocket, his gaze never leaving the man who had continued to irritate the hell out of him for the past three months.

Lester Crane had made the foolish mistake of purchasing landlocked acreage that could only be accessed easily by crossing Duncan's land. Without

Duncan granting Crane the right-of-way, which would happen as soon as cows flew, the hunting resort would remain just a dream of the consortium he represented . . . unless Isaac Marshall agreed to lease Crane a section of his ranch.

Isaac's ranch was next to Duncan's. Older and a close friend, Isaac loved the land as much as Duncan did, but Isaac had his own ideas and responsibilities. As a member of Elks Ridge's city council, he wanted the revenue and jobs the hunting lodge would bring. Both men knew many of their young people were leaving because they couldn't find employment.

"McBride—"

"I thought I made it clear, Crane, that my land wasn't for lease," Duncan said, his voice as sharp as a blade.

The broad smile on Lester Crane's too-perfect face never wavered. He was too calculating to show the anger he surely felt. He desperately needed access to the Double D for the real estate developing firm he worked for. Using Isaac's land was an option, but it would be extremely expensive to circle around Duncan's ranch and add months to Crane's completion date. If Duncan didn't miss his guess, Crane's job might depend on his quick success. He'd made an inexcusable mistake, and they both knew it.

"The consortium I represent is prepared to make a very generous offer to buy the land needed."

"If I wouldn't lease it, I sure as hell won't sell it," Duncan said.

"The offer would be generous," Crane told him, glancing around the front yard. "Ranching can be an exhausting and an expensive existence. You never know when unforeseen problems might occur that could make a man change his mind."

"I'm not changing mine. Now leave and don't come back."

The smile slipped for an instant. "Twenty thousand dollars an acre."

"Not even for triple that price."

Crane's blue eyes widened at Duncan's announcement. His mouth tight, the man turned toward the SUV. Just then the sound of another engine mixed with the bawling of the calves.

Already knowing he'd see Raven, Duncan turned. Her hair blowing in the wind, she pulled up behind the SUV. Smiling, she cut the engine and got out of her Jeep. "Hello."

Crane's blue eyes lit and his shoulders straightened in his gray tailored suit. Duncan had a strong urge to toss him into his SUV. "Hello, I'm Lester Crane with Anderson Real Estate Development," he greeted her warmly, extending his manicured hand. "Since I know everyone in the area, you must be new."

"Raven La Blanc," Raven greeted him. Holding up her dirt-smeared hands, she smiled in apology. "Sorry."

Crane stared at her hands, his smile faltering, his eyes widening. "You can't be one of the hands."

"You would be right," Raven said, still smiling.

"If you ever need anyone to show you around, I'd be happy to oblige," he told her.

"Thank you for the offer, but it isn't necessary. If

you'll excuse me, I need to get cleaned up. My apology for interrupting you and Duncan." Moving past him, Raven went up the front porch steps.

Crane's hot gaze followed. His tongue ran over his bottom lip. "Now, that's some woman."

Duncan jerked the Escalade's door open. "Leave and don't come back."

Crane's gaze came back to Duncan. "Afraid of a little competition?"

Duncan let his gaze slowly sweep the man, from the top of Crane's head to his Italian loafers lightly dusted with dirt. " 'Little' is right."

This time Crane let his anger show. Hate filled his eyes. Duncan met the man's hard stare head-on. After a couple of seconds, Crane got inside the Cadillac, slammed the door, and started the engine.

Before the car had turned in the driveway, Duncan had gone up the steps and into the house. When he didn't find Raven in the kitchen, he hit the stairs. He didn't stop until he stood outside of her door. He rapped sharply.

"Who is it?"

"Duncan," he bit out. Who the hell did she expect?

"I'm about to take a bath; you'll have to wait to chew on me."

He frowned. He didn't like her knowing she got to him. "Why would you think that—unless you know you deserve it?"

"Because, Duncan McBride, I seem to irritate you just by breathing." The door opened. Her irritated face appeared in the narrow opening. "Go chew on someone else for a change." The door closed.

Duncan simply stood there, fists clenched, trying to control the fierce desire clamoring though him. Air rushed in and out of his lungs. His skin felt too tight for his body.

He knew with certainty that Raven hadn't taken into consideration that the mirror over the dresser afforded the person in the doorway an unimpeded view of the door—and the person peeking around it.

She'd answered the door wearing only low-cut white panties. Her long black hair had been pulled over her left shoulder, leaving her elegant back bare. Her legs had been long, shapely, endless. They'd hold a man in her satin heat, urge him on to his pleasure, and give in return.

Lust rode Duncan hard. If he could have laughed at the double entendre, he might have. He couldn't recall ever wanting a woman this fiercely. And he couldn't have her.

Spinning, he started back down the stairs. Perhaps hard work would obliterate her from his mind. He took the stairs two at a time.

Trouble had come to the Double D. And it wasn't leaving anytime soon.

Darkness had fallen when Raven hurried from her room. She had every intention of staying out of Duncan's way the rest of the day, but she'd become engrossed in inputing data into her laptop and making phone calls. If she were lucky, he would have already eaten and left.

A few feet from the kitchen's door, she heard Rooster's gravelly voice followed by Duncan's low-pitched one. Her steps slowed. Well aware of how she'd lost track of time, she'd adjusted the timer on the slow cooker after she'd taken her bath. She could go back to her room and wait, but there was nothing worse than overcooked chicken.

Throwing her shoulders back, ready to give as good as she got, she entered the kitchen and stopped short. Duncan and Rooster were standing over her slow cooker.

"Smells good," Rooster said. "She told me after she got back this evening that she'd cooked enough to share."

Duncan leaned closer. Sniffed. "What is it?"

"Some kind of chicken," Rooster said.

"I prefer beef." Duncan turned to take his seat and stopped on seeing her.

Not the way Rooster cooks beef, Raven thought. *Deliver me from stubborn men.* "Hello, Duncan, Rooster," she greeted them, and prepared the water for the spaghetti.

"I was beginning to think you might have called it a night," Rooster commented. "I was wondering what to do about that pot thing of yours."

"Sorry. I was caught up in working." Out of the corner of her eye she saw Duncan take a seat. Opening the refrigerator, she pulled out a package of mozzarella cheese. She removed the top of the slow cooker. A mouthwatering aroma filled the air as she layered the cheese, then sprinkled Parmesan cheese on top, and replaced the lid under Rooster's watchful observation.

"What are you having?"

"The rest of the stew," Rooster said, slowly going to take his seat. "No sense throwing out good food. The way I figure, with just me and Duncan eating, we have enough for a couple more days."

Duncan solemnly looked down at his bowl of stew. Rooster hadn't sounded too pleased, either. Going to the refrigerator, she pulled a loaf of garlic bread from the freezer. "Mind if I use the oven?"

Duncan finally looked up. "You didn't ask before."

"Yes, she did, boss," Rooster said, staring at the slow cooker. "I told her we didn't mind. Oven is already on. I made a can of biscuits. I didn't have enough cornmeal for the corn bread."

"Thanks." Raven glanced at the table. The small biscuits looked no bigger than half-dollars and were almost as burnt as the corn bread. She put the loaf on a cookie sheet she located beneath the cabinet and placed it in the oven.

Duncan picked up his spoon and dipped it into the stew. The lifted spoon wavered and then continued to his mouth. Raven inwardly winced each time he took another spoonful.

After working all day, he had to be hungry. So he was terse with her. Anyone would be if they worked all day and had to eat a leftover meal that was inedible even freshly prepared. He was taking care of those on the ranch just as he had helped her.

Duncan took his responsibilities seriously. Because of him, she had a good shot at permanently settling down in one place, making lifelong friends, and eventually thinking about marrying and starting a family.

The timer went off on the slow cooker. She checked the bread. It was ready. Rooster's and Duncan's gazes centered on the pot and stayed there. Raven came to a quick decision.

"Rooster, I hope you and Duncan will help me out here. I think I cooked too much as well. You can freeze stew, but not spaghetti." She picked up the strainer she'd placed on the counter earlier. "What do you say to helping me out by eating some of my chicken parmigiana?"

"Well, I guess it wouldn't hurt," Rooster said.

She drained the spaghetti, then looked at Duncan. "How about you helping me out here?"

"If you have enough," Duncan said.

"There's enough." Rinsing the spaghetti, she scooped a portion onto three plates, then put the chicken breast and sauce on top. "I'll get the bread." Placing the bread on another plate, she took her seat. "I'll say my blessing, but you two go ahead."

Raven lowered her head and when she lifted it she looked straight into Duncan's implacable face. She couldn't tell what he was thinking.

"Thank you," he said.

"Perhaps you better wait until you taste it," she said, hoping to tease him into good humor. The man simply needed to smile more and lighten up.

"It's almost as good as my cooking," Rooster said around a mouthful of food.

"I take that as a compliment," Raven said, her gaze on Duncan as he tentatively took a small bite of chicken, then closed his eyes. She watched his body relax.

"You might be right, Rooster," Duncan said, cutting a larger slice of chicken.

She was about to cut into her chicken when there was a light knock on the back door. Duncan's head came up. He quickly went to the door and opened it. Billy stood there, his hat pressed against his chest.

"Is Belle ready to foal?" Duncan asked.

"No." Billy shook his head. "I was talking to a friend who works at the Marshall ranch. He said it looks like one of their horses was badly scratched by a mountain lion. Ramon said cats are territorial, but he thought you should know."

Duncan hissed an expletive. "When? Where?"

"Yesterday. Near as they can tell, it was on the eastern part of the ranch," Billy answered.

"Ramon is right, but tell all the hands I want them to keep an eye out," Duncan said. "The problem might be a young male who has been pushed out or one trying to find his own territory. He'll prefer elk or deer, but he could be a nuisance."

Billy nodded. "I'll tell them."

"Thanks, Billy, for passing on the information," Duncan said.

The young man seemed to stand taller. "Night, boss. Miss. Rooster."

Duncan closed the door, and took his seat. "You know anything about mountain lions?"

Raven picked up her fork. "Enough to know that, as you said, they're not generally a threat to humans—unless they're sick or unable to hunt game. They might be a threat to a small animal, but not to people."

"We have no way of knowing that isn't the case," he answered.

"We also don't know if it is. Your food is getting cold." She smiled across the table at him and took a bite of her chicken. "I know if I spot one to back away slowly, and I have my bear spray."

"You're smart for a city woman," Rooster said, finishing off his slice of garlic bread and reaching for another.

"Why do you say that?" she asked, well aware that Duncan still watched her and afraid he was going to put the cave off-limits.

"'Cause," Rooster said, just as the phone rang. He pushed up from the table and waved Duncan back into his seat. "Probably one of those pesky telemarketers. Don't people know it's supper time?" He snatched the receiver up. "Double D," he said, then frowned at Raven and held the phone out to her. "He wants to speak to you."

"Me?" Raven asked, her own frown forming. "I didn't give anyone the phone number here. Who could it be?"

"Only one way to find out."

She crossed to take the phone. "Raven La Blanc." Her frown cleared. "Mr. Crane."

Duncan's head came up and around. She knew that look of censure. "Thank you, but I'm afraid I don't have any free time while I'm visiting. Thanks again, good night."

Hanging up the phone, she took her seat and picked up her fork. The silence was so thick it could be cut with a knife.

"How'd you meet that snake Crane?" Rooster spit out the question.

"This afternoon," Raven answered. Both men gazed at her with disapproval. Whatever was going on, she wasn't getting involved. She'd learned in moving so much never to become involved or take sides. "It will be the first and last time, I'm sure."

She sought to change the subject and get the men eating again. "How does pot roast sound for dinner tomorrow night, Rooster?"

He picked up his fork. "The boss likes beef."

That was what she was counting on. She finally looked at Duncan. His beautiful eyes were narrowed; anger shimmered in them. She hadn't thrown him off-track. "Excuse me; I want to make a few phone calls."

Rooster shook his head as Duncan left the table. "Leave it to a polecat like Crane to turn a man's stomach and throw him off his food."

Duncan had barely touched his dinner. There seemed to be a person who annoyed Duncan more than she did. And Crane's phone call might have put her in a precarious position. "I just met the man."

"He wants to buy land from the boss and is making a nuisance of himself. He's done a lot of talk about how much money the town would make—if the boss wasn't in his way." Rooster jabbed his chicken.

Raven was silent. Duncan had misjudged her; perhaps he had misjudged Crane as well.

"None of us can prove it, but he's the one who started the rumor that the reason the boss's wife left was that he abused her." Rooster snorted. "He wanted people to turn against him. A man needs his neighbors and friends more so in these parts. Good thing folks know the boss is a good man."

Whatever his faults, Raven would never believe Duncan would abuse a woman.

"Treated her like she was spun glass. Nothing was too good for her. Didn't do no good. She hated the ranch and us. Treated us like dirt. The boss—" Rooster snapped his mouth shut. "I talk too much." Hunching over his plate, Rooster continued eating.

Raven didn't know what to think. The deceit and deviousness of people never ceased to amaze her. Faith had only mentioned Duncan's ex-wife once. Her eyes had glittered with anger that promised retribution if she ever saw the woman again. Raven wondered how could she have had Duncan, the home, everything, and thrown it away? Hadn't she realized how blessed she was?

"Before you leave tonight, please tell Duncan that his plate is in the refrigerator," Raven said. "He can warm it in the microwave."

Rooster nodded. "Appreciate it. He don't take care of himself. Didn't hardly eat the grits and bacon I fixed this morning."

"He probably had a lot on his mind," Raven offered, then looked at Duncan's barely touched plate. "We're going out early in the morning together. Why don't I cook breakfast for all of us? Pan sausages, eggs, fried potatoes."

"In that pot?"

She laughed. What Rooster didn't know about cooking would fill a library, but his heart was as big as the Montana sky. "No, a skillet."

He sopped up the last bit of tomato sauce on his plate with his garlic bread. "Since you can cook almost as good as me, I guess it's all right this time."

Chapter 5

Duncan's booted feet hit the stairs a little after six the next morning. His stomach growled. He smelled coffee and wanted to whimper.

It might smell good, but the way Rooster fixed it, it tasted like gall. Duncan wasn't sure how much longer he could go on without solid meals. He'd warmed up the chicken last night that Raven had left in the refrigerator, but it hadn't put a dent in his hunger or his anger.

He came off the stairs, his mouth set in a straight line. He'd come close to taking the phone from Raven last night and telling Crane to back off. He hadn't for two reasons. It would have been extremely rude, which didn't bother him as much as the second reason: he'd been jealous.

The knowledge still rocked him. He had to get Raven out of his mind. He alternately worried about her and wanted her.

Angry with himself, he burst into the kitchen, and a slice of heaven greeted him.

"Good morning, Duncan," Raven greeted him. "Have a seat. I was just about to take the biscuits out of the oven."

"I'll get your coffee." Rooster picked up the coffeepot and poured. "Go on and sit down. Me and Raven got this."

Still in a bit of a shock, Duncan pulled at a chair, noticing again that he had a place mat and flatware. Raven's doing. He wanted to cry tears of joy at the plate Raven sat in front of him with fluffy eggs, brown pan sausages, and golden fried potatoes. His mouth watered. Rooster placed a mug of coffee that wasn't as black as coal by his plate.

"I'll say grace so you can eat and go take care of the ranch." She blessed the food, then handed him a fork, and scooted the pitcher of syrup closer. "Enjoy."

He dug in. He took two ravenous bites before he thought to pour syrup. The biscuits were golden and baked to perfection. "This is good," he said, then quickly amended, "almost as good as Rooster's."

Raven placed another plate in front of the chair where Rooster usually sat. "It should be. He helped."

Rooster proudly took his seat and promptly placed three biscuits on his plate. "Making biscuits ain't that hard. I've got to take care of the boss."

Duncan rose to hold Raven's chair. "Thank you," he said, aware that she'd understand he was thanking her for being sensitive to Rooster's feelings and not hurting the older man.

"What time do you want us to leave this morning?" she asked.

She looked eager and cautious. Raven was no

fool. Duncan wouldn't have put it past her to have cooked the meal to soften him up. "I spoke to Isaac Marshall, the owner of the ranch Billy referred to last night talking about the mountain lion attack."

"We both know that mountain lions are territorial," she said, not bothering to pick up her fork.

"Unless they're pushed out of their territory," Duncan told her. "And who's to say there isn't another one around here?"

"I'll take whatever precautions you want, but please don't forbid me to continue," she said. "It's important for several reasons."

"Your safety comes first." The thought of her being hurt made his stomach churn. He'd seen what the sharp claws of a bear and a mountain lion could do to human and animal flesh.

She leaned closer. "I appreciate your concern, but please, let me do my job."

How could a woman tempt a man, make his body hard, his insides soft? He picked up a biscuit and put it on her plate. Rooster had already downed four. "We'll take it one day at a time."

"One day at a time it is." Smiling, she finally picked up her fork.

The ride to the cave later that morning was completed in silence. Raven had a sneaky suspicion that Duncan might regret his decision once they arrived, but he wasn't about to go back on his word.

She dutifully stayed on her mare and out of the way as he searched the area for mountain lion tracks. She was relieved when he didn't find any. She didn't want to encounter a mountain lion, she just wanted to do her job.

"All clear."

Urging her horse forward, she dismounted and helped remove the brush from the mouth of the cave, then grabbed her high-beamed lantern and entered first. She'd set up the base camp a few feet from the entrance. She didn't even slow down as she passed her supplies, this time leaving Duncan to follow.

Reaching the inner chamber where they'd kissed, she shook off the shiver of awareness and increased her pace.

Duncan caught her arm. "You really didn't go any farther, did you?"

She looked up at him, fought to keep the slight trembling she felt in her body in response to his touch from increasing. She wanted to lean closer, to touch, to mold her lips to his. *Bad, bad idea.* "I told you I wouldn't."

"Sometimes people think lying is all right if it gets them what they want."

She held his gaze. "I value my word as much as you do. I don't give it lightly."

He nodded, one quick jerk of his head. "Let's get this done."

"I appreciate you taking time this morning," she told him, aware that he'd brushed her thanks aside.

"It's necessary, but don't forget, we take this one day at a time."

"Of course. As you said, let's get this done."

Once past the large chamber, they went another twenty feet and came to a stop. The only visible passage was an opening too narrow for humans to have passed through, at least now.

"It's a dead end."

Raven stepped around him and started to reach her hand with the high-beamed lantern through the foot-wide opening. Duncan's unyielding hand on her arm stopped her. "What are you doing?"

"Trying to see if there are other drawings on the walls, bear follows, the deep grooves they make during hibernation, on the floor," she told him. "I need to know if this blockage is a recent one."

"I'll do it." He stuck his hand holding his lantern though the opening.

"Duncan," she began, then slipped under his outstretched arm. There was no sense in reminding him that he was too big for her to see around. She straightened, felt his body tense behind her, the incredible heat. He surrounded her. She felt slightly light-headed.

"Raven."

It occurred to her that this was the first time he'd said her name. It had come out husky, needy. Neither of them could afford another kiss. She shook her head to clear it. "Please make a slow arc of the walls, ceiling, floor, expanding the area each time."

After a second, he did as instructed. It took three very long minutes, but at the end she had her answer.

Duncan stepped back. "You hoped for more."

She smiled sadly and turned. "I did, but what we've already seen is incredible. The drawings might have been hidden for centuries. I want to look at the main chamber again." She started back the way they had come.

Reaching the area, Duncan shone the light on the floor beneath their feet and beyond. "I don't see any evidence the cave might have been used by hibernating bears."

"Me, either." Lowering the lantern, she squatted by the last pictograph. "The floor is often studied as well for residue that falls from the drawings because the residue can be easier to radiocarbon-date." She stood and nodded toward a drawing that followed the rough outcropping of rocks. "Because of the angle of the pictographs they will be more difficult to get a clear picture of."

"Would it be easier if you were working with someone?" he asked.

Raven was surprised by the concern she heard in the question and understood what it had taken to ask it. Duncan wanted his privacy, but he also wanted the caves studied. "Perhaps, but it's not unusual for one person to work alone. I can take shots of the drawings and reproduce them on my computer to study," she told him. "In some caves they keep workers to a minimum for fear of disturbing the ecological balance or creating carbon dioxide."

"Maybe you should call in every hour," he said.

She shook her head. "If you had to report in every hour, how much would you get done?"

"I'm not working by myself in an unknown area," he told her.

"It won't be unknown for long." She started back toward the front of the cave. "I won't keep you."

He didn't say anything until they were outside. "I'll go, but I expect you to call Rooster every two hours."

"I have the alarm clock, water, a couple of granola bars," she said.

"Then you plan to return after lunch?" he asked.

Too late she realized she should have kept her mouth closed. "As I said, I don't like to stop working. I seldom eat while I'm working in the field."

"Is that the reason for the Crock-Pot?"

"Partly." She smiled. "Rooster and I have a bet on how good my pot roast will turn out."

"His letting you cook surprised me."

"He wants to take care of you," she said. "He's willing to let me help if you benefit. He's waiting to see if I can continue to do it better."

"I think we both know that's a given."

She grinned. "Why, thank you."

He caught himself before he smiled back. "Since we're eating your food, feel free to get what you need at Harold's, the grocery store in town, and put it on the Double D bill."

"Thank you." She looked back into the cave. "I better let you get to work."

He found himself reluctant to leave her. He glanced at his watch. "Ten thirty."

"I'll set the clock. Good-bye, Duncan." Turning, she walked back into the cave.

Duncan watched her disappear into the cave, wondering why he suddenly felt bereft.

What was he doing here? He had work to do. They were still in the midst of branding the calves. His prized mare had yet to foal, yet here he was checking on Raven. The first day she'd called thirty minutes late the first time, almost an hour late the next time.

Three days had passed and she wasn't much better at calling in on time. As much as he wanted to berate her, he knew that once you were busy time got away from you.

He also knew that during that stretch of time in between accidents happened. He'd been with the search party that found the campers after a black bear attack. One hadn't made it.

Dismounting and tying Black Jack's reins to the back of Raven's Jeep's bumper, Duncan told himself he was just doing his duty; the need to see her had nothing to do with his being here. He'd scouted the area that morning and again now. He'd seen a few coyote and rabbit tracks but no sign of any large animals.

Head bent, he entered the cave and picked up his lantern. He wasn't sure why he didn't call out to her until he saw her. He liked watching her without being obvious. Intent on working, she hadn't heard him.

"Hello."

Her head came up, around. She frowned. "I'm sorry I didn't call on time today, but this is simply fantastic." She motioned him over to the drawings in the main chamber. "I want to make some notes, then trace it tomorrow."

Her face was smudged. Her hands dirty. She looked incredibly beautiful. "Don't you wear gloves?"

She laughed, a slightly husky sound that echoed in the chamber, made his blood rush faster through his veins, and to the wrong place. "At times. That's why

I keep my nails short. I think there is a good chance of finding artifacts here. I had planned to look, but it would take time from the cave drawings."

"And now?"

"I'm not sure if I'll have the time," she said. "Usually it's done by a geologist and floor specialist. It's an exacting and tedious process, but I have a feeling that it will be worth it. Once I finish the tracings and notes, I'll know."

"I'll let you get to it. Bye."

Her smile died. "Bye. I'll be more conscientious about calling next time."

He picked up the alarm clock. "It might help if you set it."

She wrinkled her nose. "I guess I forgot last time."

"Don't forget again." Turning, he walked away. He was just doing his duty. She was his responsibility. Mounting Black Jack, Duncan took one last look before wheeling his mount and riding away.

Raven was in for it from Duncan this time. After a week of working in McBride's Lost Cave, as she'd named the outer chamber, she'd missed more and more call-in times. Last night Duncan had come into the house while she and Rooster were eating to tell her not to let it happen again. Before she could offer an explanation, Duncan had walked out the back door.

She didn't need Rooster's comment that the boss didn't like repeating himself to know she was on thin ice. That morning she didn't see him at breakfast. Rooster said the boss had gone to an auction, but that he wanted her to check in on time.

She had every intention of doing just that, but she'd been so excited about a new discovery that she hadn't called in until almost ninety minutes past the due time.

The conversation with Rooster fifteen minutes ago on her way back to the ranch house had been terse and to the point. The "boss" hadn't liked it that she had called in only twice. Her walkie-talkie going on the blink was no excuse. When she was late, people worried.

Raven understood and, although she was self-sufficient, she took a small amount of comfort in knowing there was someone concerned about her, albeit only because of duty.

As the middle child, she'd grown up with parents who believed in raising independent children. There was never anyone waiting for then when they came home from extra-curricular activities, dates, or the home of their few friends.

Besides always being told never to bring dishonor to the La Blanc name, they were pretty much left on their own. Raven and her sister's older brother was much more vocal in telling them what boys wanted. At fifteen he was six-feet and could bench-press 150 pounds. No one messed with them.

Raven pulled up into the yard, grabbed her bag, and hopped out. It was half past six. She hurried up the front porch steps.

As soon as she took a shower, she planned to check and see if she had the ingredients to bake a cake to go along with the trout Rooster had found in the freezer last night and challenged her to cook. It wouldn't hurt to make Duncan aware she had her uses.

Going inside, she made it to the stairs before she heard her name. "Raven, you gonna make my job harder tomorrow?"

Raven turned. Rooster's eyes were narrowed in his bearded face. "The radio died on me."

"Then you should have come back and gotten another one." Raven almost rolled her eyes until he continued. "You're our responsibility. This country is unforgiving. It don't suffer fools. You could get distracted and get into trouble. How would we know?"

Since she tended to block everything out when she was working, she came back down the stairs. "I'm sorry."

"'Sorry' don't cut it."

She almost smiled. He certainly didn't give an inch. Just like his boss. "I'm going to do my best to keep both of us out of the doghouse from now on."

He folded his arms. "The boss has a saying about trying."

"I'm sure he does." She started back up the stairs and then paused. "I planned to bake a cake."

His arms unfolded. Interest sparkled in his eyes. "Chocolate?"

"If you have the ingredients?"

"I'll go check."

Raven continued up the stairs, hoping he did, and that Duncan would listen before he chewed on her again.

* * *

Duncan arrived back at the ranch to see Billy running toward the house and his heart jumped in his throat. He touched his heels to Black Jack, easily overtaking the young hand. "What's the matter?" he asked, dismounting before the stallion came to a halt.

Billy whirled, flushed. "Boss. I, er—"

The back kitchen door opened. "Is everything all right?" Raven asked, quickly coming down the back steps.

Billy looked at her, then back at Duncan. "I, er—"

"Billy, I'm waiting."

The young man's head lowered for a moment before he lifted his head. "I was going to get the cake Ms. Raven baked."

Incredulous, Duncan looked at Raven. She smiled at him. "It's chocolate. I promised a cake for Billy and the others at the bunkhouse since Rooster had to get sugar and flour from them."

He'd just lost ten years off his life because of a cake. "Glad everyone is having a good time. Billy, I hope you and the others finished the fence, and are ready to work the heifers tonight."

"Yes, boss." Billy turned fully toward him. "I just checked Belle and put fresh straw in her stall, just like you want every evening. You want me to put up Black Jack for you and tell the others to meet you at the outer corral?"

Billy was like an eager, frisky puppy. Duncan shouldn't have taken his bad humor out on him. He was a good, loyal hand. "I'll take care of him. The heifers will wait until after you've eaten your cake."

"Thanks, boss." He faced Raven and Rooster, who

had joined her at the back door. "I can smell it from here."

Raven laughed and stepped aside. "It's on the counter."

Duncan looped Black Jack's reins over an iron hitching post and went inside the kitchen. He had to agree with Billy; it did smell good.

"It's three layers," Rooster said to no one in particular. He didn't sound pleased.

Rooster loves chocolate, Duncan thought as the older man watched Billy pick up the larger cake, leaving two layers on the counter. "Thank you again. I better get this back to the bunkhouse." He went to the back door. "You sure I can't take care of Black Jack for you, boss?" He grinned. "The fish smells good, too. You might want to stay and have your dinner."

"I'm sure."

The young hand nodded. "I'll let Ramon know you're back, and that we're working the heifers tonight." One-handed, he tipped his hat. The door banged shut behind him.

"I still don't see why they had to get the biggest one," Rooster groused.

"Because there are more of them." Raven walked over and picked up the platter of fried trout, steak fries, and hush puppies. "And because we get to eat this."

The older man perked up instantly, took the platter from her, and plopped it between his and Duncan's plates. "Wash up, boss. We just finished cooking a while ago."

Duncan doubted the "we," since nothing was burnt. "Let me take care of Black Jack first."

"Your food will be cold," Raven said. "Would he let me unsaddle him and brush him down?"

The request stunned Duncan. He simply looked at her.

"My grandfather is Cherokee and has horses on his small ranch in Canada," she said. "We used to visit in the summer when my father was on a location where we couldn't go."

"Guess I was wrong to call you a city girl," Rooster said.

"You were right for the most part. I grew up in the cities all over the world," she said, then to Duncan, "I don't mind. You still have a lot to do before you call it a night."

"So do you," he told her.

"On the computer."

"Still work," he said, wondering when he'd ever figure her out. She'd just put his welfare ahead of hers, and it wasn't the first time. She might be doing it to win points, but he didn't think so. His ex certainly wouldn't have offered. She always thought of herself first. "Thanks. It won't take long. You two go ahead and eat." Leaving the kitchen, he pulled Black Jack's reins free and headed for the barn.

Once he settled Black Jack in for the night and checked on Belle, Duncan planned on going back to eat, but he'd heard the men in the back corral and knew it would have to wait until they finished separating, then inseminating the heifers.

Perhaps it was for the best. The less time he spent

around Raven, the better. He walked out the back of the barn toward his men.

"You might as well sit down and eat." Rooster forked another filet into his plate beside the remnants of his huge second slice of chocolate cake. "The boss probably decided to work with the heifers."

"What can they be doing at night?" she asked, continuing to gaze through the kitchen window toward the barn as she had for the past ten minutes.

"Ranching business," he said gruffly.

Raven glanced over her shoulder at him. He'd tucked his head as if he was embarrassed. She suddenly had a good idea of what might be going on. Her grandfather and mother had been extremely strict about either her, her sister, or her brother witnessing the horses' breeding. "How long do you think the business will take?"

"Don't know." He looked up. "You just let the men do their jobs. He'll probably stop by and visit Belle once he's finished. You can put the boss's food in the refrigerator like you did last night."

"All right." Raven finally took her seat. She'd escaped being chewed on by Duncan, but she also missed him. Too much. Seeing less of Duncan was probably for the best.

So why wasn't she happy about it?

Today Duncan had planned to do a flyover of the range and check out the ranch, especially the fence line, and later talk to Old Man Johnson about leasing his land to graze more cattle. The price of beef was down, and in Duncan's opinion it was the perfect time to expand his herd. The prized Angus he'd purchased at auction would help, and he wanted to buy more.

The calves born from last night's work would help his bottom line as well. They would have a shorter gestational period, which meant his herd would increase faster.

His focus was on building his ranch, making his mark. Yet here he was checking on Raven, a woman he didn't understand and couldn't ignore. She'd done a better job of calling today.

Her call had been impatient and abrupt, Rooster had said, but Duncan understood. He didn't like being interrupted, either.

He caught a movement at the mouth of the cave, then Raven fully emerged, bending and stretching. She tilted her face upward toward the sun. Taking his binoculars from his saddlebag, he saw the sheer joy on her face as she lowered her eyes and scanned the area.

Moments later, she unhooked the radio from her waist and held it to her mouth. Wind tossed her hair, dirt smeared her face and clothes, but she didn't seem to notice or care. After a few seconds, she rehooked it.

Almost immediately there was static, then Rooster's voice came through on Duncan's radio: "Raven checked in. Over and out."

Used to the static and voices from the radio, Black Jack swatted an insect with his tail. She was an hour late in calling in.

With her hand shading her eyes, her gaze spanned the area. She was looking for Duncan. Lifting her arm, she waved, then reentered the cave.

Duncan lowered the binoculars, wondering if she'd seen a reflective glint on the binoculars lens. In any case, he had seen what he'd come for. She was safe; there was no reason to go any farther. He could leave.

Yet he didn't move. He knew better than most how quickly the unexpected could happen. Predators still roamed the area.

Her need to authenticate the drawings overshadowed any fear she might have. She was gutsy, but she wasn't invincible. In the short time she'd been on the Double D, she'd made her presence felt.

She'd all but taken over cooking dinner in that slow cooker of hers. The days were getting longer, and he and his men used every minute to work. There were times he didn't get home until after nine.

He'd taken to looking for the light shining from her window when he returned home at night. He'd wonder what she was doing, if she was in bed, and try to ignore the desire to join her. In the refrigerator he always found a plate of food.

Duncan replaced the binoculars. Raven wasn't for him. Gathering the reins, he headed back to the ranch.

Raven packed away her equipment for the day, careful to pull the waterproof tarp over everything to protect it from curious animals and the elements. She'd seen a couple of coyotes today but, thank goodness, no mountain lions or wolves.

She had four panels of the total thirty already scanned and in front of their respective drawings. Once she had all of them completed, she'd moved to the inner chamber where she and Duncan had found the colorized drawings.

Sighing, she stood to her feet. Once she left the ranch she knew she'd always think of him when she remembered that initial moment. She snorted and walked out of the cave to her Jeep. Who was she fooling? She'd think of him regardless.

Duncan was a man who defied explanation. If he wanted, he could send her on her way, yet he hadn't. He cared for his ranch, the people, and everything that walked on it. He'd gone to help a fawn because he was in distress. Duncan ate burnt food because he cared. He took precious time to check on her.

As Rooster had said, Duncan was a good man, but at times he could be hard.

Getting in the Jeep and starting it, Raven turned south, away from the ranch. She'd purposefully stopped an hour earlier today. She'd walked the perimeter outside the cave, but she wanted to explore farther. The area surrounding a find often gave insight as to why the inhabitants had been there.

As she'd told Duncan, the caves were seldom dwelling places, which meant the people probably had lived nearby. And although there was skepticism about the ability of people to have a light source to go deep into caves and make the drawings, lanterns with animal fat as a base had been found in several caves in Europe and around the world.

Raven stopped to admire a shimmering patch of

wild daisies, breathe in the crisp, clean air, and take in the bluest sky she'd ever seen. Duncan and the people who lived here were blessed beyond measure.

Putting the Jeep into gear, she continued over the bumpy terrain. It had rained the week before, Rooster had said, but you couldn't tell since the land soaked up water like a sponge. But there were creeks here. The Ancient Ones had followed their winding paths to hunt game and survive.

Raven came over a rise, careful to look back to get her bearings. She was her own GPS system. Smiling at her humor, she stared down the slight incline. Her excitement grew as she saw a winding stream.

She stepped on the gas. If the maps she'd gone over were correct, this was Bitter Creek, a source of water for the Ancient Ones. She planned to cross it and see what was on the other side.

As she hit the creek, water splashed up into the open door. She shifted into second gear, expecting to continue. Tires spun.

"Come on, Buddy," she urged, shifting into low, then finally four-wheel drive. Her back tires spun, spitting out mud, but the Jeep didn't move.

"All right, let's try this again," she murmured, then shifted into reverse, then forward. Pressing on the gas, she repeated the maneuver over and over, trying to get a rocking motion for the tires to get traction.

Nothing.

She couldn't feel one bit of forward motion when she pressed on the gas. She was stuck. Closing her eyes, she leaned her head on the steering wheel.

She started to reach for the radio on her belt until she remembered Duncan's words: *I don't have time to babysit.* She had told him she could take care of herself.

Even knowing there was no one in sight, she glanced around. "Looks like you're it."

Placing the radio on the passenger seat, she opened the door and stepped out into the muddy creek.

Chapter 6

Duncan drove the truck into the shed and closed the door. He enjoyed riding horseback, but there were times, like today when he helped deliver salt licks to the herd, that a horse wouldn't do. A horse couldn't carry the number of steel fence posts and barbed wire needed to repair a break. Ranching was changing and Duncan wasn't sure if it was all for the better.

Too many of the men and women he knew had sold or died, leaving their ranches to uninterested relatives or kids or, worse, at the mercy of estate taxes and speculators like those Crane worked for. That wouldn't happen to the Double D.

Duncan had no children, but he did have one wonderful nephew, Joshua, who would almost certainly follow his father into NASCAR racing. However, Duncan hoped that there would be other nephews and nieces. He was going to give it his best shot to ensure that one of them would grow to love the land as much as he did.

For him there would be no children.

He rounded the corner of the larger equipment shed and stopped, his brow furrowed. Raven's Jeep wasn't in front of the house. She'd called in—late as usual—almost three hours ago. It was past seven. She should have been at the ranch.

He increased his strides. The one day when he hadn't gone to the cave to check on her, and look what had happened. Snatching open the door, he hurried inside. "Rooster. Rooster."

The older man met him in the great room. "Yes, boss."

"Where is she?"

Rooster shook his head. "I don't know. She called about an hour ago to say she'd be late."

"You didn't ask her why?" Duncan asked.

Rooster's neck stuck out, illustrating the reason for his nickname. "I did."

"Well?" Duncan asked.

"Said she had something to take care of."

"It will be dark in an hour," Duncan said.

"She's all right, ain't she, boss?" Rooster asked, his eyes and voice worried.

"Yes," Duncan answered, wanting to calm the man's fears. He'd deal with his own later. "She's just trying to annoy me." Duncan turned toward the back door.

"You gonna go look for her?" Rooster asked, hard on Duncan's heels.

"Yes," Duncan bit out, heading for the ATV. It would get him to the cave faster than on horseback.

A group of his men, laughing and talking, came out of the barn. Duncan opened his mouth to tell them to stay close by in case he needed them—then he heard the sound of the Jeep's engine. He whirled around.

"She's back, boss," Rooster yelled unnecessarily.

Duncan's eyes widened. The Jeep was covered almost totally in mud. Raven braked sharply and climbed out.

The only reason he knew it was her was by the shape of her body. She didn't stop until she reached the water faucet on the side of the house. Unrolling the hose, she closed her eyes and pointed the spray of water into her face.

"What happed to her, boss?" Ramon asked from beside him.

"How would I know?" Duncan snapped, but he intended to find out. He passed Rooster on the way to her.

"She looks like she took a mud bath," Billy said. "Her Jeep, too."

"I know a mad woman when I see one," Rooster said. "Walk easy, boss."

Duncan dismissed Rooster's warning. Raven was the one who had better walk easy after scaring him half to death.

"Where have—" He jumped back, barely being missed by a spray of water.

Raven moved the water to her arms. Water ran in muddy rivulets down her legs to her bare feet.

"What—"

"I'd advise you to leave me alone, Duncan," she hissed.

"Tried to warn you," Rooster said.

Duncan ignored Rooster and studied Raven. She didn't appear hurt, just mad, as Rooster had pointed out. Duncan took a wide berth around her and looked into the Jeep. The driver's seat, gearshift, and pedals were just as muddy. Mud coated the tires, beneath the fenders.

He came back to her. "Why didn't you call if you got stuck?"

"Leave me alone, Duncan." Bending from the waist, she sprayed water into her hair.

He stepped forward. "Let me—" Water hit him in the chest. His stare promised retribution.

"I don't need your help." Her clenched fist tightened on the water hose. "You don't have to babysit me and I can take care of myself." Dismissing him with a look, she sprayed water on her shirt, trying to get the thick layer of mud off.

It wasn't happening anytime soon. All she was doing was making a mud puddle on the front lawn and creating a strangely erotic scene.

He looked over his shoulder. Several of his ranch hands stood in rapt fascination, watching as the mud washed away bit by bit, leaving her clothes plastered to her body. "Don't you have work to do?" he asked.

The men scattered. He turned, gritted his teeth. He could actually see Raven's nipples. He might get the water hose from her, but not without a struggle. He started for the house. Rooster followed. "You're gonna leave her?"

"I'm going for some towels and she doesn't need an audience." Grabbing the towels out of the half bath off the kitchen, he went back outside. She was still at it and finally making a dent in the mud clinging to her.

He waited another five minutes and silently held out a towel. He knew the spurt of water that hit him in the face wasn't an accident. He continued to hold out the towel.

"I don't like you at the moment," she said, glaring at him.

"Take the towel, Raven."

A tear tolled down her cheek. His gut clenched. He closed the distance between them. "Are you hurt?"

"Mad as hell. It took over an hour to get Buddy unstuck." She snatched the towel from his hand, held it in front of his face with her clenched fist. "Do you know how many times I put brush and sticks in front of the back tires, hoping to get enough traction to pull free, only to hear the tires spin uselessly? Do you?"

"Ra—"

"Twenty-three times, that's how many, but I did it." She clutched the towel in her hand. "I proved I don't need you, Duncan McBride. I wonder if you can say the same thing about me." Tossing the water hose aside, she turned off the water, then went to sit on the porch steps. She dried her legs and feet, then stood and went up the steps. The door slammed shut behind her.

Duncan looked at the closed door, then picked up the water hose and turned it back on to wash her Jeep. She was wrong. He didn't need her. Lust wasn't need.

* * *

Raven washed her hair five times and then soaked in the tub for an hour before she felt human. During it all, she had time to think and calm down.

She'd blamed Duncan for what had happened. If he hadn't kept throwing in her face that he didn't have time to babysit her and didn't have a spare man to watch over her, she would have called for help.

However, as she put on a fresh pair of jeans and a sweatshirt, she had to admit her own stubborn pride was the root of her problem. She'd wanted to prove she didn't need him. All she'd proven was that she could be as stubborn as her grandmother, who didn't forgive or forget, to Raven's grandfather's everlasting regret. Grandma Eagle had an irritating habit of bringing up the past instead of letting it go and moving on.

Raven had sworn she didn't want to be that way. As her mother always said, holding grudges made you and everyone around you unhappy.

Dressed, Raven started back downstairs. She still had to clean up the Jeep and buy new tires. She winced thinking of the expense. She probably should have asked Blade to outfit the Jeep, but he'd done enough. She'd thought they would last.

Opening the door, she couldn't believe what she was seeing. Duncan, Rooster, Ramon, and Billy were washing her Jeep. Duncan looked up. "You feeling better?"

Regret and embarrassment hit her. She'd been horrible to him. Yet, despite her outburst, he was seeing to her welfare. Again. "Yes, I'm sor—"

"Why don't you go eat and call it an early night," he interrupted. "We'll take care of this."

She was tired. "Thank you. Rooster, Ramon, Billy, thank you."

"You're welcome," they chorused.

Raven closed the front door and went to the kitchen. Perhaps today would be the turning point in her and Duncan's relationship. If so, the Jeep getting stuck might have been worth it.

After they cleaned up the Jeep, Duncan personally checked under the hood, filled the gas tank, and replaced her worn tires with new ones. He kept a supply of tires on the ranch for all the vehicles. The rocky terrain demanded it, since it chewed up tires. He wanted the ranch as self-sufficient as possible.

Ensuring the Jeep was in good shape didn't help keep the angry words she had tossed at him from returning again and again. *I proved I don't need you, Duncan McBride. I wonder if you can say the same thing about me.*

At the time, he'd been so sure she was wrong. He didn't need her. He enjoyed the meals she cooked, but he'd made it before she showed up and he'd be all right once she left.

Or would he?

In Belle's stall, he stroked the mare's huge belly. She carried her first foal. Black Jack, the sire, shifted restlessly a few stalls over. "She's all right, boy."

Duncan took care of his own. He didn't know any other way.

But he hadn't taken care of Raven. He had been so

set on remaining detached that she had been in trouble and wouldn't call for help. Twenty-three times she'd knelt in the mud to get the Jeep unstuck. Twenty-two times she'd failed.

He wasn't sure he would have had the fortitude to keep going. He would have walked back to the ranch—where he knew help waited. Raven hadn't been sure of that. His fault.

"Duncan," came a quiet whisper.

His head came up. He peered over the stall's door. Raven slowly walked down the aisle, stopping to peer over the doors. "Here."

A tentative smile on her face, she slowly walked to him. "Rooster said you'd be here."

Duncan came out of the stall. "Are you all right?" he asked, his gaze sweeping over her.

This time the smile was more natural. "Yes. A bath and a nap can do wonders."

"I'm sorry, Raven. Don't ever hesitate again to let any of us know you need help." His gaze held hers. "I hope you believe me."

"Seeing you and the others wash Buddy went a long way to convince me." She leaned back against the stall door. "I wasn't looking forward to getting muddy again. The Jeep probably hasn't been this clean since my father purchased it secondhand for me when I was a sophomore in college."

Duncan recalled the imprints of her nipples in the blouse and shifted restlessly. "What happened?"

She blew out a disgusted breath and straightened to peer over the stall door. "I wanted to scout the territory around the cave. I was excited to see water in Bitter Creek—until I get stuck in it."

"And decided to get yourself unstuck," he said, disgust in his voice.

"My own stubborn fault." She reached out a hand and rubbed the blazed face of the mare. "Believe me, the next time, I'm calling for help."

"Hopefully, with the new tires, that won't happen."

"What?" She spun to him.

"You needed new tires," he told her. "Ruth placed you in my care. I faltered once; I don't plan to do so again."

"Thank you," she said. "I'll pay you back."

"You already have by cooking supper."

She pushed away from the stall door. "Thank you. I better get back to the house."

"Good night."

She took a few steps and paused. "Are you coming?"

"Foals are born at night. I want to watch over Belle a while longer." *And try to clear you from my head.*

"All right, Duncan. Good night."

"Good night, Raven."

Raven whistled as she drove Buddy into town. She'd been on the Double D two weeks. After the creek incident, she and Duncan had declared a truce.

He still checked on her and the perimeter around the cave. She cooked dinner and occasionally breakfast. She didn't always see him in the evenings. She often thought of going to the barn in the evenings to see if he was there, but something always stopped her.

Stopping in front of Harold's, the main grocery store in Elks Ridge, she climbed out of the Jeep. It was as if both she and Duncan were aware that their relationship was at a crossroads. It could stay on a business level or deepen into an intensely personal one. She wasn't sure which she wanted.

Entering the store, she grabbed a basket and began to move down the aisles. The small store was nothing like the supermarkets in Santa Fe, yet somehow she felt more at home shopping here. People nodded and spoke, and she returned the greeting.

Pulling out her list, she went in search of baking products, her mind wandering back to Duncan. She could tell by the way he looked at her that he wasn't any more sure of which way he wanted things to go than she was.

A couple of times this week he'd looked at her as if he wanted her gone. But, she mused as she paused in front of the sugar, there were those magical, unguarded moments when she'd caught him unaware. His gaze was hot enough to incinerate, the desire frank and compelling.

Wrinkling her nose, she picked up a ten-pound bag of sugar. He wanted her, but he wasn't about to act on it. Which might be for the best. When she finished authenticating the find, she was going back to Santa Fe, to write her paper, send it off for publication, and move one step closer to realizing her dream of tenure.

She moved to the flour. She'd promised Rooster fudge and Ramon and Billy another chocolate cake. She smiled, remembering their jubilance. If only Duncan were so easily pleased.

"Hello, Raven. Today must be my lucky day."

Raven glanced up to see Crane. This time she looked beyond the expensive suit, the charming smile on his handsome face. She watched his gaze dart over her body, pausing briefly on her breasts. Rooster and Duncan were right. Crane was all surface. She'd met his kind before—slick, charming, and self-serving. "Hello, Mr. Crane."

"Please call me Lester," he said, showing beautifully capped teeth that probably cost more than her Jeep when it was new.

She smiled, the smile she'd perfected though her years as a student and then in academia when faced with unpleasant people. It took more effort than the people were worth to tell them to take a hike off a cliff, plus it solved nothing.

Since she planned on never seeing him again, she could be pleasant for a few moments. "I was just finishing some grocery shopping."

"A beautiful woman like you shouldn't have to worry about cooking," he said with a broad smile. "Have dinner with me tonight. There isn't much to offer here, but we could go to Billings. I know the perfect place."

"That's very nice of you, but I already have dinner plans."

His smile slipped the tiniest bit. "With McBride."

"Possibly. Now, if you'll excuse me, I want to get

this done." She stepped around the man and saw Duncan. The condemnation in his dark gaze seared her. But it was a thousand times worse for Crane. If looks could kill, he would need an undertaker.

Continuing to the cashier, Duncan checked out, then left with the bag clutched in a tight fist.

"I didn't know I was stepping on anyone's toes," Crane said, a snide grin on his face.

"Please don't worry about it," she said, waiting a few seconds before adding, "You aren't."

Her comment effectively wiped the smile from his face. "Good-bye, Mr. Crane." Walking away, she went to the cashier. Finished, Raven picked up her groceries and went outside.

Once at her Jeep, she placed the bag on the floor in front of the passenger's seat, then went around to the driver's side. Instead of getting inside, she glanced around, searching for and finding Duncan's truck parked a few spaces down from hers. There was no sign of him.

She dragged her hand though her unbound hair in frustration. It wasn't her fault he'd jumped to conclusions. She didn't delude herself into thinking Duncan might be jealous. He just intensely disliked the man.

She should just go, but she remained. Besides the anger, there had been something else, something indefinable, in Duncan's eyes. If she didn't know better, she'd say it was hurt. "You're losing it, Raven, my girl."

On the other side of the busy street, Duncan emerged from the post office. He'd taken no more than two steps before he stopped sifting through the handful of mail. His head came up. His gaze locked with hers. For a split second, she thought she glimpsed a softening of his features, and then his gaze went beyond her. His face turned rock hard.

She glanced over her shoulder to see Crane. The man was really beginning to irritate her. She turned to open her front door. Crane, grinning as if he'd won the lottery, beat her to it.

"Allow me." Opening the door, he stepped back only enough to let her pass. As she did so, he dropped an ecru business card into her open handbag. "My private cell phone number, in case you change your mind."

"I won't. Thank you for the door," she said, sliding into the Jeep.

When she stopped at the signal light, she looked in her rearview mirror. A big black truck was behind her.

Duncan.

She wasn't surprised to see him. He probably couldn't wait to lecture her again. Seemed the unspoken truce was over.

Why she just didn't tell him she wasn't interested in Crane she wasn't sure. Aware that she was probably in for another lecture, she drove slowly all the way to the ranch house. Although it was Saturday, she knew Duncan probably had things to do. Yet he remained a car length behind her.

At the ranch house, she grabbed her groceries and went inside. Duncan was right behind her. He slammed the kitchen door so hard the house shook.

"Crane is a liar and a cheat. Stay away from him!"

Tired of Duncan thinking she had the brain cells of a flea, she casually folded her arms across her chest. "It is none of your business whom I date."

"Date," he snapped incredulously. "You're going out with him?"

"I do as I please."

Duncan's eyes narrowed dangerously. "We'll see about that." He swept her into his arms. Her startled protest was cut short when his hot mouth closed over hers. The instant his lips met hers, pleasure, not protest, ruled her.

She felt her back against the wall, her hands over her head, as Duncan ravaged her mouth, the curve of her face, her neck. All the while his hungry lower body rocked against hers.

He released her arms to shove up her T-shirt. She pulled his shirt out of his pants, wanting, needing, to feel his naked skin.

Need swept though Duncan like a stampede, wild and dangerous. His hand closed over her breasts. He felt her press against his palm, her nipple bud. His hand lowered with the full intention of taking the point into his mouth . . . until he heard the clump of Rooster's boots on the back porch.

Duncan almost whimpered. He stared down at Raven. Her lips were moist and slightly parted from his kiss, waiting for another. Picking her up, he rushed out of the kitchen and into his office. Once there he was reluctant to put her down.

Her arms were wrapped trustingly around his neck. She stared up at him with open desire and complete trust. No woman had ever gotten him so hot so fast.

She occupied his thoughts during the day, made sleep impossible at night.

He didn't like it, didn't understand or want it, but there was nothing he could do about it. He was tired of fighting the explosive attraction.

His head bent, found her waiting lips, and inhaled her soft sigh of surrender. He took his time, coaxing the cooling embers back to red-hot life, nibbling her lower lip, the lobe of her ear, teasing, enjoying the way her body twisted against his, showing her growing need, her frustration. When she was tired of it, she palmed his face, bringing his lips to hers, pressing her breasts against his chest.

She was heat and desire in a tantalizing, explosive package.

Standing her to her feet, he pulled her flush against him, letting her feel his blatant arousal. Undaunted, she pressed her woman's softness against him. His eyes almost crossed.

His hands slid up under her T-shirt until they cupped her high, generous breasts again. Her nipples pushed against his palm. She whimpered. Her hands, soft and exploring, worked their way under his shirt.

"Boss, you in there?" Rooster called out on the other side of the door.

Chapter 7

Raven jumped. Her eyes widened. She made a motion as if to step back, but Duncan's arm tightened.

"Boss?"

"Yeah," he called, staring down at the top of Raven's tucked head.

"Everything all right? You left your truck door open."

"I was in a hurry," he said. He felt Raven tremble and wasn't sure if she was fighting embarrassment or laughing.

"Miss Raven must have been in a hurry, too," Rooster mused. "She didn't put up her groceries. I went up to her room and knocked, but I didn't get an answer."

"She's probably in the shower," Duncan said, which was the wrong thing to say. He recalled too clearly seeing a near naked Raven.

"I suppose." Rooster didn't sound too convinced.

"If you don't mind, put the truck up," Duncan called. "I want to finish what I'm doing."

"You're sure?" Rooster asked.

Duncan recalled the man's poor eyesight, thought of how much he loved his truck, how just last week Rooster had banged the fender of his own truck. Then Duncan felt the warmth, the incredible softness, of Raven in the shelter of his arms. "I'm sure."

"Sure thing, boss. I'll be real careful."

In a matter of seconds, Duncan heard the back kitchen door slam. Raven must have heard it, too, because she gently pushed against his chest. Again he refused to release her.

He waited until she lifted her face. Beautiful, exotic, tempting. "I want you."

Her eyes widened at the gritted-out words. "I don't—"

"The only mistress that I'll ever have is the Double D. I'll give you pleasure to heat up the night, but when it's over, it's over."

Raven had been propositioned before, but never by a man who made her body hum and burn for his touch. *He wanted her just as she wanted him.* Even now the blatant proof of his desire kept nudging her. She could be sensible or angry. She had an analytical mind that sought answers. "Why me?"

Duncan frowned, obviously as taken aback by her question as she was by his proposition. She watched his face become shuttered. "The reason seems obvious."

"Not to me." She pushed against him and this time he let her go. "We could have just kept going and let it play out. Why the need to set the ground rules? Why are you so sure it will be enough for either of us?"

"It's always best to know where you're going."

And you're stalling, she thought. She recalled the ex-wife. Or was it another matter entirely? "Surely you don't think there's any validity to the McBride curse? Especially since your brother and sister are so happy."

"We're just met and you want to talk about forever," he said gruffly, shoving his shirt back into his pants.

He didn't want to talk about it. She'd bet her prized Jeep that there were few things that Duncan feared. Obviously failing at another relationship was one of them. He wasn't being callous. He just didn't believe in happily ever after for himself. She didn't know if this was forever, either. What she did know was that she wanted to honestly explore the possibility, that she wanted and deserved something more than lust.

Watching him, she imitated his motions and stuffed her T-shirt back into her jeans. "I think not. If I go to bed with a man, I'd like to think it meant more than scratching an itch."

"I can change your mind," he challenged, his black eyes filled with such sensual promise that her nipples tightened.

"You're welcome to try." At the door, a safe distance away from temptation, she glanced over her shoulder. "But be warned, Duncan. All women aren't so easily forgotten."

Duncan glared at the closed door. Why did women always want the last word? In this case, she wasn't telling him something he didn't already know. He couldn't stop thinking about her, wanting her. One one thing he was sure of.

It had to be his way or no way. He didn't even want to think of going through the hell of another ruined relationship. He only had to think of his father, still in love with Duncan's mother and afraid to open himself up to the pain again, for Duncan to realize that some women were impossible to forget. He had a feeling that Raven was one of those women.

It was better his way, a simple affair where both parties knew the rules. Her way was unthinkable.

Raven might have an analytical mind, but she also realized that there were situations that couldn't be analyzed or explained. Such as the intense sexual attraction between her and Duncan.

With the slightest touch of his hand, his body against hers, her normally intelligent mind shut down. The body that she thought she knew so well yielded control to a man she had just met. She became consumed by a desire, a need, so fierce that it blocked out everything else except the hunger for fulfillment.

This wasn't supposed to be happening to her. She had her life mapped out. It did not include a man and a burning hunger that swept reason aside.

Her hand trembling, she paused while icing the cake she had just baked, her thoughts on the man she could see though the kitchen window. Hands on his hips, Duncan was talking to several men on horseback with blanket rolls tied to the backs of their saddles. Another man was sitting in a small truck with the motor idling.

If she weren't stronger, her tongue might be hanging out. Duncan moved with the sensuous grace of a large cat, his body perfectly conditioned. Although the corral was fifty yards away, she had no difficulty picking him out. The hard thump of her heart alerted her.

She realized why she hadn't told him the truth about Crane. She wanted Duncan to be a little jealous. Pure teenage mentality. And deep down she'd wondered if he'd lose control again if he kissed her.

She ran the tip of her tongue over her lips. She vividly recalled his hot, damp mouth over hers, the first pressure, and the ball of heat that had rolled through her, exciting and tempting. Recalled the spark that had jolted her when his tongue touched hers, swirled around hers, suckled hers.

Her hand clenched as the heat swept through her, her body yearning for their mouths, their bodies, to be fused again.

He was also a gentleman.

It hadn't occurred to her befuddled brain until she'd left Duncan in his office and her mind began to function normally. Then she realized he'd taken her to his study to protect her, not to continue his seduction of her.

"You finished?"

Raven started, turning around to find Rooster's speculative gaze aimed at her. She barely kept from tucking her head in embarrassment.

When he'd returned from putting Duncan's truck in the garage, Rooster had found her putting away groceries. He hadn't asked where she'd been, but his steady gaze had made her a bit nervous, just as it did now. He might have poor eyesight, but there was nothing wrong with his brain.

"Almost." She dipped the knife into the chocolate icing she'd made from scratch. Her mother abhorred any type of prepared food. She even had made her own pasta, had grown spices, and had a garden whenever possible. She had taught Raven so much about cooking and little about life.

Her mother would follow Raven's father wherever he wanted with a smile on her face. She let her love for him overrule her own happiness and that of her children. Raven had promised herself that she'd never be so easily led by a man.

Her mind leaped to Duncan's proposal of a hot, no-strings affair. If two people ever had completely different outlooks, it was them. He said it himself; the Double D was his only mistress. Raven wanted tenure and stability, not to be a man's plaything.

"At least, if I stay here, I can probably have another slice," Rooster mumbled.

"Were you planning on going out?" Raven asked.

"Yep. Monthly poker game with friends at the Marshall spread."

"Isn't that where the mountain lion was spotted?" she asked.

"Yeah. One of their hands spotted a cat yesterday near our connecting property line, but none of our ranch hands have seen signs of a cat," he said.

She hoped it stayed that way. She turned and began icing the top of the cake. "You driving?"

"A friend of mine is pickin' me up. The games sometimes last most of the night." Rooster's eyes searched hers. "I was planning on continuing my winning streak from last month, but I could stay."

Not wanting to read too much into his offer, Raven casually swirled more icing on the cake. "Do Ramon and Billy or any of the other hands go with you?"

He grunted. "Ramon is too busy chasing women. He's teaching Billy to be the same useless way. They're going to camp out tonight to get an early start on the section of fence in the southeast corner of the ranch."

Her head came up. "They're working on a Sunday?"

"No choice. The fence has got to be fixed," he said. "Lot of ranchers don't care 'bout letting their hands off on Sundays, but not the boss. It's a long way from the ranch. That's why they're going tonight. Once they're finished they can come on back and have the rest of the day off." Folding his arms, he stepped around so he could see her face. "The boss is staying to watch Belle."

Her hand didn't jerk, but it was a near thing. Did that mean they would be at the ranch alone? "So how far is Marshall's ranch?"

"Like I said, our property lines connect. Marshall hopes the ranches will be joined one day."

A frown creasing across her brow, she glanced up. "Joined? How?"

"His daughter," Rooster explained. "She's another one after the boss."

She can't have him, Raven thought, her fingers curling around the knife. She relaxed her fingers, hoping Rooster hadn't caught her reaction. Opening the drawer, she picked up a cake knife and cut a generous slice of the cake.

Faith had said the kitchen was well stocked with cooking utensils. She had seen to that. She'd looked sad for a moment and whispered that she wished one day there would be a woman in Duncan's life to use them.

"Do you have time for pork chops with mushroom sauce? It's one of my best dishes."

"Hoagie is fixin' rabbit stew."

Raven glanced up from wrapping the cake in foil. "I think I'd rather have pork chops."

Rooster took the cake she handed him. "Don't knock it until you taste it. There's nothing like it."

The back door opened, and Duncan came in. Their gazes met, held. Heat and desire arched between them. Her breathing altered; her breasts felt heavy. She was the first to look away. *You might say the same thing about Duncan*, she thought.

"I was just leaving, boss, if you're sure you don't need me?" Rooster said.

"Go on." Duncan closed the kitchen door. "You haven't missed a game in ten years. There's no need to start now."

"Well," Rooster began, glancing between Raven and Duncan. "Most of the men are out on the range or off."

"It's not the first time. Harvey and Pete are at home with their families. Stew and Otis at the bar in town. If needed, they can be here in twenty minutes," Duncan said just as a horn blew. "There's Redman to pick you up."

"I guess. I'll have to hear his mouth all night if I keep him waiting too long. Well, good night." With one last look at them, Rooster went out the kitchen door.

Raven felt nervous and unsure. The idea that she and Duncan were virtually alone was as unsettling as it was exciting. "You want dinner now?"

Duncan's black eyes burned with an intensity that sent shivers racing though her. "You think we could eat it in bed afterward?"

Heat lanced through her at the thought. The idea appealed to her. Too much. He stepped closer. "Tell me no before I kiss you and take it out of both of our hands."

The thought was tempting and so foolish. She stepped away. "I'll fix your plate." She quickly prepared his food and placed it on the table with hands that refused to steady.

He caught her hand, studied the fine tremors, then lifted his head.

"Why are you fighting this so hard?"

"Because I value myself and you." She flexed her arm and she was free. "There's cake for dessert. I'm going to my room."

"You're also running," he said to her retreating back.

Since he was right, she kept walking.

Wanting a woman shouldn't make you this damned restless, Duncan thought as he walked to the barn. He hadn't been this messed up when he first went out with Shelley. They were in bed by the end of the second date.

Females shouldn't be so unpredictable. Just like

the one he was going to see. Belle should have foaled by now. The vet had been out the day before to check her and said things looked good. He expected a normal delivery. Horses did most of the work. It wasn't anything Duncan hadn't gone though before.

But this was Belle and Black Jack's first. Duncan had raised Belle from a filly and she'd never acted the way he expected. She'd been a scrawny runt and had grown up to be graceful and beautiful. For some odd reason he thought of Raven. Perhaps not so odd. She had grace and beauty in abundance, and she also kept him guessing.

His mare wasn't giving any of the signs that labor was imminent—she wasn't off her feed or acting unusual. He was just going on a gut feeling that her time was near. He'd been out to check on her at least twice in the last hour, and each time she'd been fine.

As he entered the barn, his gaze went to the fifth stall on the left, and he expected to see her head. When he didn't, he took off running. Opening the stall's door, he saw Belle on her side, in labor.

Raven couldn't concentrate, and it made no sense. The cave drawings were everything she had hoped for and so much more. If her calculations were correct, and she was sure they were, she was on the verge of a major discovery.

Yet here it was, almost midnight, and she hadn't made any significant progress in the past hour. She should have completed the day's notes hours ago and been in bed. Instead, she sat, still dressed, thinking about a man she had no business thinking about.

His proposition was certainly insulting, but his kisses made her wonder what other things he might be good at.

Her cell phone sitting on the desk by her laptop rang. This late at night, she was sure it was a wrong number. But thankful for the interruption of her wayward thoughts, she quickly picked it up. "Hello."

"Come to the barn. I need your help with Belle." The line went dead.

Raven shot up from her chair, jammed the cell phone into the pocket of her jeans, and took off running. Duncan's voice had been calm, but she knew he wouldn't have called her unless there was a problem. She raced out of the house and to the barn.

"Duncan," she called when she didn't see him.

"Belle's stall. Hurry."

Raven took off. She opened the door to the stall, not knowing what to expect, just hoping the mare was all right.

"Her water broke thirty minutes ago. She should have progressed further by now. Finish wrapping her tail," Duncan said. He was on his knees in the straw at the mare's head. "Easy, Belle."

He threw a quick glance at Raven. "We're going to have to help her. Neither the vet nor my men can get here in time."

We. Raven swallowed. The mare's stomach was enormous. It rippled with a strong contraction. Belle groaned. Raven shuddered, then took a deep breath. The horse and Duncan both needed her.

On her knees, Raven did as Duncan instructed. "What do you want me to do now?"

"Stand back for the moment. I'm going to get her to stand and walk to hopefully reposition the foal." Sliding a halter on the mare, Duncan urged her to her feet. "Come on, girl."

Raven stood to one side, watching for several long minutes that seemed to go on forever. Belle groaned again. Raven clenched her fists.

"All right, Belle. Easy, girl," Duncan murmured as the mare lay down. "I'm here."

Minutes ticked slowly by—then the hind feet appeared. Raven wanted to sag in relief until she heard Duncan curse softly under his breath. "What?"

"The foal is breech. The hooves are flexed upward."

"What do you want me to do?" Raven asked, wanting to help the mare.

"Go to her head and stay with her," he told Raven.

Raven gladly went to the horse's head and tried to comfort the mare. She heard Duncan murmuring, his voice soft, calm, reassuring, and the whinny of Black Jack, as if he sensed a problem.

Duncan glanced at a clock on the wall. "It's been twenty minutes. We should have seen the foal by now. I can't wait any longer." Duncan washed and lubricated his arm. "I'll have to reposition the foal myself."

Raven nodded, stroked the mare's head. "Easy, Belle. Duncan is going to help you and your foal."

"You're almost there, Belle," Duncan murmured a short while later; then the mare began to struggle and groan.

"What's wrong?" Raven asked, her heart thudding.

"The hips are the widest portion and the most difficult to deliver," Duncan said. "Hand me the towel over there."

Jumping up, Raven retrieved the towel and gave it to Duncan. As she turned she caught a glimpse of Duncan using the towel to grasp the foal's wet, slick feet and pull downward toward the mare's hind hooves.

The head and shoulder appeared. Belle whinnied. Raven went back to the mare's head.

"Everything is going to be all right. You're going to be a mother soon." Raven glanced around again to see the foal in a white sac. Duncan used a pair of scissors to free the foal. Finished, he positioned the foal near the mare.

"She's out of the woods now. She'll rest, and then stand," Duncan said, looking at Raven. "We might have to help her foal to stand. Thanks. You did good."

"I didn't do anything," she said, still a little in awe of the whole thing.

The mare made a motion to stand. Raven came to her feet and stood back, watching as Belle stood. After a few tries her foal stood beside her. Duncan cut the umbilical cord and dipped the foal's navel in a liquid solution.

"Boss, I'm coming!" called a man's voice, quickly followed by that of another man. "The vet is right behind us."

The stall door opened and Pete and Harvey came in, quickly followed by the vet. "We missed it."

"Looks like you woke me out of a sound sleep for

nothing," said a middle-aged man with rumpled white hair and a black medical bag in his large hand.

"Sorry, boss. There was a traffic tie-up on the road. The ditch was too steep for us to go around," Pete said.

"The state trooper wouldn't even let us try," Harvey added.

"Raven was here." Duncan urged the foal to his mother's teat.

Raven wanted to squirm under the men's scrutiny. "Duncan did all the work."

With his hand on the mare's rump, he looked at her. "I couldn't have done it without you."

"I've seen grown men keel over at the birth of a foal," commented the man with the medical bag.

"I didn't look most of the time," she said honestly.

The men laughed. Duncan simply stared at her, his hand still on Belle's rump. "Doc Harrington, Raven La Blanc, a houseguest doing research for a book."

The man stuck out his hand. "Pleased to meet you. Always a pleasure to meet a woman who is as strong and courageous as she is beautiful."

"Duncan did all the work," she repeated. She glanced at the foal and smiled. "He's beautiful and hungry."

"It could have gone differently if you hadn't helped and stayed calm," Duncan said.

"You were calm, and I never doubted that you'd bring mother and foal through," she said, her warm gaze on Duncan.

She became aware of the silence, could feel the men looking from her to Duncan, speculating. Afraid she hadn't been able to hide the sensual undercurrents between her and Duncan, she moved toward the stall door. "I was glad to help. Good night."

"Good night, Miss Raven."

"Good night, miss."

"Nice meeting you."

Raven closed the stall door and looked back over the top. The men were crowded around the mare and foal. She shouldn't expect Duncan to look at her one last time, but she wanted him to.

Just as she was about to turn, his gaze shifted to hers. She'd seen his eyes angry, annoyed, aroused, but this was the first time they'd ever been tender. Her heart thumped hard in her chest. Together, they'd brought a new life into the world. An extraordinary feat, creating a shared bond.

Turning, she started for the house. *Be careful, Raven*, she thought, *or you might be the one who won't be able to forget.*

Duncan rolled out of bed Sunday morning earlier than his usual time. He wanted to check on Belle and her foal before he took his Cessna and flew over the section of fence that Ramon and the hands were repairing and to check on the men watching the newly bred heifers to make sure they were all right.

Although there had been no sign of the mountain lion on Duncan's land, he wasn't taking any chances, especially after a ranch to the east of him had lost a calf to a cat a couple of months back. If that weren't enough, he worried about Raven being alone in the cave, but there was nothing he could do until tracks or signs were actually spotted. Wild animals roamed the area. It was a fact he had accepted and lived with—until Raven arrived and worked alone.

He admitted that he was being overly cautious and protective of her. He reasoned it was because he owed her after her Jeep had gotten stuck and she hadn't called. The thought that if she was in trouble again she wouldn't call was never far from his mind.

Dressed, he left his room. He'd stayed with Belle until early that morning, watching mother and son bond. He'd even taken Black Jack to see his family. It had been a silly thing to do, but Duncan hadn't cared.

At the top of the stairs, he stopped and looked down the hall at Raven's closed door. She was a unique puzzle he'd never figure out. Last night, when he saw Belle in trouble and realized his men and the vet would arrive too late, she was the first person he'd thought of. He hadn't a doubt that she'd be able to handle the birth.

And he'd been right. He trusted her. Raven had guts. Which could present a problem. Like the vet said, it was always a pleasure to meet a strong, courageous, and beautiful woman.

Duncan hit the stairs. Midway down, his nostrils twitched. Coffee. Not the too-strong brew that Rooster made, either. Duncan's steps increased. It had been after one when he'd seen her light go out. After the vet had checked out Belle, he and his hands had left for home, and Duncan went back to the house to shower and change clothes before returning to Belle for the rest of the night.

Entering the kitchen, he saw Raven at the table with a cup in her hand, probably hot chocolate, since he smelled it as well as the coffee. She looked up.

As always, she looked beautiful. This morning she wore a simple tan short-sleeved blouse. "Are Belle and her foal all right?"

"They're fine." He stopped by her chair. "You all right?"

A smile curved lips he wanted to press his against. "Yes. I just keep thinking about the birth."

His hand squeezed her shoulder; he understood a little of what she felt. "The awe of bringing a new life into the world never gets old."

She nodded. "Duncan McBride, you have just about the perfect life."

"Shock" was a mild word for what he felt at her unexpected statement. He gazed down at her upturned face. Sincerity stared back up at him. "You haven't seen the winters with six feet of snow and the temperature below zero when you have to go out and check on livestock and mend fences."

"No, but facing the elements is part of the price you pay for what you've been blessed to have, don't you think," she said, a statement, not a question.

Her thoughts were so close to his own that his hand clenched. He felt the fragile bone structure, but there was strength there as well. "Who are you, Raven La Blanc?"

She laughed, a sultry sound that stirred his body, slithered down his spine. "Just a woman."

He shook his head before she finished. "I've met women before and you're nothing like them."

She looked up at him through a sweep of lashes as black as coal. "It takes more than age and gender to make a woman. A man like you should know that by now."

Desire to close his mouth on hers curled though him again. This time he had no intention of not satisfying the urge. His head bent until his lips were inches from hers. "I'm beginning to find that out."

"Dun—"

His mouth on hers cut off whatever words she had been about to say. Drawing her warm, willing body to his, he took his time relearning the exotic taste and texture of her lips. His hand swept up and down the elegant curve of her back, learning her shape, shaping her to his hardness.

His head lifted. "I want to take you to bed."

"So I gathered." She pushed out of his arms and went to the oven. "I thought you might be hungry and cooked a sausage pie."

"I don't suppose we could eat—"

"You would be right." She removed the pie and placed it on a wire rack. "Grab a cup. Rooster isn't here to serve you coffee."

Duncan's eyebrows lifted. People didn't order him around, especially women. They tended to want to wait on him, try to gain his attention. Raven wouldn't cater to any man unless she wanted to. Yet she gladly took care of him and Rooster, even cooked special treats for the other hands. She was a woman a man could depend on.

He took a cup out of the cabinet, filled it with coffee, and poured her more hot chocolate. "You must have been up a long time to do this."

Putting their plates on the table, she took the seat he held. "I decided to stop tossing and turning and get up to do some research on a discovery I made yesterday."

He cut into his pie. Delicious, as he expected. Wasn't there anything Raven couldn't do well? "What kind of discovery?"

"Just a drawing," she said.

Duncan reared back in his chair. If he hadn't been watching her, he wouldn't have seen her blush. The woman had decimated him with a kiss, talked frankly about desire, yet she she'd just blushed about a drawing.

"Why are you up so early on a Sunday morning?" she asked, sipping her hot chocolate.

He could push for an answer, but he decided to let it go. "I need to check on a few things."

"You taking Black Jack or the ATV?"

He finished off his pie. He liked it that she was learning about the ranch. "I'm taking the plane."

"Really?" She leaned across the table. "Could I go with you? I'd love to get an aerial view of the area where the cave is located—if you're going in that direction."

He hadn't planned on it. "We could swing by."

"Great! I hate to ask another favor, but do I have time to go by the barn and see the foal?"

"I would be surprised if you hadn't asked." He

nodded toward her untouched food. "Eat up and we can leave."

She picked up her fork. "Thank you."

"I'm the one who should be thanking you," he said, meaning it. "You were there when I needed you the most. You didn't let me or Belle down, just as I knew you wouldn't." He hadn't intended the words to sound so needy but couldn't for the life of him think of trying to negate what he'd said. She had made a difference.

She looked across the table at him, her face softening. His chest felt tight for some odd reason.

He came to his feet. "I'll be at the barn when you finish." Not waiting for an answer, he continued out of the house.

If he wasn't careful, he'd forget that Raven was here just for the summer.

Chapter 8

Sitting beside Duncan in the cockpit of his Cessna, Raven had a new appreciation and understanding of the vastness of his ranch. The Double D sprawled over mountains, flatland, and valleys.

In his face she glimpsed the determination and pride it took to manage property that far-reaching. His roots were deep, his responsibilities innumerable.

"I had no idea the Double D was this large," she murmured as he flew over Ramon and the other men repairing the barbed-wire fence.

It was almost inconceivable that one man could take on so many responsibilities and not buckle under the weight. "How do you do it?" she asked.

"I love the land, love what I do," he answered, waving to the men below, who waved back. "As long as I can remember, I wanted to be a cowboy, to own a ranch in Montana."

She turned to him. "Why not Santa Fe? Faith said you grew up there."

"Perhaps it was those Western movies I saw as a kid," he said, banking left. "Montana, with its beauty and its harshness, has always appealed to me."

"It couldn't have been easy buying this much land," she said, then quickly added, "I'm sorry, that was rude. I didn't mean to pry into your personal business."

"That's all right. It wasn't easy, but I had an ace in the hole," he said. "We're nearing the cave. Follow the crop of trees to your left in a straight line and it will lead you to the mouth of the cave."

Raven was surprised how reluctant she was to look away from Duncan. She wanted to hear more about how he had acquired the ranch, hear about his life as a child. Sighing inwardly, she looked below. "I wish I had a pair of binoculars."

"Here."

She glanced around and took the binoculars, recalling the glints of light she sometimes caught in the trees when she came out of the cave. Putting them to her eyes, she scanned the area, thankful when he circled again and took the plane in closer. "I don't see anything."

"Did you have reason to believe there might be other caves?" he asked, continuing east toward the ranch house and landing strip.

She placed the binoculars in her lap. "No, but I wanted to check out the possibility. I didn't see anything when I checked the area out in my Jeep the day before yesterday."

Duncan's fingers flexed. "If you decide to look again, remember to stay away from the bushes."

"Will do. The Jeep makes enough noise to scare any animals, predatory or otherwise, away."

Lowering the wheels, Duncan smoothly landed the plane and taxied to a hangar. As soon as he shut off the motor, she handed him the binoculars. "How many of these do you have?"

Frowning, he placed the binoculars in a case. "What do you mean?"

She unfastened her seat belt. "Because you're a man who plans ahead. You didn't have them when you got on the plane. You must have another pair."

He unbuckled his seat belt and followed her off the plane. "How would you know that?"

"Because I've caught the glint of the sun on the binoculars' lenses," she said. "After this morning, I realize a little bit of what a huge responsibility you have. Yet you check on me every day."

"As long as you're on the Double D, you're my responsibility."

Raven was silent on the way back to the house. They were in the kitchen before she had enough courage to ask the question that had been nagging her. "What if I wasn't on the Double D? How would you feel about me?"

His hand curled around the back of her neck, bringing her closer. "We would have been in bed long ago."

The back kitchen door abruptly opened behind them. Raven jumped. Duncan whirled.

"Why am I the last to know?"

Raven bit her lip and tried not to look at Duncan, who remained silent.

"I might not ride the range anymore, but I'm still a part of the Double D," Rooster continued, glaring at Duncan. "I deserve to know when something important happens. Everyone is talking about Miss Raven helping with Belle's foal. One of you could have told me."

Raven almost wished he had been talking about the attraction between her and Duncan. Not for anything would she have wanted to hurt Rooster's feelings. Without thinking, she looked to Duncan for help. He moved to Rooster.

"Did you check your cell phone for messages?" Duncan asked calmly.

Rooster's gaze faltered. "You know I don't know how to do that yet. You got me the dang thing in case I was away from the house and needed to contact you or the boys."

"I'd hoped you'd hear it ring and pick up," Duncan said. "I called you shortly after Doc and the men left. I'll show you again how to check your cell phone for messages." Duncan placed his hand on Rooster's slightly stooped shoulder. "You're an important part of the Double D. You taught me more about this land than anyone else. Without you, I wouldn't have made it that first year or the next, and we both know it."

"Well." Rooster worked his shoulders. "You never acted like you knew it all. You might have owned the land, but you were willing to learn from the bottom, willing to work as hard as any of us, the first one up in the morning, the last one to go to bed."

"I learned from you," Duncan said. "I couldn't have had a better teacher or friend."

"Well," Rooster repeated, running the back of his hand across his eyes; then he looked at Raven. "I suppose you've already taken care of the boss."

Raven's gaze flew to Duncan; she saw his mouth quirk. "Partly," he murmured.

Raven wanted to kick him. "We've eaten. I cooked a sausage pie and made coffee. Are you still full of rabbit stew or do you want a slice of pie?"

"Hoagie's stew didn't taste like I remembered. I'd appreciate the pie." He went to the cabinet and picked up two mugs. "Boss, I'll get us some coffee and you can give me a firsthand account while I eat."

Raven slid the rest of the pie, almost half, on a plate and put it on the table. Rooster might be small, but he could pack away food like a lumberjack. "I'll leave you to it and go get dressed for church."

"You can go with us." Rooster forked in a bite of pie, nodded his graying head. "After last night, you're one of us."

Raven's gaze went to Duncan, but his expression was unreadable. "I don't mind driving myself."

"Makes no sense," Rooster said around a mouthful of pie. "The boss can introduce you to our neighbors. Afterward he can take us out to eat. After cooking all week, we deserve the day off. Ain't that right, boss?"

"Yes," Duncan agreed, but the teasing man of moments ago was gone, leaving Raven to wonder what had caused the abrupt change.

"If you're sure, Duncan. I don't want to take up your time on Sunday, too." She wanted to give him an out. Obviously Rooster hadn't noted the difference in Duncan's demeanor.

"Why should Sunday be different than any other day?" he asked, picking up his cup and taking a drink.

Raven's eyes narrowed. Had he been just making a statement or being pithy? Last Sunday, she had worked at the cave half a day before returning to the ranch house to do research. On the way back to the ranch house, she had spotted Duncan.

Rooster stood with his empty plate. "Better hurry, Raven. We want to get a good seat."

Raven stopped trying to figure out a pensive-looking Duncan and headed for her room.

Duncan wanted to stuff a biscuit in Rooster's mouth. Make that two biscuits. Because of him, Duncan was wedged in the church pew with Raven pressed against him from her delicate shoulder to her delectable knee.

Every time he drew in a breath, he inhaled her perfume, a sweet, spicy scent that made all of his male hormones pant for mercy.

And if that weren't all, the hem of the skirt of the celery-colored suit stopped a good five inches from her knees. The large handbag in her lap didn't help; neither did her discreet tugging. He wished she'd stop. Her rubbing against him was having the wrong effect. His hat might be in his lap now, but Reverend Radford paced back and forth in front of the wooden podium and the organist played, sure signs that the reverend was winding down and that meant Duncan would have to stand.

God knew man was weak and would forgive him. Duncan wasn't so sure about the people in the congregation. Even now, Duncan could feel the blatant stares and hear the hushed whispers speculating on the relationship between him and Raven.

Rooster's doing. Like a proud father, he had introduced Raven, retelling the story of her helping with the foal's birth. Each time the story was told, the situation grew more dire, Raven more heroic. To give her credit, Duncan had seen her lips twitch a couple of times. She'd mouthed "I'm sorry" to him.

She accepted the praise and always managed to reiterate that Duncan had been the one who deserved the credit, not her. Rooster called her modest, then instructed Duncan to seat "our newest hand."

More than ready to get out of the spotlight, Duncan had done as instructed, finding them a seat at the farthest end of the pew. He hadn't thought so at the time, but as Reverend Radford asked everyone to stand and gave the invocation the seating had been intentional.

Duncan hadn't wanted another man as close to Raven as he was and definitely not to see that much of her legs. A couple of times he'd almost driven off the road looking at her instead of where he was going.

Too many men were looking already. If Jack Stewart looked around one more time, grinning like he'd been thrown from his horse one time too many, Duncan wasn't going to be responsible. The shiftless man wasn't getting near Rav—

"Will all of our visitors please stand," Reverend Radford requested.

Duncan's attention snapped back, felt Raven try to make herself smaller. At five-seven, it wasn't going to happen.

"Raven, stand up," Rooster said, in a voice loud enough for half the church to hear.

Reverend Radford smiled benignly and stared straight at Raven. "I think we have a shy visitor, but one I've heard a lot about. Rooster, perhaps you can encourage your guest to stand."

Rooster sprang up like a jack-in-the-box and reached across Duncan for Raven's hand. She placed hers in his and came to her feet immediately. Duncan knew inwardly she might want to bop Rooster on the head, but she would not want to embarrass him.

Heads turned. Jack Stewart smacked his lips. Duncan wanted to smack him in his rude mouth. They acted as if they'd never seen a woman before.

"This here is Miss Raven La Blanc. She—"

Raven squeezed Rooster's hand, smiled at him, and then sat back down, drawing him with her. Not to be outdone, Rooster said, "She's modest, as becoming a fine woman."

"The Psalms say it is better for someone else to brag on you," Reverend Radford said. "Let us stand."

Duncan grasped Raven's elbow and drew her to her feet. The moment the reverend said, "Amen," Duncan urged Raven out the pew and into the aisle near the wall. They didn't even get a foot.

Jack Stewart was the first of many men to introduce themselves. It took over thirty minutes for Duncan,

Raven, and Rooster to work their way out of the small wooden church. On the steps, Pastor Radford waved them over. Another seven minutes, complete with the retelling of the birth of the foal.

By the time they were heading for Duncan's truck, his teeth ached from clenching them to keep the words locked in his mouth.

"Duncan! Duncan!"

Duncan increased his pace, muttered beneath his breath, heard Rooster do the same. Raven, however, balked, giving Cynthia Marshall and her father, Isaac, enough time to catch up with them. Isaac spoiled his youngest child, who thought all she had to do was point and her father would get her whatever it was she wanted. It was no secret that Cynthia, a recent college graduate, had pointed to Duncan.

"Hello, Duncan," she said, staring at him as if he were the last designer bag on the Last Call table at Neiman Marcus and she intended to have it. He supposed she was pretty enough, but he had absolutely no interest in the woman, whose thoughts went no deeper than shopping or spending money.

"Hello, Duncan, Rooster, miss," Isaac said. He was a big man with a wide chest, bowed legs, a startling contrast to his slim daughter. If he had a fault, it was not saying no to her.

"Hello, Isaac, Cynthia," Duncan said. "Raven La Blanc, Isaac Marshall and his daughter Cynthia. Her father's ranch is next to mine."

"Hello, Mr. Marshall, Cynthia," Raven greeted

them, but Cynthia barely noticed. Her attention and affection were obviously on Duncan.

"You haven't RSVP'd to my party Saturday night, Duncan." Cynthia trailed a finger down the front of his white cotton shirt. "Surely you won't disappoint me or Daddy."

Isaac chuckled. "I told her you were just busy." He circled his daughter's shoulders with his arm. "My friends will be there to help my little girl celebrate finishing college. I can't believe she's all grown-up, but my credit cards tell me she is."

Cynthia made a pretty face. "Women should do their best to look good at all times." Her gaze slid to Raven. "Some women try, but they can't quite pull it off."

Duncan saw Isaac frown as his gaze snapped to Raven. She smiled, a siren's smile, as if she knew the secrets of the world. "You're so right, Cynthia. That's why I never try." She extended her hand to Isaac. "Nice meeting you. I think I'll wait in the truck."

Obviously not knowing how to handle the situation, Isaac quickly pulled his hand out of his pocket to shake her hand. "Same here. You're welcome to come as well."

"Daddy," Cynthia wailed. "I'm sorry, but I've already turned in the number to the caterer."

He cut his daughter an impatient look. "He'll add one more. Duncan is a friend. I can't ask him nor should he have to leave his houseguest."

"Houseguest!" Cynthia's eyes snapped. "You're staying at the Double D?"

"Doing research for a book," Rooster interjected into the growing silence. "She's becoming indispensable to me and Duncan. Last night she helped him deliver a foal."

Cynthia's expression said she wasn't impressed. "When are you leaving?"

"Summer's end," Raven said. "Good-bye."

To Duncan's annoyance, she didn't make it two feet before four men, who had obviously been biding their time, surrounded her. Her laughter was a goad in his side.

"Like Reverend Radford said, it's best to let others brag on you," Rooster said. "I guess I'll go escort Raven to the boss's truck; otherwise she might not make it. I can't remember another woman ever creating this much excitement, and to think, she didn't even try."

Cynthia's sharp intake of breath cut through the air. Duncan smiled. If he hadn't respected Isaac, he might have slapped Rooster on the back. "Good-bye, Isaac, Cynthia."

"Duncan, I'd like to talk to you a minute." Isaac turned to his daughter. "Excuse us for a moment, please."

Cynthia looked as if she might protest, then said, "Yes, Daddy." She smiled flirtatiously at Duncan and lightly touched his arm. "I'll see you at the party."

Not if I can help it, Duncan thought.

"Duncan, I wanted you to hear it from me that me and Crane are moving closer to a deal. My ancestors helped settle this land." Isaac tugged the brim of his black Stetson. "I can afford to take care of my family, but some can't. Ranching isn't for everybody. As a member of the city council I have to think of what's best for the majority of the people."

"You don't have to explain anything to me, Isaac. You can do what you please with your land," Duncan told him.

Isaac hitched up his pants. "I know, but I don't like to think of anything coming between our friendship. You're a good friend and neighbor."

Duncan respected the older man. He clasped Isaac's shoulder and looked him straight in the eye. "I count myself lucky to be your friend. Nothing is going to change that. You do what you feel is right, but I'll tell you straight out, I'm hoping you'll find out what a snake Crane is before you sign anything."

"I've had to deal with snakes before," Isaac said. "See you at the party. Good-bye."

"I hope this time you don't get bit," Duncan murmured, then turned to search for Raven. His eyes narrowed on seeing her surrounded by several men. He didn't stop until he helped Rooster extract Raven from the crowd of eager men. "Sorry, fellows. Breakfast was a long time ago."

"Good-bye," Raven said, shaking each of the offered hands before allowing Duncan to lead her to the truck. Helping her inside, he tried not to watch her skirt slide up her thighs and failed. If he hadn't, he might not have seen her open her purse and drop several pieces of paper inside.

He started the engine. "What are those?"

"Nothing," she said, staring straight ahead.

" 'Nothing' is right," Rooster said. "As if Raven is gonna call any of them."

Duncan's hand tightened on the gearshift. "They gave you their telephone numbers?"

She shifted in her seat beside him. "Once I took one, I had to take all of them." She glanced at Rooster. "I should have *you* call them. They all think I'm some kind of superwoman. You have to promise me not to tell that story again."

"You should be pro—"

"I was thinking of making a double batch of chocolate chip cookies tonight," she said. "I'll prepare pot roast for supper tomorrow night—if I'm not fielding phone calls."

"The ranch always has to come first," Rooster said.

"Glad you agree."

Duncan had listened to the exchange with interest. Rooster had met his match.

Something told Duncan he might have as well.

Chapter 9

Raven, her chin resting on top of her hands, stared over the stall door at Belle and her foal. It was still hard to believe that she had helped bring a life into the world.

"Can't stay away?"

Raven didn't start. Somehow she'd known that Duncan would find her. They hadn't talked much since that morning. He didn't want his emotions involved with her. She was afraid it was already too late. Somehow helping Belle had brought them closer. They were less guarded, more relaxed, around each other.

He braced his arms on the top of the stall door beside hers. She felt the faint touch radiate all over her body, felt his go still. It just remained to be seen if either of them could resist the sensual pull. She wouldn't take any bets on it.

"I thought the proudest day of my life was the day I walked across the stage and received my Ph.D. But that was before last night."

Duncan was quiet for a moment, then, "What do you think we should name him?"

Surprise lifted Raven's head; joy widened her eyes. "We?"

He smiled, making her heart beat wildly. "You earned it."

She looked back into the stall at the foal, jet-black and all legs, nursing. "Did you have any names picked out?"

"Not really. I'm not usually a superstitious man, but I wanted to wait," he confessed.

"Rooster said you raised Belle from a filly," she told him.

"The man I purchased the ranch from warned me to look at the livestock as a business, first, last, always. That way when you lost one, you wouldn't feel it as deeply."

Somehow she knew he hadn't been able to do that. "Without caring, they become a burden instead of a joy. When that happens, you don't take pleasure or pride in what you do. You love the land, the life you have, and it shows."

"You're right," Duncan agreed. "I can't imagine any other life for me."

"Then you're doubly blessed to have found your dream and be able to live it. Very few people can say that." One day she'd be among the blessed ones. Opening the stall's door, she went inside and stroked the foal now that he had finished eating.

"What's your dream, Raven?" Duncan asked softly from behind her.

"To have permanence and roots so deep they can never be pulled up," she answered. She'd never revealed her dream to anyone except Ruth. "As I said, my father traveled all over the world. Everyone in the family except me saw the traveling as a wonderful experience. I intensely disliked it."

"Where do you plan to put down those roots?"

"Santa Fe." And that was the fly in the ointment. Her life was over a thousand miles away; his was here. She looked up at him over the foal. "My findings at the cave will give me my dream."

Entering the stall, Duncan closed the door and went to stand on the other side of the foal. "The Double D will give both of us our dreams."

But not together, she thought. Sadness coursed though her. She felt the warmth of the colt beneath her hand. Life went on. You made choices in life and hoped and prayed they were the right ones.

"How about Midnight? He was born near midnight and his coat is jet-black."

"Midnight it is."

"I better get back," she said. "We both have to get up early."

"Just not together."

At least he was persistent in what he wanted. "No. Good night, Duncan." She quietly left the stall while she had the strength to do so.

During the following week, Raven did her best to call in on time. She didn't want to give Duncan any reason to search her out. Since it didn't get dark until late, he and the ranch hands didn't stop until they had to. There were times she didn't hear him on the stairs until after midnight.

No matter how deeply engrossed she was in her work, she'd always hear his footsteps. She'd listen for his pause at the top of the stairs and grow still herself, wondering if he'd come to her room.

He never did.

And afterward she'd feel restless, on edge. And no matter how hard she worked, the thought of Duncan was never far from her mind.

One night she gave in to the need to see him and waited on the front porch. The full moon added to the loneliness she felt. She'd almost talked herself out of waiting when she saw him coming from the barn.

Her lonely heart raced. Even with only the moon, she easily identified him. The wide breadth of his shoulders, his proud carriage, the easy gait. The closer he came, the more dangerous her idea became.

When he was several yards away she stood with the intention of slipping back inside. She turned to flee.

"Raven."

Caught. She slowly turned back around and waited for him to reach her.

He placed one foot on the steps beside hers, his hand on the rail next to hers. "You all right?"

"Yes. You're working late."

She thought she saw his mouth quirk. "Goes with the territory. How are things at the cave?"

"I'm making progress, but it's slow," she admitted.

"You'll get it done."

His faith in her meant a lot. "Thank you. I should be going to bed."

He stepped closer, his eyes searching hers. His hand lifted to brush his knuckles down her cheek. Awareness rippled though her. "I think you haven't been sleeping any better than I have. It doesn't have to be that way."

She shivered, wanted. "For me it does."

"I thought you'd say that, but at least I can have this." His head lowered, his lips finding hers, as he brought her body flush against his. Fire and need zipped though her. Her arms went around his neck and drew him closer. Her mouth was as ravenous and greedy as his, her tongue as daring.

His hand molded her hips against his hard arousal. She moaned into his mouth, unable to keep from pressing closer. She shifted, bringing her more deeply into the valley of his thighs. Instinctively she rubbed against the hard ridge.

Abruptly his dark head lifted. She wanted to drag his mouth back to hers, continue to explore the sensual hunger he created in her. Their labored breathing sounded harsh in the night.

"One night. Please give me just one night with you."

Her eyes closed, her body ached for the release she knew Duncan could give them both. All she had to do was lift her face to his and he'd take it from there.

And then what? She had a feeling that making love to Duncan would create more problems, not solve them.

She also realized something else. She wanted the decision taken out of her hands and felt ashamed. Duncan wasn't that kind of man. He might initiate the seduction, but in the end he'd want her willing, with no regrets.

Opening her eyes, she stepped back. "You have a strong code of honor."

His hand drifted through her hair; she pressed her cheek against his hand. "And it seems I'll have another long lonely night."

"If it's any consolation, mine will be the same," she said. At least she could give him that. "I want you."

"But not enough."

She placed her hand over his heart, felt the erratic beat that mirrored her own. His hand clasped over hers, squeezed. He was so strong and yet so gentle. "You tempt me more than I ever thought possible. You want one night because you don't believe in forever. I do."

His hand fell. "People toss out words like 'forever' and 'love' to get what they want. It doesn't mean anything."

He was thinking of his ex-wife. "I admit some selfish people do, but not everyone." Raven placed her other hand on his chest. "Just look at Faith and Brandon. Cameron and Caitlin couldn't be happier."

"And my parents couldn't be more miserable," he told her. "Even when people mean the words, it doesn't work out."

Her hands clenched. "So you're afraid."

He stiffened and then pushed her hands from his chest. "Maybe you should go to bed."

Stubborn, proud, and running as fast as he could from the truth. "The next time you talk to Faith and Cameron, you might want to ask them if they had doubts, if there were moments they wanted to run in the opposite direction."

"You can't compare them to us," he snapped.

His words sliced her heart. She cared for him and he wanted only a no-strings affair. "No, I guess not. They were in love. You just want a bedmate for the night." She turned for the door.

An expletive sizzled from his lips. He caught her before she took two steps, dragging her back against him. "Maybe you should know something. I haven't been with a woman in more than two years, and it hasn't been because I haven't had the opportunity. I want one night with you, but I'd barter a piece of my soul for more."

"Duncan."

He released her and stepped back. "Forever isn't for me. I forgot once and suffered the consequences. I won't forget again."

Raven finally understood the promise of retribution in Faith's voice when she spoke of Duncan's ex. Raven wouldn't mind having a "chat" with her, either. "I'm not like her."

"No, you're not. You're everything she wasn't, and it changes nothing." His hand swept up and down her arm. "Why can't you accept what I can give you, give both of us?"

"Because we both deserve more." She went to the door. "Don't stay up too late."

"The same goes for you."

She wondered what he'd do or say if she told him she never went to bed until she heard him come upstairs. "Good night, Duncan." She slipped inside just as she heard him bid her good night.

Telling Rooster good-bye the next morning, Raven hurried out of the kitchen. She had a lot of work to do that day. Putting the sleepless night to good use, she'd tracked down the information she needed on cave drawings of female sex organs.

There were few caves where human forms were repeatedly seen. Humans were more often depicted by the sketch of an anatomical picture. She'd been stunned when she'd seen the drawing in the last chamber, McBride's Wall of Panels.

For those with an educated eye, it wasn't particularly difficult to identify the wall drawings. As expected, she didn't find any drawings of male organs, because they were rarely depicted.

She blushed on recalling Duncan asking her about her latest discovery. There was no way she was telling him any of this. She ran down the steps and hopped into the front seat of the Jeep.

She heard an engine and saw Duncan coming up the road behind her. Her heart did its usual flutter despite his unsmiling face. "Good morning," she greeted him when he pulled up beside her. "I was just about to leave."

"That's not possible."

Shock and worry swept through her. "Did something happen at the cave?"

Switching off the ignition, he climbed off the ATV and went to her. "Pete spotted a mountain lion when he was chasing strays this morning."

The event that Raven feared finally had happened, but she had no intention of letting it ruin her plans. "How far away?"

"Close enough."

Raven studied him. To Duncan's way of thinking, that could mean one mile or twenty. "I have bear spray, and I'll go back in the house for my portable radio."

"Getting a radio station can be hit-or-miss, but it doesn't matter because you aren't going anyplace," he said, his voice final.

Raven climbed out of the Jeep, undaunted when he didn't step back. "You can't do this."

"We both know I can."

"Duncan, don't do this, please," she pleaded. "The cat might never come near the cave, and if it did, there is nothing to indicate it might present any danger."

His eyes narrowed under his hat. "This is not open for discussion." Turning, he started back to the ATV.

She grabbed his arm, felt the muscled hardness, the warmth and strength. "Please reconsider."

"We agreed to take one day at a time, that you'd follow my orders or I'd call Mrs. Grayson to send someone else," he told her, studying her. "Is that what you want me to do?"

Her fingers unclamped. She stepped back. "You'd do that after . . ."

"You'd be safe in Santa Fe." He got back on the ATV. "I don't want you going anywhere near the cave until I give you permission."

How could this unbending man be the same one who had held her last night, kissed her, turned her world upside down?

"Raven, give me your word or I'm calling Mrs. Grayson," he said, his words flat.

Raven felt her dreams in jeopardy and, as the last time, a man was the reason. "I loathe you."

His expression didn't change. "Your word."

"I won't go to the cave."

Starting the motor, Duncan pulled away. He didn't look back.

Angry and hurt, Raven snatched her satchel out of the Jeep and returned to the house, slamming the door. "He makes me so angry!"

Rooster came rushing into the room. "What's all the commotion? I thought you were leaving."

"The great Duncan McBride has decreed that I can't," she said. "Pete saw a mountain lion."

Duncan's voice came on Rooster's radio: "Raven is staying at the ranch house today."

Rooster's gaze locked on a fuming Raven as he picked up the radio from his belt. "She just told me about the cat."

"We'll discuss it later. Out."

"Out." Rooster hooked the radio under the dish towel, his concession to an apron.

"How can he dictate to me like that?" she asked, her voice trembling. "It's not fair!"

"It's been my experience that a lot of things ain't

fair, but I've never known the boss to be anything but," Rooster told her. "You're a friend of the family, and even if you were some greenhorn stranger, he wouldn't let you roam over the ranch when you could put yourself in danger."

"But he has no way of knowing I'd be in danger," she argued.

"You have no way of knowing you won't be," Rooster came back. "A friend of ours tangled with a cat and has the scars to prove it. The boss cares about all of the people on this ranch, some more than most. Mad or not, you're safe. I got washing to do."

Raven watched Rooster walk away and, with him, her anger. She hadn't missed his statement of "some more than most." If even the hint of danger was there, Duncan wouldn't allow her to continue. Ruth's four sons would feel the same way about their wives. Raven shuddered to think of what Blade would do to anyone who threatened Sierra; his fury would have no equal.

Of course, Duncan didn't feel the same way about her that those men did about their wives, but he did care. He'd protect her even if it meant earning her anger.

And she'd just hurt him. Misery knotted her stomach. She went in search of Rooster, finding him in the middle of sorting bath towels, sheets, and clothes, with a bewildered frown on his face. "I'd like to call Duncan on the radio."

Rooster scrutinized her features, then handed her the radio. "We're all on the same frequency so the boss knows what's going on."

In other words, be careful what you say. "Thank you—for everything." She turned on the radio. "Duncan, come in, please. Over."

"Duncan," came the terse answer.

"You were right. I'll be helping Rooster today. Over," she said, accepting he had a right to be a bit put out with her.

"Thanks for the call. Over."

"Over and out," she said, and handed the radio back to Rooster. "Let's get this laundry sorted; then I have to make a phone call."

Chapter 10

Sorting laundry with Rooster hadn't lasted long. The first time Raven picked up Duncan's T-shirt, Rooster had declared he could do it himself. He'd actually blushed. She'd made a huge chart on how to sort whites from dark and on water temperature, made sure he knew how to measure detergent. Then she'd gone to her room to call Blade Navarone. She paced as the phone rang, once, twice.

"Blade."

"Good morning, Blade. Raven La Blanc. . . . I've run into a situation here. There's a possibility of a mountain lion in the area of the cave. Duncan put it off-limits this morning."

"As well he should have."

Raven had expected the answer. "I'm aware of the expense you've already incurred, but I wondered if you were able to contact someone who could set up a perimeter around the cave to alert me if a large animal approached the mouth of the cave. I could work inside, and Duncan wouldn't worry."

"Have you discussed this with Duncan?" Blade asked

"No, I wanted to see if it was possible first," she said, already knowing it was. A billionaire and powerful man like Blade had to have top-notch security. She'd learned a lot more then just self-defense from her brother, who was an Army Ranger.

"I wouldn't like it if anyone made a security decision for my property without consulting me."

Duncan wouldn't, either. She'd accept the veiled reprimand if it would allay Duncan's fears and get her back into the cave. "I'll talk to him when he returns to the ranch house, but that might not be until late."

"If you don't mind, I'd rather talk to him. If he has any questions, I can answer them."

She'd been pushed out of the loop. *Men.* She idly wondered if he tended to push his wife, Sierra, out of the loop. Probably not. Sierra wasn't the kind of woman to be pushed, not even by the man she loved. "Of course. I'll get his cell phone number and call you back."

"I'll look for your call."

"Thank you, Blade. Bye."

"Bye."

Raven hung up the phone and headed downstairs to get the information from Rooster, hoping he wasn't in the midst of sorting Duncan's briefs. She paused on the stairs thinking maybe he wore boxers. Shaking her head, she continued. No, Duncan was definitely the briefs type.

If she and Duncan kept being at odds with each

other, the chances of her ever finding out if she was right were slim to none.

A short while after Duncan spoke with Raven, he watched his cattle graze contentedly. The bone-chilling, snowy winter that had made life so difficult a few months back had also provided water from the snow melting in the mountains and helped the lower grasslands flourish in the summer.

When winter arrived again, the hay and alfalfa he'd planted would see the livestock through. He'd planned for every contingency in his life, except one. Raven La Blanc. She was passionate, stubborn, and fiercely independent.

She probably didn't realize how much the call from her meant. Her angry words to him at the ranch house had cut deeply. No matter how hard he tried, he hadn't been able to get the stinging announcement that she loathed him out of his mind. His hands clenched on Black Jack's reins, causing the stallion to sidestep. Reaching down, he patted the horse's strong neck in reassurance.

"We both know how a female can mess up your day, heck, your life."

Duncan wasn't sure when it had happened, but her opinion of him mattered. He cared about her. The realization didn't disturb him as much as it once might have.

Caring about a person didn't mean that there wouldn't be upheavals, words spoken in haste. Some were able to get past it; others went their separate ways. He understood that better than Raven. Whatever it was between them wouldn't endure the many unexpected obstacles life placed in their paths.

She wanted independence, her dream. He wanted her safe and accepted that her dream meant she'd leave at summer's end. When that time came, he just hoped they wouldn't part in anger.

His cell phone rang. Unclipping it from his belt, he wished again that they made an earpiece that would let his Stetson fit his head properly. "Duncan."

"Hello, Duncan, this is Blade Navarone."

A frown darted across Duncan's brow. He'd briefly met Blade when he and Sierra attended Cameron's wedding. As he knew Blade wanted, neither had spoken of Blade's intervention in helping Duncan obtain the loan from the bank to buy the Double D.

The day Duncan had gone in to sign the papers, he'd overheard the president of the bank tell the loan officer to give Mr. McBride unlimited credit and that Mr. Navarone wanted his name kept out of it. Duncan had known immediately that Faith was behind Blade's involvement.

They'd been in her office at the hotel the day before when the bank had called to tell Duncan his loan had been denied. He was heartsick. He didn't have any other options to obtain the money. He certainly wasn't going to let Faith take a loan out on the family hotel.

The next day, he'd received a call from the chief loan officer saying the bank had reevaluated his application and his loan had been approved. At the time he'd been too grateful to question his good fortune. Arriving at the bank, he thought they were falling over themselves to be nice to him because of the size of his loan.

He owed the real estate mogul a huge debt of gratitude. "Hello, Blade."

"Through Mrs. Grayson I became Raven's sponsor for her to authenticate the cave drawings on your property. She contacted me this morning to tell me that a mountain lion was spotted in your area, and your very appropriate way of handling the situation," Blade said.

Duncan's grip on the phone eased. He had been waiting for Blade to say he had overreacted so he could tell him that he didn't run his ranch, but there had to be more to the phone call. Blade Navarone didn't do chitchat. "And?"

"I'd like to propose a proven way to ensure Raven's safety, which will allow her to continue working on the cave," Blade said.

"She doesn't want anyone watching over her," Duncan said, although he was considering the possibility. He didn't think Raven would comply with staying at the house for more than a couple of days. Then all bets would be off.

"Strong, independent women don't like depending on a man, and luckily for us in this case, a man won't be needed after everything is in place," Blade said.

"Everything?"

"With your permission, I'd like to send my head of security out to set up a secure perimeter around the cave. The wiring will be hot, but not enough to injure, just deter. If anything over fifty pounds touches the wire, an alarm will sound that will be heard as well as registered in the cave."

It sounded high-tech, elaborate, and expensive. "I'll foot the bill."

"I appreciate the offer, but it's part of ensuring Raven has what she needs to authenticate the caves," Blade responded. "I understand you have a landing strip. We can be there by this afternoon and get started immediately."

"You're coming as well?"

"With Raven's permission, I'd like to see the cave. Naturally, Sierra is coming with me, and Ruth would disown me if I didn't let her know so she can come. I've a feeling that Luke might want to come, and thus Catherine," Blade said casually.

Duncan had counted five people at a minimum. But what really stuck in his mind was that Blade and Luke expected and wanted their wives with them whenever possible. Both men were blessed and they knew it.

"I'll pick you up at the airport in Billings," Duncan said, heading toward the ranch. He wasn't sure what kind of shape the bedrooms were in. He *was* sure that Raven hadn't prepared enough in her slow cooker to feed that many people.

"We'll take the small jet and fly directly to your ranch, then off-load the equipment and drive to the cave," Blade explained. "I estimate our arrival time around six. Ruth has a class this afternoon."

"That won't give you a lot of time to work before dark." Duncan topped the rise and saw the ranch house and buildings.

"We work best in the dark. See you at six."

In a much better mood than when he had left, Duncan shut off the cell and continued down the hill. He owed Blade another debt of gratitude. He couldn't wait to see Raven's expression when he told her.

"I knew Blade would come through," Raven said, grinning up at Duncan.

Duncan's smile slowly ebbed. "You knew?" She bit her lips. Her gaze darted away. "Answer me."

"It was just a suggestion I made to Blade," she finally told him.

He shook his Stetson-covered head. "Here I thought I was telling you something you didn't know and it was your suggestion. I guess Blade is right. Strong, independent women don't need men. I better get back on the range."

Raven caught his arm. "Strong, independent women might not need a man, but it's wonderful having one in our lives who worries about us. With Sierra for a wife, I bet Blade would be the first person to agree."

Duncan relaxed. He was too sensitive where Raven was concerned. He didn't want to be around a woman who couldn't think for herself, but he admitted he wanted Raven to rely on him just a little bit. "Whatever is in your slow cooker isn't going to be enough to feed all the people who are coming."

She smiled up at him again. "Leave it to Rooster and me. We'll make you proud."

His knuckles brushed down her cheek. "I haven't a doubt."

* * *

Duncan and Raven were waiting with the truck and Jeep when the jet landed at the airstrip at six. The number of people coming now included Ruth's middle son, Brandon, and his wife, Faith, Duncan's sister. The first person off the plane was Sierra, followed by her mother, then Blade. Next came Catherine, Luke, and Rio, a man Raven had met twice and had yet to see smile.

"Welcome to the Double D." Duncan extended his hand to the men, greeted the women, and hugged his sister to him. Raven did the same. "I'm glad you could come."

Faith, pretty with a round face and figure, smiled up adoringly at her older brother. "I wouldn't have missed it. I'm just glad Sierra called."

Sierra, elegant and beautiful, waved her sister-in-law's words aside. "I knew you'd want to see Duncan." She lifted a perfectly arched brow and glanced at Brandon. "Although brothers can be trying at times."

Brandon laughed and threw one arm around Sierra's shoulder, the other around Faith's. "The next time, I'll track you down and ask if I can serve the last slice of coconut cake."

"See that you do," Sierra said, but a smile curved her lips.

"See what I had to contend with growing up?" Luke said.

"And you couldn't have been happier," Catherine, his wife, commented.

Ruth beamed proudly at her children. "Life was interesting."

"And even more so now." Sierra curved her arm around Blade's waist and stared up at him with complete love.

"I couldn't agree more." Blade turned to Duncan. "As soon as we finish unloading the equipment, we can go to the cave." He glanced at Rio putting a box in the back of the truck. "If he left us anything to unload."

"Ruth, wait until you see the drawings." Raven clutched the other woman's hand as the men moved to help Rio. "You'll get goose bumps. The presence of The People is still strong."

"I can't wait," Ruth said.

When they reached the cave, the women waited in the Jeep as Luke, Duncan, and Rio made a wide arch around the cave, checking for cat tracks.

"Duncan was right to be concerned. This is quite a distance from the ranch," Ruth said from the front passenger seat as they waited and watched.

Faith scooted forward in the backseat until she was inches from her mother-in-law. "Please don't worry. Every morning Duncan checks on the cave before Raven comes out."

"What?" Startled, Raven jerked around, barely noticing Sierra waving to the men that everything was all right.

The panicked expression on Faith's face was priceless. "I gather you weren't aware of what he was doing."

"No," Raven said, thinking of the extra time it took to come out to the cave twice a day. She looked at Duncan and experienced the familiar tug of her heart. "You have a wonderful, caring brother."

"I happen to think so," Faith said.

At the mouth of the cave, Duncan waved the women forward. They scrambled out of the Jeep. Raven felt the familiar surge of excitement as she and Duncan entered the cave ahead of the others. She and the men carried high-beamed lanterns, with Rio bringing up the rear.

No one spoke, as if in reverence of what they were about to see. Raven paused and reached her hand back for Ruth's. As soon as the other woman was beside her, Raven continued, holding the light waist high. Without her telling Duncan her intention, he followed suit.

In the midst of the drawings, Raven slowly raised her lantern. Images appeared. Ruth's hand clenched in Raven's.

"You were right, I can feel the Old Ones," Ruth said softly.

"The rock formation in this area is perfect for the Ancient Ones to have followed for food and water," Raven said. "I haven't been able to search the floor, but once I do, I'm hoping to find archeological objects that might have been covered by sediment or which haven't been taken by an animal."

"Have you been able to determine the source of the drawings?" Blade asked.

Raven looked over her shoulder. "Wood charcoal."

"From that you'll possibly be able to tell what type of vegetation grew in this area at that time," Duncan said.

Raven's gaze swung to his. "How did you know that?"

"Internet," he said succinctly.

Pleased that he had researched a subject important to her, she felt it was time. "Caves are usually named; this one is McBride's Lost Cave." Catching Duncan's startled expression, she started forward. "This is one more area I want to show you."

The stunned gasps were pretty much what Raven had expected at the appearance of the red dots. "I finally figured out they were created by the right hand. The lower ones were probably done by a small woman; the higher ones, by a man.

"And this is McBride's Wall of Panels." She held up the lantern for them to see the various three-dimensional drawings of animals and human forms.

"Master of Breath and God, thank you for allowing me to see this," Ruth whispered softly, and she grasped Duncan's hand. "Thank you for giving Duncan the wisdom and the caring heart to seek answers, to honor all people. Thank you, Duncan."

"Anyone would have done the same," Duncan said, obviously a bit embarrassed.

"They might have contacted an authority on wall paintings and cave drawings, but the reason could have been financial gain or notoriety or fame," Blade said. "You did it for the good of man."

"Duncan," Faith cried. "I'm so proud of you!"

"We all are," Luke said. "This is mind-boggling."

"And Raven gets to study it." Sierra glanced over her head at a drawing. "No wonder you wanted to get back to work. You have a very important task ahead of you."

"With Blade's help, I can. Thank you," she declared.

"This is too important not to complete and share with the world." Blade handed Sierra the lamp he held. "I'm going to help Rio."

Luke gave his lantern to Catherine. "I'll see if I can help."

Brandon hugged Faith. "I know I'll be useless, but I'm going anyway. Since I can't see in the dark, I'll take the lantern," he finished with a chuckle.

"I'm glad they're gone," Sierra said, holding her lantern closer to the drawing she had been studying. "In Santa Fe, Georgia O' Keeffe paintings are everywhere. This." She pointed to a three-dimensional drawing on a rock just above her head. "Am I crazy or is this what I think it is?"

"I had the same thought," Catherine mused.

"What thought?" Faith asked innocently.

"Tell them, Raven," Ruth said.

Raven looked behind them as if to ensure that none of the men had come back. "It seems O'Keeffe was hardly the first to draw female sexual organs."

"Oh my! I see it," Faith gasped after a moment.

"Imagine that," Sierra said with a chuckle. "Man hasn't changed his obsession in centuries."

"And he never will," Catherine offered.

"You all go on. I'm not leaving until I know it works," Duncan said, referring to the alarm system.

"It works," Blade said, and not for the first time.

"I'd rather see for myself." Duncan handed Blade his truck keys. He was thankful to Blade for help with the loan, for the security system, but Duncan wasn't budging. "It's dark. The women need to be inside. I can radio Rooster once the alarm sounds and meet my foreman away from the cave."

Blade, his features set, made no motion to take the keys. "If I didn't understand the reason for your concern . . ."

"Glad you do," Duncan said. It was obvious in the touches, the tender looks, that Blade loved Sierra.

Sierra rubbed her hand down Blade's arm. "I suppose you know Rio isn't here any longer."

Blade kept his gaze on Duncan. "He's gone to give Duncan proof. I suggest we put the women in the truck where they'll be more comfortable. We'll wait in the Jeep."

Duncan frowned. "The only way to do that is with a large animal."

"You'll have your proof." Taking Ruth's and Sierra's arms, Blade led them to the truck.

Duncan took Raven's arm and followed, giving her the keys. "Say it. I'm being overly cautious."

She waited until she reached the driver's side of the truck. "As I told Faith, she has a wonderful, caring brother." Climbing in, she closed the door.

Brandon clasped Duncan's tense shoulder. "I trust Blade completely. If it were any other situation except with Raven, you would, too. Maybe you've finally put the McBride curse behind you."

"I don't know what you're talking about," Duncan said.

"Leave him alone, Brandon." Luke opened the door of the Jeep and got into the backseat. "He might be slow like you were."

"Ha. Ha," Brandon mocked, but he joined Luke in the Jeep, leaving Blade and Duncan alone.

"I wish I could tell you that once you stop fighting it, your gut will settle, that you'll feel better when she's out of your sight, when she acts before she thinks," Blade said. "You won't, but you'll know happiness this side of heaven that few men have ever experienced."

Duncan, tired of people assuming because he cared about Raven that that was all it took for them to grab the brass ring of forever, walked to the Jeep and got in. Brandon, Luke, and Blade had found their fulfillment with the only women for them.

Duncan never would.

Less than fifteen minutes later, there came a loud yelp. Almost instantly, a piercing alarm sounded.

"You have your proof," Blade said, almost sounding bored. "We would have installed lights if we knew a demonstration was needed."

Duncan stared at Blade in disbelief. "That was a coyote."

"Yes, it was." Blade fastened his seat belt. "Let's go or the women will get too far ahead of us."

"What about Rio?" Duncan started the motor. After the equipment was unloaded, both vehicles were moved out of the perimeter of the alarm. The Jeep was left closer to the cave.

"In the back of your truck," Luke answered.

"Which is leaving us," Blade said.

"Sure hope you're not one of those men who dislike women driving their vehicles," Brandon lazily commented.

Duncan was, or he had been until Raven had barged into his life—despite it all, he had to admit as he followed the truck to the ranch, he would be forever grateful that she had.

Aware that they'd want to discuss the findings and could do so openly because Rooster had eaten early and gone to his place to give Duncan time to spend with his "company," Raven elected to serve hot roast beef sandwiches, buttered creamed potatoes, steamed broccoli, salad, and tomato soup. Among the buffet-style offerings were two desserts—bread pudding and a chocolate pie with a four-inch meringue top—because she couldn't decide which to prepare.

Making sure everyone was taken care of, Raven almost felt as if she and Duncan were a couple. He'd even sat by her as everyone ate scattered over the great room. She was pleased that whatever earlier tension between him and Blade was gone.

She thought everyone was having a good time—until she looked up and saw Rio off to himself, his expression unreadable. She would have thought him lonely, but there was a self-assurance about him that said he wouldn't be bothered by a weak emotion like loneliness.

But hadn't she thought she was self-sufficient and hadn't she been lonely?

"Thank you for a wonderful meal, but we better be getting back." Blade came to his feet, pulling Sierra with him.

"I know Ruth had called to say you were going back tonight, but since it is so late I thought you might change your mind and stay." Raven stood as well.

"I've logged a lot of hours flying at night since a certain woman came into my life." Blade's arm circled Sierra's waist.

"I'm learning to fly as well." Sierra grinned. "It will let us be able to do things at the spur of the moment without interrupting the pilot's life."

"I have to be at work in the morning," Faith said. "Brandon can sleep in."

He kissed her lips. "But I won't."

Ruth crossed the room to hug Raven and Duncan. "I'm proud and thankful for both of you."

"Thank you," they said.

"Thank you for allowing us to see the caves." Luke extended his hand to Duncan. "And remember what I said."

"Bye, Raven. You've been given an incredible opportunity." Catherine glanced at Duncan standing close to Raven. "I know you'll take advantage of it."

"I will. Bye." Raven felt Duncan shift restlessly beside her. She certainly planned to try. It remained to be seen how it would turn out.

Chapter 11

"Are you going to the party tonight?" Duncan asked. He stood a few feet away from Raven in the cave. Even with the security device, he continued to check on her daily. The alarm had sounded earlier that day, but when she'd gone to investigate she hadn't seen what had tripped the system. Since Duncan always checked the perimeter of the cave, the fact that he didn't seem worried and hadn't mentioned any concerns told her she was safe.

"Raven?" he urged.

Knowing Duncan was definitely going because of his friendship with Isaac, Raven had debated with herself all day whether she should go to Cynthia's party. "The only reason her father invited me is because I'm your houseguest."

"Isaac is a good man," Duncan said. "And you didn't answer my question."

She pushed up from the panel on the cave floor she'd been making notations on. "We both know she doesn't want me there."

"There'll be so many people there, you probably won't even see her," Duncan said. "You need a break."

"The same could be said for you," she said.

"Isaac is a friend. I'm going, but I'll also do my best to stay out of Cynthia's way," he admitted, his mouth compressed into a hard, flat line.

"She won't be the only one after you," Raven said, unable to keep the annoyance out of her voice.

"We both know there's only one woman I want." He tugged his Stetson. "I checked the perimeter and didn't see any cougar tracks. If one does wander into this area, the security system will scare it off."

She followed him out of the cave and watched him mount Black Jack. Duncan was always concerned for her. It went deeper than obligation, deeper than lust.

"Think about the party. You might have to come to my rescue again." Wheeling his stallion, he took off at a fast clip.

Raven realized she was smiling. Duncan had actually joked with her. Despite his wanting to keep their relationship compartmentalized, they continued to grow closer.

She'd done a lot of thinking about Duncan's statement that he hadn't been with a woman in over two years. There would be a lot of women at the party. A good number of them probably had designs on him.

He wasn't the kind of man to substitute one woman for another, so she didn't have to worry about that aspect. Still, she knew she wouldn't have a moment's peace if she stayed at the ranch. Perhaps in a social setting she'd help him see that he could take a chance on them. Looked like she was going to a party.

* * *

Duncan couldn't help but stare. In his lifetime he'd seen some awe-inspiring sights, but none compared to the woman at the top of the stairs. The white sundress, with slices of red and yellow, flared at the waist and stopped just above her knees, showing off incredible legs that he thought of more and more clenched around his waist, drawing him into her moist heat.

"You're beautiful."

Happiness swept through her. She wanted to be beautiful for him. "Thank you. You look incredible yourself." She stopped at the foot of the stairs. "Is Rooster going with us?"

"No, he left a little bit ago with friends." Duncan took her arm with a hand that wasn't quite steady. He had accepted that Raven affected him as no other woman ever had or would. She drew him with her strength, her caring nature, her stubbornness that rivaled his. "It will be just the two of us."

"Oh," she said

He grinned at her. "I'd promise to behave, but I don't like to lie."

"I never want to be the reason for you to lie." She grinned up at him.

Since Duncan didn't see any reason for waiting until they reached his truck, he pulled her into his arms and kissed her, his hand running over her soft skin and silken hair. He studied her. "You're going to create a sensation."

She laughed and pushed against his chest. "No one will even notice I'm there."

* * *

Being right wasn't any consolation to Duncan. Partygoers converged on them before they had gone ten feet. People, make that men, wanted to meet her, dance with her, get her a drink.

Her polite "no, thank you" didn't move them along. In less than thirty minutes, she had two plates, four glasses of wine.

"Excuse me, fellows, but Raven and I were about to dance." Not waiting for an answer, he led her to the dance floor, an area off the immense patio, and drew her into his arms. As always, she fit perfectly, as if she had been created just for him.

"I told you you'd create a sensation."

Her delicate brow lifted. "And women are waiting to get their chance with you."

He tsked. "Except for Cynthia, you're imagining things."

She shook her head, her unbound hair blowing in the slight wind. He caught the strands and curved them behind her ear, captured again by the silkiness of her hair, her skin. "Just look around you."

He kept his gaze trained on her. "I'm looking at the only woman I want."

The sudden softness in her face, in her eyes, made his gut clench. He'd give anything to keep this woman, to find the secret to keeping her happy. He wished he could kiss her, just a brush of his lips to let her know how much she appealed to him.

The music stopped. He'd never been much for dancing, but to keep Raven in his arms he'd dance all night.

"Duncan. Raven," Isaac greeted them. "Glad you made it."

Reluctantly Duncan released Raven and slid his arm around her slim waist. "Hello, Isaac. Half the county must be here."

He laughed jovially. "Probably more than that."

"Good evening, Isaac," Raven greeted him. "It's a wonderful graduation party. You must be so proud of Cynthia."

A moment of sadness touched his round face. "I am. I just wish her mother could be here."

"Millie would be proud," Duncan said, referring to Cynthia's mother, who had died of pneumonia when Cynthia was a senior in high school.

"That she would," Isaac agreed. "I'd better circulate, like Cynthia wanted."

"Good-bye, Isaac, and thanks again," Raven said.

A fast song ended and a slow one began. Duncan swung Raven into his arms.

"You already had one dance," Rooster greeted them, placing his hand on Duncan's arm. "If you don't mind, boss, I wanted to introduce Raven to some of my friends."

He did mind, but Raven had already turned to Rooster. "Rooster, remember our conversation."

He waved her words aside. "I never forget a thing. Ain't that right, boss?"

"Never," Duncan agreed, accepting that he wasn't going to be holding Raven anytime soon.

Rooster held out his arm. Raven curved hers through it. "We'll see you later."

Raven spoke over her shoulder: "Save me a dance."

Duncan watched Rooster, like a proud father, squire Raven across the wooden dance floor to a high table surrounded by several men from the Double D. In a matter of minutes, at least six other men joined them. One led her out onto the dance floor, then another and another as one song ended and another began.

Looked like he'd have a long wait before his dance . . . if he got one at all.

"She's making a spectacle of herself," Cynthia said. "People will talk."

Duncan whirled around so fast the young woman stepped back. He had been so engrossed in watching Raven that he had sent women on their way who wanted to talk, been less than friendly with ranchers. His entire focus had been Raven. He hadn't even heard Cynthia approach.

"If I hear one word, I'll know where it came from, and you, me, and your daddy will have a talk that you won't like," he warned.

Lips painted a shocking red tightened. "I can say what I please. This is my house. My daddy—"

"Should have said no to you long ago," Duncan said, cutting her off. "If he had, you wouldn't be so mean-spirited. You've changed in the past couple of years, and it hasn't been for the better. You're jealous because men are paying attention to Raven instead of to you."

"If anyone is jealous, it has to be you," she said, her voice quaking. "You can't take your eyes off her, and she hasn't looked your way once."

The truth didn't bother him as much as Cynthia pointing it out to him. He never wanted to be the target of gossip and speculation again. "Just remember what I said."

Not giving her a chance to answer, Duncan went to the jovial crowd surrounding Raven. She looked ethereal in the white strapless sundress, her hair flowing free. He wanted to strip the dress from her to see and taste the soft skin beneath, see her hair spread out on his pillow.

He was well aware that conversation abruptly ended when he approached. "I'm leaving. You ready, Raven?"

"She promised to teach me how to do the two-step," Billy said, his smile missing for once.

"I'll bring her, boss," Ramon said, slapping Billy on the back. "Billy dances like he has three left feet." All the men, including Billy, laughed.

Duncan kept his gaze on Raven. "Raven?"

She casually held up her full glass of wine. "It would be a shame to waste this. Plus I promised Billy, and I always keep my word."

Duncan had an urge to grab her by the arm and take her anyway. The thought shocked him, made him ashamed. He didn't manhandle women. "Stay as long as you want. Good night."

Duncan put one foot in front of the other and kept walking. If Cynthia had figured out he was jealous, there was a good possibility others had as well. One woman had stomped his pride in the mud in front of his friends; he wouldn't let another.

* * *

Surreptitiously Raven watched Duncan fade into the darkness. She had watched him most of the night, became jealous when woman after woman kept approaching him, especially Cynthia. She might be young and spoiled, but she had something Duncan valued, a connection to the land he loved and honored.

He wouldn't use the young woman to get to the land, but it could be a bridge, a starting point for them to build a relationship. Raven had nothing to offer but herself—and she wasn't even willing to give that.

"Ready to give me that lesson now, Raven?" Billy asked, his handsome young face anxious.

This was important to him. Raven thought she knew why. He'd been following Cynthia with a morose expression all night.

"Of course."

"I'll hold your wine until you get back," Ramon said. "Then it's my turn at a dance."

"Then mine," Terry, another hand at the Marshall ranch, said.

Raven never felt less like dancing. She smiled and allowed Billy to lead her to the wooden floor that had been erected for dancing. Duncan wasn't for her. For a while she had forgotten and let herself believe he was. She mustn't forget again.

"Billy, I think if you paid more attention to what you're doing, this would go a lot better," Raven said, trying not to wince as she felt the brush of Billy's boot against her foot. She certainly had picked the wrong time to wear sandals, but she had wanted to look feminine and desirable for Duncan.

That was her first mistake. Riding in the truck with just the two of them to the party was her second. She thought it would be fun. It was, but it made her more aware of him. Leaving with him would have been strike number three. She was too conscious of him.

If he kissed her like his eyes promised when he came for her just now, she would be in his bed before the night was over. A fission of heat coursed though her, causing her to tremble.

"Sorry, Raven." Billy lifted his contrite gaze to hers. "Maybe this was a bad idea."

"Depends," Raven said, trying to think of something else besides Duncan and the incredible way he made her feel. "Did you want to ask Cynthia for a dance or see if she'd notice you?"

He shook his head. "Dad always said women were smarter than men."

"Smart man, but you didn't answer my question," Raven said.

Billy scrunched up his face and finally gave up all pretense of dancing. "Can we walk over there?"

Raven started toward the end of the immense patio, away from the crowd of people and his friends. She stopped by a metal bench.

"Please have a seat," he said.

Raven sat. Billy was courteous, hardworking, and loyal. Cynthia could do worse.

"I met her in town a couple of weeks ago. She seemed interested and impressed that I graduated from the University of Texas until Ramon walked up and said we had to get back to work." He took off his hat to run his hand over his close-cropped black hair. "The other girls with her made disparaging sounds. She couldn't get to her convertible Benz fast enough. I haven't seen her again until tonight."

"I'm sorry, Billy, but if she's that superficial, you're better off without her," Raven said gently.

He plopped down beside her. "I know. I thought of telling her my dad is as rich as hers, maybe richer."

"Billy, lies never help."

He looked at her, then burst out laughing. Several people turned toward them. "You really don't know?"

She frowned. "Know what?"

"Both my parents come from oil and real estate," he told her with a smile. "They're partners in one of the top law firms in the state. I'm here for the summer; then I start law school in Dallas at SMU in the fall."

"You always wanted to be a cowboy," she said, recalling Duncan's story.

"Yeah. The wife of one of Mom's biggest clients heard me talking about it at a party and said she knew just the place." He shook his head. "A few days later I was on a plane to Billings. Mrs. Navarone works fast."

"What? Sierra, Blade's wife, is the reason you're here?"

"You know them?" he asked, the surprise on his face mirroring hers.

She laughed. "Meet a fellow benefactee. Blade is funding my research. I'm leaving at the end of summer as well."

"At least the boss will miss you. Cynthia could care less," he said, his shoulders slumped.

Raven thought of denying that Duncan would miss her, then decided it was probably best to let it pass. She placed her hand on Billy's shoulder. "I hear there are a lot of pretty girls in Texas, and just think, they're going to meet a real cowboy."

"Why didn't you say you liked them young and green?" Crane sneered. An almost empty glass of bourbon in his hand, he swayed unsteadily on his feet. "Does McBride know?"

Billy came to his feet. "You have a foul mind, Crane. Take it someplace else."

"Whooo, I'm scared," Crane said, and laughed.

Raven caught Billy's arm. "I only care about people's opinion of me that I respect. Let's join the others."

Crane's face harshened. "You—"

"Say it and you'll wonder what mountain fell on you," Raven said, her voice flat and cold.

He stepped back, glanced around. Several people were watching. Ramon and Rooster quickly closed the distance and positioned themselves in front of Raven. When Raven couldn't budge them, she stepped around them. "Good-bye, Crane. Walk away while you can."

Whirling, he quickly left. Raven faced the three angry men. "If one of you says a word to Duncan, you'll have me to deal with. Understood?"

"The boss would tear him apart if—"

"Ramon, I don't like repeating myself," Raven said.

"Menfolk take care of—"

She rounded on Rooster. "I am not some helpless woman. I can take care of myself. I thought we'd settled that."

"We know that, Raven, but when the boss hears about this, and believe me he will, Crane is going to wish he had never been born," Billy said, his gaze locked on Crane's fast-retreating back.

Since there were a couple of men from the Marshall ranch within hearing distance, she knew the story would eventually reach Duncan, but by then she hoped Crane would have the sense God gave a goose and make himself scarce.

"I'm going to thank the hostess and then we can leave." She looked each man in the eyes. "Crane might be an idiot, but we have better sense and more respect for Cynthia, her father and friends not to start a fight and mar a night they're celebrating."

"Leave it to a woman to tie a man's hands," Ramon said with regret. "We'll be good. The boss deserves the honor of putting Crane in his place."

"Ramon is right," Billy said. "I'm just hoping I'm there when it happens."

There it was again, the inference that she and Duncan were an item. Or was it simply because, as she was his houseguest, he was expected to take care of her? To her surprise, from Rooster there was nothing, which made Raven a bit uneasy.

Deciding not to look at Rooster to gauge his reaction, she went in search of Cynthia.

It took some doing, but Raven finally located Cynthia in her room. Raven knocked on the door she had been directed to by Cynthia's older sister, Michelle, who said Cynthia had gone upstairs to freshen her makeup.

"Come in."

Raven opened the door to find Cynthia with her back to the door, staring out a large window. Raven thought the pose odd. "Thank you, I'm leaving. It was a wonderful party."

The younger woman faced her, her dark eyes misty. "I knew you weren't any good when I first saw you. You want all the men after you." She sniffed. "This was my party and you ruined it for me."

Apologetic, Raven softly closed the door behind her. "I'm sorry, Cynthia. It wasn't my intention to cause you any distress."

Cynthia moved to stand in front of her. "Duncan will never love you."

Just hearing the words pierced Raven's heart, made her ache inside, left her without a comeback.

"You'll soon be gone and I'll still be here, my father's ranch still next to his," Cynthia said, her lower lip trembling.

Perhaps because her family had been cordial to Raven, perhaps because Cynthia had said nothing about loving Duncan, Raven said, "I'll be gone, but you can't make a man love you no matter how hard you try. A good man will let you down gently; a bad man will use you until nothing is left."

Raven opened the door. "Keep gauging a man by his bank account and not by his character, you'll have only heartache ahead. Good-bye."

Closing the door, she paused on seeing Michelle in the hallway. There was no way she hadn't heard.

"Thank you again. Good night." Quickly passing Cynthia's silent sister, Raven hurried down the stairs.

Going out the open door, Raven started down the lit path leading back to the patio. It looked as if she should have taken the advice she had given Rooster and the others and kept her mouth shut. She had made things worse, not better.

She heard a noise behind her a split second before a punishing hand grabbed her arm. She acted instinctively, kicking her foot backward. She connected solidly with something and heard a man's cry of pain followed by a curse. Free, she whirled to find Crane a few feet away from her on the flagstone path. Cursing, he held his leg.

"I should have aimed higher," she said.

"You almost broke my leg," he moaned.

"You shouldn't have grabbed me."

His head came up. He stared at her coldly and then came unsteadily to his feet. "You need a real man to teach you how to treat a man. Obviously, McBride doesn't have what it takes between the sheets."

Raven took a menacing step toward Crane. "Like Billy said, you have a foul mouth. Take it someplace else."

"Or what?" he challenged.

"Stay and find out," she said.

He stared at her a long time. "You're not worth the effort." Turning, he limped away.

"Nicely done."

Raven whirled to find Michelle on the path. One thing overrode everything else. "Please don't tell Duncan."

"I have to tell Father. What he does with the information is up to him," Michelle said.

Raven groaned.

"But since I followed you to ask you not to think harshly of Cynthia and to apologize for her bad behavior, I'll wait until the morning to tell Father," she said.

"Thank you, and you have nothing to apologize for," Raven said.

"We both know there is. We've spoiled Cynthia since Mama died, but the sweet young girl is still there," Michelle said softly. "She's still learning that beauty and money aren't a woman's most important assets."

Raven winced. "I shouldn't have spoken to her that way."

Michelle shook her dark head. "The truth sometimes hurts, but it's still the truth. I didn't speak when you came out of her room because it stunned me for a moment that Cynthia had changed so much. After tonight things are going to be different."

Looking at the tall, no-nonsense woman, Raven believed her. "Cynthia is lucky to have you."

Michelle laughed. "After our talk tonight, I hope she feels that way in the morning. Good night, and thank you for coming."

"Thank you. Good night." Raven continued down the path to the patio. At least she had tonight. Tomorrow, once Duncan learned about Crane, all hell was going to break loose.

Duncan stepped off the porch when he saw the headlights of Ramon's truck in the distance. In the past ten minutes Duncan had received three phone calls. With each one, his temper had accelerated.

He stopped in the middle of the driveway. The paved drive was wide enough for Ramon to go around him, but Duncan knew he wouldn't. Sure enough, the Silverado stopped. Doors slammed as the four people Duncan had been waiting to see climbed out of the truck.

"Problems, boss?" Ramon asked.

"Is everything all right?" Raven asked, reaching him seconds behind Ramon and Billy, and only because they were on the driver's side. Rooster reached them last.

"Come inside." Duncan went back into the house without waiting for them, knowing they'd follow.

Duncan faced them in the middle of the great room. He controlled his temper by sheer force of will. "Is there something one of you would like to tell me?"

They traded worried stares. All three men looked at Raven.

"We had a great time at the party," Raven said.

His hands flexed. He'd bet their silence was Raven's doing. He wouldn't have put it past her to threaten them. "Rooster, Ramon, Billy, do you have anything to say?"

Their eyes darted to Raven again. His men were loyal. Yet Raven seemed to have eclipsed their loyalty. "I'm not going to ask again."

Raven threw up her hands in obvious annoyance. "I can't believe it. Men are bigger gossips than women around here."

Duncan waited.

"It might help if you'd tell us what you're referring to," she said.

Duncan looked at Rooster.

"Crane was drunk and shot off his mouth," Rooster said. "Raven put him in his place."

Duncan moved fast. "Where were you? Why didn't you protect her?"

"Because I can take care of myself," she said, stepping in front of Duncan, ignoring his hard glare. "And I made them promise not to. Crane might be a jerk, but I didn't want anything to mar Cynthia's night."

"He insulted you."

"And I insulted him right back, which, to a coward like Crane, will hurt a lot worse," she said.

"You should have let them take care of it," he said, his anger escalating again.

"Duncan, listen to me for once. My brother is an Army Ranger. He taught my sister and me how to take care of ourselves." She stepped closer, into his space. "Crane came out the loser. When he sobers up and remembers that he tucked his tail and ran from a woman, he won't be able to hold his head up."

"I plan to give him another reason for not being able to hold his head up." To the men Duncan said, "I don't want Crane near her again."

"Dun—" Raven began.

"Yes, boss."

"You got it."

"I told her."

Raven glared at Rooster for that last comment. Like Duncan, it bounced off the older man.

"Good night, men."

"Good night, boss," they said, and then quickly filed out of the house.

Raven knew she wouldn't get off so easily. She didn't even want to think of how Duncan would react when he learned Crane had grabbed her.

"When will you learn that you are not invincible?" Duncan lectured.

She was ready for him. "I never thought I was. But I have a black belt in karate, and can shoot a handgun or rifle with accuracy. Crane would have come out the loser."

Duncan moved with startling speed, his hand reaching for her. Her hand came up, deflecting his, then coming up with her other hand toward his face. The maneuver was blocked.

Raven crouched, spun, her left leg sweeping outward, knocking Duncan's feet from beneath him. She smiled in triumph, then had to scramble backward as he managed to balance himself. She bumped into a table, looked around, and he was on her. They tumbled onto the leather sofa, Raven on the bottom.

Air rushed in and out of her lungs. She didn't know if it was because of the brief fight or because her dress had come up to the middle of her thighs and Duncan lay between them, his hands holding hers over the top of her head.

"If I hadn't bumped into the table you would be on your back by now," she predicted.

"If you didn't have on a skirt and distracted me with your long, endless legs, you would have been exactly where you are now, but quicker," he told her.

"Get off," she said, bucking her body.

Air hissed though his teeth. "If you don't want me buried deep inside you in the next five seconds, don't do that again."

Raven was caught between temptation and annoyance. Annoyance won. "Then get off me." She tried to put some bite in her words but knew she failed miserably. With each breath that seemed to grow more labored, the arousing scent of him, the heavenly weight of his body pressed against her, lured her and teased her senses.

Muttering, he stood, turning his back to her. It took her a moment to regain her equilibrium. When she did she shoved her skirt down and stood.

"Go to bed, Raven."

She started to tell him that nothing was settled, but then he turned. In his eyes she saw the barely leashed passion he'd spoken of earlier. He'd held himself back from making love to her with the sheer force of his will.

If it slipped . . .

Grabbing her purse, she hit the stairs running.

Chapter 12

Raven left her room shortly after ten the next morning. She'd overslept. After leaving Duncan, she hadn't been able to fall asleep. After putting on her nightgown, she'd simply sat on the side of the bed.

She heard his steps on the stairs a little after two that morning. She'd finally crawled under the covers, aware that she had been waiting for the sound. Part of her wanted to go to him, to ease the almost constant ache deep inside her, but common sense prevailed.

Until Duncan believed in what they had more than his past failures or any curse, they were doomed.

She wasn't sure what time she finally fell asleep, but it hadn't been a peaceful sleep. She'd awakened after nine feeling restless and on edge.

In jeans and a top, she went downstairs to cook breakfast. She had no idea if work on the ranch allowed Duncan to attend church weekly, but if he did go today she planned to be with him. She didn't think she could keep Isaac from telling Duncan what

Crane had done, but she hoped she could deflect Duncan's anger.

He was leaving Crane alone.

Crane was a fake. She didn't recall seeing him last week at church, and the chance that he'd wake up with a hangover and decide to attend this morning wasn't likely. But he might put in an appearance later that day in town. Last Sunday they hadn't left the restaurant until after three. If he did show, Raven wanted to be with Duncan.

She had just taken the biscuits out of the oven when Duncan, followed by Rooster, came into the kitchen. Seemed she wasn't the only one who planned to stick close to Duncan today.

She placed the biscuits on the bread tray she had ready and picked up the platter of meat and fried potatoes. "Good morning."

"Morning," Duncan greeted her, his eyes watchful as if he'd figured out what she had planned and he didn't like it.

Tough.

Rooster rubbed his hands and then went to get mugs for him and Duncan. "Smells good, Raven."

She placed the food on the table. "I'll get the coffee, Rooster."

"I'll get it," Duncan said, going to the cabinets. "Where is your chocolate?"

"I ran out," she said, taking her seat.

"She used it to cook that chocolate pie the other night," Rooster said.

Duncan paused. "You always take care of us."

She shrugged. "Cooking relaxes me."

His hooded gaze studied her a long time. "You want coffee?" He frowned. "Is there juice?"

Rooster's face was just as puzzled. "Don't know."

Raven smiled. They'd be lost when she left. Her smile vanished. She tucked her head so Duncan wouldn't see her face. "There is apple juice. I'd like a glass please."

Duncan placed the tall glass of apple juice by her plate, then got his and Rooster's coffee. She didn't relax until he said grace.

Picking up her fork, she looked across the table and straight into Duncan's eyes. Her breath caught. For a split second, his eyes were unguarded. She glimpsed the same hot passion in his eyes she'd seen last night, as though he'd like to taste her skin all over and start again—like—

"Raven, you all right?"

Startled, she glanced at Rooster. "I— I— Yes." Putting her fork down, she picked up her juice. "I was just thinking."

Rooster looked doubtful, but he gave his attention to the platter of food Duncan stuck under his nose. "These sure are good biscuits."

Raven mumbled thanks and kept her head down. Duncan was too compelling, the strength and the power of him too great, the fierce need he incited in her to give in to him growing stronger each time she saw him.

She wondered how much longer she could withstand the growing need to yield to those desires.

* * *

Raven thought it couldn't happen, but even more people came up to her at church to introduce themselves. With each handshake or hug, congratulating her on how she'd put Crane in his place, Duncan grew stiller. All Raven could think of was that she was glad they didn't seem to know about her second encounter with Crane.

Thankfully, Raven and Duncan didn't see Isaac and his family until they were seated. Reverend Radford might have spoken on turning the other cheek, but from Duncan's clenched jaw he wasn't listening.

Afterward, she had tried her best to get him to return to the ranch, but Duncan insisted on buying her and Rooster lunch. Since the last time he hadn't wanted to stay in town to eat, she knew he was waiting on Crane.

From the watchful looks of the other diners, they were waiting and hoping for the same thing. Even Ramon, Billy, and Pete from the Double D were in the restaurant, which was considerably busier than last Sunday.

She was glad to see Rooster finally scrape the last crumbs of apple pie from his plate so they could leave. She didn't release the death grip on her purse until they were in the truck heading back to the ranch.

Duncan abruptly pulled into a parking space in front of Harold's. She sat up arrow straight. "Why are we stopping at the grocery store?"

"Cocoa," he said, opening his door.

"I can do without," she said. His door closed and he started inside.

Rooster opened his door. "Might as well get a few things." He sauntered into the store behind Duncan.

Raven got out of the truck to hurry Rooster along. A promise of anything sweet should do it.

She closed her door, stepped on the sidewalk, and couldn't believe her eyes. Crane, strutting as if he owned the world, was coming down the street toward her. She jerked her head in the direction of the store in front of her. Duncan was at the cash register.

Indecision held her still. Would it be better to warn Crane or to keep Duncan busy?

Apparently Crane recognized her, because his strides increased. The door of the store behind her opened and Duncan came out.

"Raven!" Crane cried, increasing his strides.

Raven couldn't believe any man could be that stupid. "Duncan, let's go."

"Hold this." Duncan shoved the cocoa into her hands. She held the sack with one hand, Duncan with the other.

Perhaps Crane wasn't as stupid as she thought. He stopped several feet away and visibly swallowed. "I said some things last night that I regret. I ask your forgiveness. It was the alcohol."

Duncan started for Crane, stopped, and stared down at Raven holding his arm. "Let go of my arm."

"No," she said.

"Let him take care of the polecat," Rooster advised, a paper sack clutched in his arms.

"We're going back to the ranch." Raven tugged at Duncan's arm. It would have been easier moving a mountain.

"McBride, I hope we can still do business," Crane said, trying to smile.

"You're either a fool or stupid," Duncan rasped. "Maybe both. I'm giving you warning, set foot on the Double D at your own risk. Bother Raven and there won't be a place on this earth you can hide from me."

Crane swallowed hard. "You can't mean that. No woman is worth—"

Duncan started for Crane. Raven dropped her purse and the sack Duncan had given her and held on to his arm with both hands. "Turn me loose."

He tried to pry her hands away, but the moment she said, "Ouch!" he jerked his hand away. Raven didn't mind playing dirty. He was not getting into a fight.

"Once you wipe up the sidewalk with him, then what?" she questioned.

"I'll let you know when I'm finished."

"What he said doesn't matter," she said. "If you hit him, it will."

"That doesn't make sense," he said.

"It's the way I feel." She took a chance and let him go and said for his ears only, "Does what he says or what I think matter most?"

Duncan's chest heaved in and out, his black eyes narrowed. He spun toward Crane. Raven clenched her hands to keep from grabbing him again. She'd gambled and lost.

"You get a pass today because the woman you thought to belittle has more compassion in her than scum like you can imagine," Duncan bit out. "But don't press your luck. Stay off my land and out of both of our way."

"That goes for me, too." Isaac Marshall stepped beside Duncan. "You insulted a guest in my home. Worse, it was a woman. We honor and take care of our womenfolk here. You crossed a line."

Crane's eyes widened. "Isaac, let's talk about this. Elks Ridge and you stand to make a great deal of money."

"Money don't mean squat without a man's self-respect," Isaac told him. "I can't do business with a man I don't respect, and that goes for his company as well."

Raven watched as several men and women gathered around them. The community of Elks Ridge had closed around Duncan. She slipped her hand into his, felt his tighten.

Crane visibly gulped. "You-you can't mean that. We were about to sign contracts. I've already advised my company. They are expecting—"

Isaac turned his back on Crane while he was speaking. "I'm sorry, Miss La Blanc, for everything."

"Please call me Raven, and there is nothing to apologize for," Raven quickly said, hoping this was the end of it and he wouldn't tell Duncan about Crane's second attempt to bother her.

"Thank you, Raven." Isaac faced Duncan. "You were right about Crane. He fooled me."

"Because you wanted what's best for the town," Duncan said. "You'll find another way to help the economy."

Isaac nodded, tipped his hat. "I better get home."

People around them moved away. She and Duncan started back to the truck. Rooster handed her her handbag and held on to the package Duncan had thrust at her. As Duncan pulled away from the curb, she glimpsed Crane standing in the street alone.

Pure hatred stared back at her.

Monday afternoon Raven answered the front door and saw the last person in the world she expected. "Hello, Cynthia. Duncan isn't here."

"I came to see you."

Puzzled, Raven stepped back and closed the door behind the young woman. "Can I get you anything to drink?"

"No. I'd just rather say what I have to say and leave," she said, her hand clamped on the small black Dolce & Gabbana handbag.

"All right." Raven waved the young woman to a seat in the great room.

She shook her head. "This won't take long. I'm sorry for the things I said Saturday night. I ask your forgiveness."

Raven studied the younger woman. It wasn't difficult to see she was there under duress. "Did your father or sister make you come?"

Her chin lifted. "Both."

"The consequences must have been dire," Raven said.

"You might think me spoiled, but I love my family." She momentarily looked away. "Neither my father nor my sister was happy that I had been rude to a guest. Father was annoyed with me and furious with Crane. He was ready to track him down and tell him off. Duncan gave him the opportunity to do just that."

Raven wrinkled her nose. She'd like to forget the incident. Duncan still wasn't pleased with her because he hadn't been able to hit Crane. He hadn't spoken two words to her after they'd returned Sunday afternoon.

She hadn't seen him at all today, although she had caught a flash of light in the trees and had known he was checking on her. He might be annoyed with her, but he'd never shirk his duty.

"Crane's bad behavior made me see how badly I had behaved. I don't want my family turning against me."

Raven looked at the other woman with growing respect. "They aren't likely to call to ask me if you apologized. You didn't have to do it."

"They'd know."

Raven had to smile. "Parents have a way of knowing. I accept your apology. You're sure you wouldn't like something to drink before you leave?"

"No, thank you. Good-bye."

"Good-bye." Raven followed Cynthia to the door. She started down the steps, then stopped. Raven's gaze followed the direction of Cynthia's gaze and saw Billy, his shirt off, rolling a wheelbarrow from the stable. Raven made a quick decision.

"Would you like to see the new foal? He's beautiful."

"The one everyone is talking about that you helped deliver?" she asked, a hint of annoyance in her voice.

"Rooster's doing," Raven confessed. "The truth is Duncan did all the work. It won't take but a minute."

"I suppose."

Cynthia might not sound interested, but her gaze remained on Billy as he worked. Together, the two women walked to the stable. The moment they entered, they heard Billy whistling as he worked. "Hello, Billy. Look who stopped by."

The young man's head came up. He started toward them, then stopped as if he remembered he had a pitchfork in his hand and the job he had been doing. "Hello, Cynthia."

"Hello, Billy." She moistened her lips. "Where's the foal?"

"The fifth stall," Raven said. While Cynthia walked ahead, Raven motioned for Billy to wash up and then join them. Finally, he seemed to understand.

"Excuse me." Leaning the pitchfork against the wheelbarrow, he headed for the back of the barn to the sink. Raven noticed Cynthia paid more attention to him than Midnight.

"I suppose you've been around horses all of your life and have your own?"

"What? Oh yes, a thoroughbred named Sheba." She glanced toward the direction Billy had taken. "Daddy bought her for me for my eighteenth birthday."

"You're fortunate to have a father who cares about you and wants the best for you," Raven said. Her father loved his children, but each one of them had to find their own way and that was exactly what she was doing.

"My sister reminded me of that yesterday."

Raven saw Billy come running back to them, buttoning his shirt. "Good timing, Billy. I need to finish doing some research. Billy can walk you to your car."

"Sure," Billy said, a wide grin on his face.

"Good-bye, Cynthia. Come back anytime."

"Good-bye," she said, but her attention was on Billy.

Raven left them alone. Billy had another chance. She hoped he was smart enough to capitalize on it. Glancing over her shoulder, she saw them standing close. Yep, Billy was a smart young man.

Duncan dismounted and led Black Jack into the barn. It had been a long, tiring day, yet he couldn't get Raven out of his mind. He still couldn't understand why she wanted to protect scum like Crane.

He took his hat off to any man who understood women. He was afraid he never would.

He took two steps inside the barn before he saw the open stall door. He took off running, knowing Belle and Midnight would be gone.

He turned in a circle, hoping against hope that Billy had moved them while he cleaned the stall. They weren't there.

Jerking his cell phone from his belt, he called Billy. After five rings it went into his voice mail: "Belle and Midnight are missing. Call me." Putting his cell phone away, he picked up his radio.

"Ramon. Where's Billy? Belle and Midnight are missing."

"Missing? Billy completed his chores an hour ago and went to the movies on a date," Ramon said. "I'm on my way to the barn."

"Alert all the men." Duncan looked at the full moon. "We're going to go after them. Tell the men to bring their rifles." Duncan dragged the saddle off Black Jack, then started for the shed and the ATV. He glanced toward the house and pulled up short.

Raven's Jeep wasn't there. That was all he needed. Pulling his radio from his belt, he hurried to the shed. "Rooster, I thought you said Raven came home. Her Jeep isn't out front."

"She lent it to Billy to go on his date," Rooster answered. "What's the matter?

Seated on the ATV, Duncan started the motor. "Bring my rifle and a lantern and tell her to meet me in the front. Belle and Midnight are gone."

Ramon entered the shed and got on the other ATV. "The men are saddling up. I called the rest of the men off-duty and told them to come back. We'll find them."

Duncan didn't say anything. Midnight was still unsteady. If he broke his leg— Duncan roared out of the shed and saw Raven running toward him.

"Oh, Duncan, I'm sorry. What happened?"

"Do you know where Billy went?"

"The movies. I let him take my Jeep."

"Call until you find him. I want to know the last time he was in the barn," Duncan said.

"About thirty minutes before he left," she told him. "He was hurrying to get through so he wouldn't be—" Raven stopped abruptly.

Duncan's mouth flattened in a hard line. "And left the stall door open."

"Duncan—"

"Here are your rifle and the lantern," Rooster said. "I can go with you."

"Stay here and take care of things." Duncan put the rifle in a specially built holder. "When you find Billy, tell him—," he muttered, then sped off, Ramon and the men following.

"The boss doesn't blow often, but when he does, it's best to stand back," Rooster said from beside her.

"Billy wouldn't have left the stall door open for anything," she said, worried about the mare and foal, concerned for Duncan and Billy.

"He might if his mind was on something else. We both know it was."

"We've got to help."

"They took all the automobiles and the horses in the barn except Black Jack, and no one can ride him except the boss," Rooster grumbled. "Leaving me here like I can't help. I should be there with him."

"I'm not sitting here doing nothing when Duncan needs me," she said, going back into the house. "I'm finding Billy."

"You do that. I can try to find some of my friends, but if you can find Billy, he might be closer. With your Jeep, we could go help search," he said, following her into the house.

"It's worth a try." She ran up the stairs for her cell.

"I don't remember closing the stall door, but I'm sure I did," Billy said. "The boss has to believe me. He loves that mare and foal."

"It's not your fault," Cynthia said from the backseat, shining the high-beam flashlight into the thick darkness on the right side of the Jeep. Billy shone his on the left side.

Raven didn't say anything, just continued. Rooster had insisted on searching in her Jeep. With his poor eyesight, she couldn't allow him to go by himself. Billy wasn't about to stay, and neither was Cynthia.

Raven had radioed Duncan that they were all out searching. Her hands gripped the wheel. He'd tersely told her to go back to the ranch house and take Billy with her; he'd done enough. The thought of complying never entered her mind.

She went over another rut; down and out of a shallow ditch, glad she had new tires. A sudden growl in the darkness cut through her.

"Cat," Rooster muttered. "Over there."

Raven turned the Jeep in that direction, then turned up the radio, hoping to scare the animal away, praying Belle and Midnight were all right. "Cynthia, call Duncan on the radio, then keep your lights high in the trees. Rooster, you and Billy shine yours to the right and left of the headlights."

"I see headlights," Cynthia said. "Duncan didn't answer. That could be my father and his men coming to help."

"Keep trying to get Duncan on the radio." Raven kept her hands gripped on the steering wheel. Isaac was a good man, as Duncan had said. Out here when a man was in trouble, his neighbors came without being asked.

"There!" Billy shouted. "Belle."

Raven jerked the steering wheel, jostling everyone. The mare was running all out. Midnight wasn't with her and couldn't have kept up if he were.

The radio crackled. "Hello," Cynthia answered.

"The boss said to stop and cut your motor," Ramon ordered.

Raven wanted to ask why, to argue. She did neither. This was Duncan's area of expertise, not hers.

As soon as she did, she heard a piercing whistle. Belle kept running. The whistle came again. The mare slowed, finally pulled up.

"Duncan trained that mare from a filly," Rooster murmured.

"But where is the foal?" Cynthia asked.

There was total silence. Raven felt tears crest in her eyes.

"My fault," Billy said. "My fault."

"We'll find Midnight," Raven said, with more assurance than she felt.

In the lights of the automobiles, she saw Duncan slowly walking to Belle, his hand outstretched. The horse kept shying away.

"Something spooked her bad," Rooster said.

Raven put the Jeep into gear. "Duncan can handle this. We need to keep searching for Midnight. Billy, did you see the direction which Belle came from?"

"Over there, due east toward those trees in the distance."

"Billy, radio Ramon where we're heading," Raven told him.

Rooster ran his hand over the rifle butt in his lap.

Billy stood up. "Through those trees." He glanced

down at Cynthia. "You scoot in front of me and stay there. And please don't argue."

Raven glanced in her mirror to see Cynthia do as she was told. They hadn't gone a mile before they heard the cat scream again.

"It's prowling and running from the noise," Rooster said.

They came to thick underbrush. Raven started to go around, but then she heard a sound and switched off the engine. This time she clearly heard the frightened whinny of a young horse.

"Midnight!"

Raven grabbed Rooster's arm as he started to get out. "You stay here with Cynthia." Raven stepped out of the Jeep.

"Billy, stay here with Cynthia." His face full of resolve, Rooster rounded the Jeep. "Two pairs of eyes are better than one. I'm going."

Raven reached for the rifle he held. With his poor eyesight she couldn't let him go alone. She didn't want to hurt his pride by pointing that out.

"I should be going. This is my fault," Billy said, his voice strained and quivering.

"And Cynthia is your responsibility, and arguing is wasting time." Raven turned to Rooster. "Let's go get Midnight."

Rooster nodded and picked up the lantern from the floorboard. Together, they entered the dense area of brush and trees.

Chapter 13

Duncan held the radio with one hand and drove with the other. "Tell Raven and Rooster to wait until I get there."

"Boss, they're already gone. I would have gone, but I couldn't leave Cynthia," Billy said, clearly upset with the way things were going.

"I could have gone," Duncan heard Cynthia say.

"Drive the Jeep as close as you can to the trees. Keep the lights on and honk the horn every thirty seconds," Duncan told Billy. If the cat they heard was anywhere around, the noise should scare it off, unless it had a fresh kill. The cat would fight to protect it.

"Is Belle all right?" Billy asked, his voice tentative and unsure.

"As far as I can tell," Duncan said. Part of him wanted to hurl blame, but the most important thing was finding Raven, Rooster, and Midnight. "I'm almost there."

Duncan came over a rise and gunned the ATV. Just behind him were his men and Isaac with a few of his hands. Duncan had sent Ramon back to the stable with Belle. He had wanted to argue, but Duncan hadn't the time.

Stopping beside the Jeep, Duncan reached for his rifle and lantern, then stepped from the ATV.

"They went in dead center. We haven't heard anything," Billy said as Duncan approached. "I've been blowing the horn."

Duncan thought of a cat protecting its kill. "Stay here." He could tell Billy didn't like it any more than Ramon had. Duncan stepped into the underbrush. "Raven. Rooster."

He hadn't gone very far when he heard a noise behind him. He turned to see Billy.

"Mr. Marshall is with Cynthia. I can hold the flashlight, just in case."

The growl of a cat pierced the night. Duncan thrust the light at Billy and took off running, fighting underbrush, jumping logs. "Raven! Rooster!"

"Raven! Rooster!" Billy called from beside Duncan when possible or just behind when they had to be in single file.

"Raven!" Duncan called. He stepped over a fallen log and heard the colt's whinny. "That way."

They hadn't gone more than fifteen feet when they heard the cat's growl again. Their light intersected with another beam of light to reveal a large mountain lion perched on a limb. "Stay here and keep that light on it."

Duncan sighted the cat with his rifle, then moved cautiously forward. "Raven, slowly back away and come around behind me."

Waiting until the beam of the other light became fainter was the most difficult thing Duncan ever had to do. If the cat decided to jump once they were out of sight, it wasn't likely it would follow them or come at Duncan and Billy. But cats were unpredictable.

The mountain lion raised on its haunches. Duncan took the slack out of the trigger. "Stay there," he whispered to the animal.

"Duncan."

Raven. Relief flooded him. "Billy, get them back to the Jeep. I'll follow."

"Dun—"

"Go!" The light wobbled, then steadied. "Billy, when I give an order I expect it to be carried out."

The light remained fixed. As the cat leaped to the ground Duncan cursed. He turned to back up slowly and stared into Raven's face. Cursing wouldn't do any good. He simply caught her by the arm and began to move, yelling and making noise. Moments later it was joined by honking horns and blaring radios.

"They made it back," Raven said, clearly relieved.

Duncan was too angry to say anything. He was furious with Raven for putting herself in danger. He didn't breathe easier until he stepped in the clearing where all the vehicles were parked.

"Dun—"

"Why can't you listen and do as I say for once! I could have handled this! All you did was get in the way and make things worse!"

Her eyes were huge in her face. "I only wanted to help."

"I don't need your help! I don't need you!"

She flinched. Wordlessly she turned and walked away. It was only then that Duncan became aware that they had an audience and there was condemnation in the eyes of those watching.

He'd never felt lower. He wanted to go to Raven and beg her forgiveness, but that would have to wait. He needed to find Midnight, but all he seemed to be able to do was watch as Raven backed the Jeep up and drove off. His gut in knots, he had started to turn toward the trees when he heard the soft whinny.

"Midnight!" He rushed over to the colt and knelt down, his eyes and hands going over the trembling animal, looking and feeling for injuries.

Rooster stood beside the colt with a belt looped around his neck. "It was Raven's idea to search for him in the direction we saw Belle run from once she saw that you could handle Belle. She was right on the money." He stared down into Duncan's face.

"Raven found him tangled up. He wouldn't lead and he was too jittery for me to carry by myself, so she helped. We spotted the cat the same time you did. A little ways back, we'd found its kill. She had a bead on it quicker than a man could blink, but she didn't panic and pull the trigger. Somehow she knew it was you before you said anything. She told Midnight that you were here and everything would be all right.

"We circled just like you said until we reached Billy. She knew Billy and me could carry the little fellow faster, so she stayed with you. She's one courageous woman. Too bad you can't see that." Rooster handed him the belt. Raven's belt. "I'll ride back with someone else."

Duncan had thought he couldn't feel any lower. He'd been wrong.

Raven vacillated between tears and anger as she hurriedly packed and ignored the ringing of her cell phone. She'd check messages later. She didn't want to talk to anyone, couldn't. She'd start crying again.

I don't need your help! I don't need you!

She cringed as she relived hearing Duncan's heated words. More than the words that sliced though her was the final acceptance that no matter what she did, she'd never be able to help him get over his fear of failure in another relationship.

She jerked the suitcase from the bed. She'd have no problem finding a replacement to study the caves. There was no way she could stay and face Duncan or any of the other men. She didn't want their pity and couldn't have Duncan's love. She stopped and closed her eyes. She loved a man who wanted no part of her.

Her eyes opened. She'd survive. But at the moment, she didn't see how the gaping hole in her heart would ever heal.

Her keys clenched tightly in her fist, she hurried out of her room and stopped dead in her tracks. Standing there was the last person she'd expected to see.

"Please don't go," he said, his voice tortured, his eyes pleading. "I'm sorrier than you'll ever know." His fists clenched and unclenched. "Knowing you were in danger scared me more than anything in my life. If you had been hurt—" His words halted abruptly, his chest heaved.

Tears sparkled in Raven's eyes.

"Don't go." He took a halting step toward her. "I'll get on my knees and beg if I have to."

Her lips began to tremble.

Duncan's knees began to bend. Dropping the suitcase and keys, Raven ran to him. Catching her around the waist, Duncan tightly held her to him. "Forgive me. Please forgive me."

Her mouth fastened on his. She loved him too much not to forgive him. The kiss rocked them both. His tongue swept greedily inside her mouth, mating with hers.

Grabbing her up in his arms, he quickly went down the hall to his room. Raven had a fleeting thought of all the nights she'd heard him go to his room and wanted to be with him.

At the side of the bed, he stood her to her feet, took her face in his hands. "You still with me?"

She tugged his shirt out of his pants. "And getting ahead of you."

Laughing, he tumbled them into bed. The laughter turned into a groan when his hand slid under her blouse, felt her silken skin. He pushed it up over her heaving breasts, his own breathing growing short and harsh on seeing her lush breasts in the provocative bit of pink lace.

He had to put his mouth there. His head lowered, placing a kiss in the valley of her breasts, then slowly moving to the dark nipple that beckoned. Teeth gently closed around the point, his tongue laved. A desperate need tore through him.

"Duncan," she moaned, her voice hoarse with arousal.

He needed to slow down and get them undressed. He wanted the first time to be special, but as he looked at her, all he wanted to do was touch, taste, bury himself in her hot sheath.

Groaning, he buried his head in the curve of her neck. "I need to take things slower, but I want you too much."

"How about we go slower the next time?"

His head snapped up. In her eyes he saw a passion as deep and hungry as his. He kissed her, deeply, thoroughly, while he released the buttons on her blouse, the snap on her jeans.

Sitting her up, he tossed her blouse aside. She tugged the shirt from his chest, then splayed her hands there. "You're so beautifully made."

He shook his head. "Not me. You." He unhooked the front clasp of her bra and slowly pulled the material away. He stared, fascinated, aroused. The back of his hand brushed across her nipple. The turgid point hardened.

"You're so responsive."

Her nails raked across his nipple, and she watched it harden. "So are you."

"Just for you." He leaned forward, brushed his lips across hers when he unzipped her jeans, then slid them off her long legs. Knowing if he touched her he wouldn't want to stop, he quickly shoved off his jeans and briefs.

She frowned.

He stopped in the midst of reaching for her. If she had changed her mind he hoped he wouldn't go stark raving mad. "What's the matter?"

She held out her arms to him. "Nothing important."

Relieved, he drew her into his arms. He kissed the curve of her cheek, the slope of her shoulder. He paid homage to her body as he kissed every inch of her skin, leaving her panting, hungry, and hot.

Duncan eased into her, felt the tight fit, and met a barrier. Shock radiated though him.

He stared down into her flushed face and felt humbled beyond belief by this one special woman. "You amaze me, make me want to be a better man."

Her hand tenderly palmed his cheek. "If you weren't the *best* man, I wouldn't be here." Her hips lifted to meet his. "Don't keep us waiting any longer."

His mouth fastened to her as he filled her. The fit was tight, exquisite as he'd known it would be. He lifted his head to look into her eyes. Her awed expression caused tightness in his chest. He promised himself that he'd never do anything to cause her pain—even though that meant eventually letting her go.

His mind and body rebelled against the idea. He pushed the unbearable thought away. Tonight she was his, and he was hers.

He began to move, bringing them together again and again. Her cry of completion mingled with his.

His breathing labored, he gathered her in his arms and rolled to the side, his hand stroking her back. He wanted to keep touching her, reassure himself she was there, that he hadn't lost the woman he loved.

Everything inside him went still. His mind circled around for a way to deny his feelings, and then he glanced down at Raven blissfully lying in his arms. His arms tightened. He couldn't deny his love any more than he could stop the sun from rising in the morning. He didn't want to.

She made each day so much better just by being there. She was as courageous as Rooster said. Nothing—not hard work, not a stuck Jeep, not a cougar—daunted her. Except him.

He rested his cheek against her forehead. For that it would take a long time to forgive himself—if at all.

"You're a man of your word, Duncan McBride."

He glanced down to see her looking up at him with an impish smile on her beautiful sated face. "I should have stopped when I learned it was your first time," he said.

As she rose up, the sheet he'd pulled up over them slid away, revealing her exquisitely shaped breasts. "Could you have?"

His hand closed around her breast, brushed a thumb across the distended peak. He felt her tremble beside him. "No, I'm not that strong or that courageous."

"Right answer." She nipped him on the chin. "Call me crazy, but I want the man in my bed to want me as fiercely as I want him. No substitutions. Ever."

"Then you have what you want." His hand drifted through her hair. "I've wanted you since you first set foot on this property."

"I guess I was a bit late." She grinned, gliding her thumb over his lips. "It didn't hit me until I stopped on the walkway."

"You could have fooled me," he said.

She glared at him. "You can make me so angry."

"You can return the favor." His hand circled her neck, bringing her face close to his. "Please don't ever do anything that will put you in danger again."

"It's not intentional," she said. "My parents raised all of us to be independent. I don't look around for someone to do something I can do just as well."

"Now you have me." He kissed her, then pulled himself up in bed and placed her in his lap. "Thank you for finding Midnight. Saving him."

"He's all right?" she asked, leaning away from Duncan. "We didn't want to take time to look him over after we heard the cat."

"Some scratches from the brush, just like Belle had from obviously trying to go to him." Duncan kissed the top of Raven's head. "Both are safely back in their stall."

"What about Billy?"

"My first instinct was to fire him, but I was too busy trying to find Belle and Midnight, then finding you and Rooster," he told her. "Billy got pushed to the back of the line."

"And now?"

His hands tenderly palmed her face. "I know how a woman can interfere with a man's thinking, how a man can make a mistake and regret it with everything within him. Billy is in the bunkhouse." He hugged her tighter. "He, Rooster, and the others there were ready to take me on for hurting you."

"Give me an hour or two on the way back to Santa Fe and I would have probably turned Buddy back around and taken you on myself," she told him.

"You wouldn't have had to turn around. I would have gone after you."

"Well, I'm glad we met here." Her hand closed over his turgid manhood. "I can tell you are, too."

He chuckled. "What am I going to do with you?"

She straddled him. "I have complete confidence that you'll think of something."

Duncan woke up with his own slice of heaven in his arms. Raven, with one arm across his chest, her leg across his, slept peacefully. If his internal clock hadn't been at work, he would have still been asleep as well. As it was, it was almost six thirty. He hadn't slept this late since he'd bought the Double D ten years ago. He couldn't recall ever sleeping so well.

The reason stirred. "Go back to sleep."

He twisted his head to see her face. "How did you know I was awake?"

She smiled without opening her eyes. "Trade secret."

He smiled. He'd found himself doing a lot of that last night. Talking, sharing. He'd missed that. Hell, he'd never had that.

"What are you thinking?" she asked, staring up at him, her eyes troubled.

Telling her would put too much on her when she had to leave. "That I was right. One night with you wasn't enough."

"Then isn't it great that I'm staying for six more weeks?" she teased, walking her fingers up his chest.

His heart clenched, but he gave her the smile she expected, then scooped her up in his arms and headed for the shower. "Let's make the most of it."

"It's good seeing them happy and safe," Raven said as she stood in the barn in front of Duncan with his arms wrapped around her later that morning, watching Belle and Midnight. "I feel the same way."

Duncan brushed his lips across the top of her head. "I intend to keep you feeling that way."

She angled her head up to kiss his chin. "I intend to hold you to that. Now, I better get breakfast so we both can get to work."

He slowly released her. "Any chance you might take the day off? I planned to go to an auction in Billings this morning." He glanced at his watch. "I wanted to be gone by now. I'm taking the trailer and it will be slow going."

"Then we can grab a bite on the road," she said. "Anything I can do to help?"

"You already have." Drawing her into his arms, he kissed her. "I'll go get the truck and hitch up the trailer. We won't be back until late tonight."

Hand in hand, they walked out of the barn. "I'll put something in the slow cooker for Rooster."

Duncan stopped. "He really likes you. He made

sure I knew you're the reason we found Midnight safe and sound."

"I kind of like him, too, even if he kind of embellishes the truth," she said with a grin.

"Not last night. He was too ticked at me." He stared down at her. "Once I had time to think and control my fear for you, I realized he wouldn't have liked being left behind. You went with him to help Midnight and to watch over him because of his poor eyesight. Even when his eyes were good, he was a terrible shot."

She shrugged. "The important thing is that we're all back safe."

"I wish— Never mind. I'll meet you in front in ten minutes. Billy is riding with us."

"Dang, I guess I'll have to keep my hands to myself," she said, and started toward the house.

Raven quickly prepared the beef stew, then ran upstairs to get her purse. She didn't experience an ounce of remorse on seeing the notebook she took with her each day to the cave. Her time with Duncan was limited. Besides, if she didn't finish, it would give her the perfect excuse to return next year.

She wasn't going to regret one moment with Duncan. She loved him. She had six weeks to get him to admit he felt the same way. A strong, proud man like Duncan wouldn't beg a woman unless he cared deeply for her. Guilt might do a lot of things, but it wouldn't have brought him to his knees

Downstairs, she went to the kitchen to leave Rooster a note. Usually he was there by now. He and the other hands were probably giving her and Duncan a wide berth until they saw how the wind blew.

The back door opened. Rooster stepped cautiously inside. She thought of his offer to chaperone. Thank goodness he hadn't. A blush heated her cheeks, but she smiled. "Good morning; I was just leaving you a note. Your supper will be ready by three. Duncan and I are going to an auction in Billings."

"Everything all right between you two then?" he asked, closing the door behind him.

"Perfect," she said, managing not to blush again. "I better hurry. I don't want to make Duncan lose time pulling the trailer."

Going out of the house, she went down the steps to Duncan's truck, hooked behind was an empty cattle trailer. Coming around the back, he opened the passenger door for her.

"Where's Billy?" she asked.

Duncan's smile was slow and easy. "Ramon said Cynthia and her father picked him up an hour ago."

"I'm sorry. I threw you off-schedule," Raven said.

"And I don't regret it one moment," he said. "There'll be other auctions." Briefly touching his chest with her hand, she climbed inside the truck. Duncan closed the door and turned to Rooster on the steps.

"Glad to see you came to your senses," Rooster said.

"I would have done whatever it took for her to forgive me." Duncan went up the steps and stopped when they were eye to eye and stuck out his hand. "Thank you for taking care of the Double D. I always know I can count on you. I let both of us down last night, but it won't happen again."

Rooster stuck out his hand. "Ain't a man livin' who ain't never made a mistake. But it takes a real man to admit it."

"We'll be late getting back. She said she'd leave your supper cooking."

The older man nodded. "She did." He looked Duncan in the eyes. "Raven's a keeper."

"I know." Duncan went back to the truck. He just wouldn't be the man blessed to always have her by his side.

Raven and Duncan laughed and talked the entire trip to the cattle auction in Billings. Sitting as close as possible beside Duncan in the cab of the truck, for the first time she felt that maybe, just maybe, they had a chance.

The parking lot outside the arena where the auction was to be held was bustling with people and every type of vehicle imaginable. Trailers were everywhere.

"We're not too late, are we?" she asked, holding tight to Duncan's hand as they made their way to their seats.

"No," he reassured her. "The cattle I wanted weren't going to be auctioned until later. There's Isaac." Duncan pulled Raven in front of him and urged her up the steps. Raven hesitated for a moment, not sure how Isaac would view them. It was obvious from the way Duncan looked at her and the way she looked at him that they were lovers.

"What is it, babe?"

There was no way she could tell him surrounded by hundreds of people. She'd been so happy to be with him she hadn't thought. Elks Ridge was a close-knit community. It would be all over town.

"Duncan, Raven, up here."

Raven looked over her shoulder to see Isaac, a wide grin on his face, waving to them and pointing to two seats next to him. Cynthia and Billy were seated in the next seats. They waved as well.

Left without a choice, Raven continued to join Duncan's neighbor and friend. "Hello."

"Thanks for saving us seats." Duncan held Raven's arm until she sat; then he and Isaac took their seats next to each other. "Later I'd like a word with you about my bad behavior last night," he said to the other man.

Isaac gazed down at the arena as a man walked a bull around the arena. "A man says some things he might regret when he's worried about people he cares about. All me and my men remember last night is helping a neighbor I'm also honored to call a friend, how courageous Raven and Rooster were, how Billy watched over my Cynthia just like he promised me when he picked her up."

He leaned over and looked at Cynthia, then straightened. "She made me proud last night. Billy told me she was ready to go with them to search for Midnight."

"In three-inch heels," Raven said, relaxing a bit.

Isaac laughed, slapped his leg. "Her mother was the same way. Once she helped deliver a calf in the pearl necklace I gave her when our oldest was born.

She was in such a rush to help she forgot to take it off. She was a special woman." He sobered and glanced at Duncan. "A man is blessed if he finds a woman like that."

Duncan held out his hand. "Thank you, Isaac."

The handshake was firm. "Neighbors help neighbors."

"If ever you need me or my men, we're there," Duncan told him.

"Daddy, they're about to start bidding on the bull you wanted," Cynthia said from beside Raven.

Isaac jerked his hat down on his head and leaned forward. "I need backup."

Out of the corner of her eye, Raven saw Duncan's mouth twitch, and she could just imagine the type of "backup" he was thinking of.

Raven couldn't understand what the auctioneer was saying. She was amazed at how fast he spit the words, how fast the bidding went. The cattle Duncan wanted to bid on still hadn't come up, and since everyone with her seemed so caught up in the process, she offered to go get drinks. "My treat."

"Let me get it." Duncan was up before she could get the words out of her mouth.

"I can handle it." When he tried to give her money, she pushed his hand away. "Please put your billfold away. It's on me. You've fed me enough. I'll be back before you miss me," she teased as she stepped past him and Isaac into the aisle.

"That's not possible," Duncan mouthed.

Raven's heart turned over. He was getting there.

Smiling, she went to the concession stand. She was next in line when the hair on the back of her neck stood up. Frowning, she glanced over her shoulder, but she didn't see anyone.

"What will you have?"

She turned back around and gave her drink order. On the way back, she couldn't shake the sensation that she was being watched. The moment she stepped into the aisle and saw Duncan, he was out of his seat and coming to help.

"I'm not helpless, you know," she said, letting him take the drink holder with the most drinks.

"I know." His gaze centered on her lips. "Told you I'd miss you."

"I missed you, too. Now, let's take our seats so you can get those Angus heifers you want." She saw his reluctance. It warmed her heart. "We'll get a late start in the morning."

He grinned. "Deal."

Smiling, she started for their seats.

It was close to ten when Raven and Duncan arrived back. Billy, who had ridden back with them, got out of the truck and opened the gate to the back corral for the newly purchased Angus heifers.

Raven climbed up on the side of the trailer to get the cattle moving. "Shoo."

Laughter floated from inside the truck. "Babe, you don't shoo cows."

"It worked, didn't it?" she told him, jumping down when the last cow entered the corral.

"She's got you there, boss."

Duncan pulled the trailer away from the gate so Billy could close it. The young man came to the driver's side. "You want me to put the truck and trailer up?"

"No, I got it. Night."

"Night, boss, Raven." Whistling, Billy started to the bunkhouse.

"Go on in." Duncan put the truck in gear. "I'll be inside in a minute."

Raven gave him a smile that heated his blood. "I'll be waiting."

Duncan headed for the shed. Usually he had no trouble backing the trailer back into the space it was kept in. Since space was a commodity, it had to fit between the tractor and the smaller truck. Instead of concentrating on what he was doing, his gaze kept going to the house.

The lights came on in Raven's room. He waited for them to go off, anticipating that she would go to his room, but they remained on. He became worried, then decided she was probably taking a bath in the oversized iron tub Faith had found at an auction a couple of years back. Which was the wrong thing, since he easily visualized Raven naked, her skin wet and soft.

He swallowed, pulled the truck up, and tried again. This time he overcorrected on the other side and almost hit the smaller truck. His gaze went to the window again. Pulling up, he took a deep breath and backed up again. If the fit wasn't perfect, at least he'd gotten the trailer parked.

Jumping out of the truck, he quickly unhitched the

trailer and put his truck in the garage. Closing the door, he sprinted to the house, praying every step that Raven was still in the tub.

He opened the door to her bedroom, quickly crossed to the bathroom, and opened the door.

One bare arm draped over the side, she reclined in the big claw-foot tub. "What took you so long?"

Chapter 14

Raven was positive that being in love was the most glorious thing in the whole world. If only . . . She crushed the thought before it completely formed. She wasn't going to spend precious time being ungrateful. At least she was going to do her best not to.

It was wonderful falling asleep in the arms of the man you loved, waking up the same way. She usually woke up sprawled halfway on top of Duncan, one of her arms across his chest, her leg thrown across both of his, as if even in sleep she wanted to be as close as possible to him.

She paused while sketching the drawing of the female anatomy in the inner cave. Sierra and Catherine were right about man's obsession with sex not lessening. Some men, like Duncan, tried to control that obsession.

She smiled to herself and continued to sketch. It was a heady feeling knowing she could test Duncan's control, just as he could test hers.

"I'm shameless where Duncan is concerned."

"Glad to hear it."

Happiness splintered through her. Whirling, she found him there. Instead of being embarrassed, she launched herself into his arms. The security she found there always made her feel cherished, blessed to have found him.

His lips brushed against her forehead. "Hi."

"Hi yourself." With her arms around his neck she stared up into his handsome face. "I thought you were going into town today."

He kissed her lips. "Been there and back." He glanced over her head. "You were intent on that drawing when I came in."

Blushing, she tucked her head.

"I noticed it the day Mrs. Grayson came with the others," he continued. "Sierra couldn't seem to take her eyes off it."

Raven's head dipped a little lower. In that case, all the men had noticed the drawing. Absently she wondered if Brandon was as naïve as his wife. "It's an important discovery."

"Is that what you found and didn't want to talk about?" Duncan asked.

"Yes."

He tilted her chin up; his thumb grazed her lower lip. "You're such a combination of innocence and sexy, and all mine."

She wished that were true with all of her heart. "You make it ridiculously easy."

"So do you." Releasing her, he picked up her sketch pad and placed it on a small folding table. "Let's take a lunch break."

Raven's happiness took a nosedive. "All I have is the granola bars and water."

He tugged her on out of the cave. "Like the old days, I've brought the food." Bending, he picked up a handled plastic bag and a blanket. "Where would you like to sit?"

"Up there." She pointed behind him to the flat outcropping of rock fifteen feet over the cave. The mountainside was peppered with smooth rocks, making it an easy climb. "I've gone up there a couple of times looking for you."

He frowned, looked at her feet encased in hiking boots. "I guess it's too late to worry."

She kissed him. "Definitely. Not a scratch on me." Her grin widened, she started for the base of the mountain to climb up. "And you should know it."

Duncan chuckled and started after her with the blanket over his shoulder, the plastic sack looped at his elbow. "I might have to check again just to make sure."

Arriving at the top, she reached for the blanket, then his hand. "As long as I get the same privilege."

Duncan hoisted himself on top of the rock, caught her to him. "I wouldn't have it any other way. We share and share alike."

She placed her head against his chest, felt the erratic beat of his heart that mirrored hers. "I can't think of anything I'd like more."

He leaned her away from him, studied her face. "You're the most incredible woman I've ever met."

"It's easy with the right man." Turning away, she

picked up the folded blanket and placed it on the flat rock where they could look out over the range.

"I've got this. Sit down." Duncan helped her sit, then sat beside her and pulled the contents out of the bag. "Sliced roast beef sandwiches, oatmeal raisin cookies, and chips." He dug back in the sacks for two cans of soda. "Although we might want to wait before we open these."

Raven took the sandwich he held out to her. "This is nice. Thank you."

"I like doing things for you," he said simply, sitting beside her.

Raven took her time unwrapping her sandwich. How could she not love such a caring man?

"You all right?" he asked, lines radiating across his forehead.

Lifting her head, she smiled. She'd said there would be no regrets. "Perfect. I get to share lunch and the beautiful scenery with you."

"That's what I mean about you," he said. "Most people see the endless range and nothing else. You see the beauty of the land, how it has endured, how it will be here long after we're gone."

"I'm an archeologist." She stared out toward the distant plains. "It's natural for me to see beyond what others might see."

"Modest like Rooster and everyone else say." Duncan bit into his sandwich.

Raven stilled. Were people talking about her?

"I couldn't get five feet in town today without people asking about you, asking me to tell you they said hello although you don't know them." He picked up a cookie. "I'd say Rooster was at it again, but a few of the people said that Marshall girl, so I think Cynthia has taken up where Rooster left off."

"Are you serious?" she asked.

"Yep." He cautiously opened a canned drink, then handed it to her. "I can't say how I would have handled it if it would have been a lot of men, but they were mostly women. Delivering Midnight was one thing, standing up to Crane another, but I'm sure what cinched the deal was saving Midnight and standing down a mountain lion."

Raven stared at him. "I only help—"

He kissed her on the lips and opened his own drink. "Might as well get used to it. You'll see for yourself this weekend when we go to the July Fourth celebration."

Mentioning the holiday made her forget to ask what he meant by "get used to it." "The Fourth is this weekend?"

"Yep. Elks Ridge might be small, but we celebrate the Fourth in a big way," he told her, stuffing the paper from his cookie and sandwich back into the plastic bag. "There's a parade around noon, then a rodeo at the fairgrounds and a big dance afterward, with lots of food.

"Then Sunday after church we're going to Old Man Johnson's place and start on his barn that was hit by lightning last month. It took a lot of talking with Reverend Radford for him to agree with that. A point in our favor was that Old Man Johnson refused any financial help. He only wanted his one-hundred-year-old barn rebuilt."

"He doesn't mind you building on a Sunday?" she asked.

"The reverend understands that in these parts it's impossible at times not to work on Sundays." Duncan nudged her hand toward her mouth. "He's also one of the best carpenters in the country."

Dutifully Raven took a bite of her sandwich. Elks Ridge was close-knit and caring. Besides Ruth and a few faculty members, Raven didn't have any close friends in Santa Fe. It must be wonderful to have that connection with so many people.

"I can see why you like it up here." He curved his arm around her shoulder. "It's peaceful, and you can see for miles. At night I bet the stars look close enough to touch."

"There's only one way to see if you're right." She picked up her drink.

"Just what I was thinking." He rubbed his cheek against her forehead. "Another reason for me to want the night to hurry so I can be with you. You have me thinking thoughts I never had before."

She put her food away and leaned into him. "Same here, and I couldn't be happier about it."

His hand clenched on her arm. "I never want you to be anything else."

Her hand palmed his cheek, turning his face to her. "No matter what, I'll never have any regrets about us being together. I don't want you to, either."

"How could I regret the happiest days of my life?

Regret you?" He palmed her face, stared into her eyes. "I didn't know what true happiness was until I held you in my arms."

"Tell me again when we return tonight and you're holding me and we're looking at the stars together."

He kissed her gently on the lips. "It's a date."

Raven had barely made it into the house when she heard a car outside. Going back to the front door, she saw Cynthia pull up in her Mercedes and get out. Raven hadn't seen or talked to her since the auction. "Hello, Cynthia."

Getting out of the sports car, the young woman closed the door and came up the steps. "Hi, Raven."

"Come on inside, or were you looking for Billy?" Raven asked.

Cynthia smiled. "Actually, both of you."

Raven recalled what Duncan had said about Cynthia singing her praises. "Cynthia, while I appreciate the good intent, you really shouldn't have discussed what happened the night we found Belle and Midnight."

Cynthia waved her hand negligently. "People deserve to know how courageous you were."

Sensing she was dealing with a person as stubborn as she was, Raven opened the front door. "Let's go into the kitchen. I need to check on dinner."

"The perfect place to talk."

Raven led the way. In the kitchen, she washed her hands. "Please have a seat. Can I get you anything?"

"No." Instead of taking a seat, Cynthia watched Raven stir the barbeque beef in the slow cooker.

"Smells good. I might have known you could cook. It will make things easier."

"What things?" Raven replaced the glass lid and leaned back against the counter.

"Michelle said men wouldn't consider this important, but you might. Every year women bring their specialty dishes to the Independence Day dance. The men supply the beef. It's kind of like the women's time to shine and for once hear their men brag on their cooking abilities."

"Duncan didn't mention bringing food."

Cynthia made a face. "Michelle didn't think he would. So I thought I'd stop by and give you the heads-up so you can start thinking about your specialty."

Raven bit her lower lip. "I don't have one."

"Well, you have the rest of the day and tomorrow to think of one."

"Chocolate cake?"

Cynthia shook her head. "Sarah Jessup. Her husband owns the feed store."

"Apple pie?"

"Absolutely not," Cynthia told her. "Mrs. Mattie Ferguson's specialty and domain. Her husband owns the largest ranch in Montana. She can be a dear woman, but don't get on her bad side. Although I have to give her credit and say nobody bakes a pie as good as Mrs. Ferguson. That reminds me. You can't bring anything another woman considers she makes or bakes the best—unless you want to enter in the baking contest."

Raven held up both hands. "No way. Perhaps you'd better tell me what's taken."

Cynthia rattled off at least twenty desserts and side dishes. "There's more of course, but those are the main ones I remember, because I've grown up going to the Independence Day celebration. Mama's specialty was deep-dish pecan pie. Now, it's mine and Michelle's." She briefly tucked her head. "I'm baking one just for Billy. He says it's his favorite."

Raven knew Duncan liked chocolate, but not what his favorite dessert was. There was so much they still had to learn about each other. Although he hadn't mentioned her bringing a dish, she didn't like the thought of somehow letting him down. "I'll think of something."

"I'm sure you will." Cynthia headed for the door.

Raven followed. "I probably shouldn't question this, and please don't think me rude, but why are you so intent on helping me?"

"You helped me and Billy get together." She quickly went down the steps when she saw Billy come out of the barn. "I might have ended up with Duncan and been miserable. See you later."

Duncan and Cynthia wouldn't have happened in a million years. Raven wouldn't let herself think that Duncan and Raven was just as improbable. Closing the door, she went in search of Rooster and found him in the great room watching the news. "What do you remember about the food at the dance for the Fourth?"

Rooster smacked his lips. "I'm eating light that day so I'll have plenty of room. The women do their best to outshine each other and the rest of us reap the benefits."

"I was afraid you'd say that." Raven plopped into a chair. "I'm out of my class."

"Now, hold on a darn minute." He sat forward in the recliner. "You're a mighty fine cook. Duncan will be proud to point out the . . ." His voice trailed off. "What are you taking?"

"I wish I knew."

"What's your favorite dessert?"

Duncan closed the kitchen door and pulled Raven into his arms. "You."

She evaded his searching lips. "I'm serious. Cynthia came by today to tell me about the women cooking the food the evening of the big dance, their men bragging on them."

"You don't have to cook anything," he said.

"I want to. I want you proud and bragging on me," she admitted honestly.

He nuzzled her neck. "I'm already proud of you and I've done my share of bragging already. I might have even surpassed Rooster and Cynthia."

Raven didn't know if he was kidding or not. It felt good knowing he felt that way about her. "What's you favorite?"

"Besides kissing you, it's peach cobbler with ice cream," he told her.

"I know how to make that," she said happily.

"But you don't have to."

"I know." Pulling her arms from around his waist, she nudged him toward the sink. "Wash up, and I'll fix your plate."

He turned on the water. "We're still on for tonight, aren't we?"

"Most definitely." Filling his plate with barbeque beef, green beans, potato salad, and corn bread, she placed it on the table.

"Good. I've got a surprise for you." He took his seat. "This looks great."

"What kind of surprise?" she asked, taking the seat next to him.

"You'll just have to wait."

She opened her mouth to ask him what again, but he bowed his head to bless his food. When he lifted his head he was just as closemouthed. "You'll just have to wait," he repeated.

He grinned at her annoyed expression. He seemed so pleased with himself she found herself grinning back. For the life of her she couldn't imagine what could have put that pleased look on his face.

"Duncan. Oh, Duncan," she repeated, her trembling fingertips pressed to her mouth. Where they'd sat that afternoon was a raised cushion covered with a blanket, a couple of pillows, and in the middle a wild daisy. Next to the raised area were a small cooler and several flameless candles.

"Does that mean you like it?" he asked, a trace of worry in his teasing voice.

"It does." On tiptoes, she kissed him. "This must have taken a lot of trips, not to mention the time and thought you put into it."

"Seeing you happy is worth it." Taking her hand, he helped her sit down, then sat behind her, pulling her back into the V of his legs, the shelter of his arms. "It was actually fun. The benefits are sure worth it."

She leaned back against him and wrapped her arms across his at her waist. "I'll never forget this. You were right about the stars. I see the Big Dipper."

"The nights in Santa Fe are wonderful, but they can't compare to these," he whispered. "It's as if you're the only person in the world. If you're still, you can hear the night sounds of the animals stirring."

"You respect the land and the creatures on it," she said quietly. "I realize what it took not to pull the trigger the other night."

"It was difficult not to," he admitted.

"Because you were afraid for me and Rooster."

"Losing cattle, at times, to predators is not something I like, but I realize we're encroaching on land they've hunted for centuries. Whenever possible, I'd rather walk away than shoot," he said.

"That's what sets you apart from most men," she said, twisting her head to look back up at him. "You see the land as a gift, an opportunity to leave it better than when you came. You want to give, not take. Even when we make love, you're never selfish."

"Because you trusted me, because hearing you sigh, the little moans you make, is pleasure unceasing for me." His lips brushed across hers. "Being with you is my greatest pleasure, my deepest desire fulfilled. You're graceful, beautiful, and you're here with me."

Raven's heart ached because she heard the loneliness he'd never admit to. But more than that, she heard the warmth, the love he might never fully admit to her—perhaps not even to himself.

She turned until she knelt in the V of his legs, her mouth a whisper from his, her arms around his neck. "Once I thought I knew what desire meant. I was young and foolish and was fortunate enough to find out that to some men words are as worthless as wheels on a fish."

His hands tightened. His features hardened.

She smiled at him, her lips brushing across his. "Don't you understand? If he hadn't been so utterly worthless, I might have stayed with him; I might have missed being loved by you, missed the pleasure of your touch, the security of your arms, and the hunger of your mouth on my skin. I would have missed this and never realized it. That would have been tragic."

"I guess I'll let him live," Duncan said tightly.

"He hasn't mattered in a long, long time." She brushed her mouth across his again and again, murmured against his lips, "This, only this, does."

She pushed him back, determined that this time she would be the aggressor, loving Duncan the way he deserved, with tenderness and warmth. Unbuttoning his shirt, she pulled it off and kissed his muscled chest, swirled her tongue across his nipples. Sitting back on her haunches, she unbuckled his belt. The entire time, her eyes were on his. Unzipping his pants, she cupped his erection, heard air hiss through his teeth.

Reluctantly releasing him, she scooted down and took off his shoes, giving brief thanks that he had changed out of his boots. She tugged his jeans down his thighs, his legs, and over his long, narrow feet.

Standing, she stared down at him, the candles burning near his head, his hard erection pushing against his white briefs. He started to rise.

She held out her hand. "No." Her hands went to her blouse, releasing the buttons one by one. Slipping it over her shoulders, she let it slide down her arms. The warm night wind brushed across her naked breasts. She shimmied out of her walking shorts and panties.

She stood before him naked and proud. Gracefully she knelt in front of him.

"Back pocket," he gritted out.

Raven found the condom package and tore it open with her teeth. Moving closer, she closed her hand around his hard length, rubbed the velvet top against her cheek, and blew across the top.

"Raven!" It was a warning.

She rolled the protection on, marveling at how rigid and long he was. Finished, she smiled at him. "Yes, I'm a very lucky woman." Her hair tumbled over her shoulder as she pressed her lips to his quivering stomach, moving up, her breasts and lower body sliding sensuously over his, inflaming both their senses.

By the time Raven straddled him, both were breathing heavily. His hands on her waist, hers firmly on his chest, she rode him hard, eagerly meeting the thrusts of his hips, gripping him tightly. Soon the pleasure overtook them both. She collapsed in his arms.

His arms closed around her, holding her to him.

He'd finally found something to rival the strength and beauty of the land he loved so much, and he was holding her in his arms.

Duncan couldn't ever remember enjoying a day more. Except for his riding Black Jack to open the parade, Raven had been with him since they'd arrived for the Independence Day celebration in Elks Ridge. As he'd expected, people had warmly greeted Raven. With her modesty and courage, she'd made herself known in the community.

He couldn't be prouder of her as they watched the parade. He'd put Black Jack in the stable and made his way to her as soon as possible. He hadn't minded the good-natured teasing of the men for rushing to get back to her. His focus had been on Raven.

He'd found her in front of the restaurant, in exactly the same spot where he'd left her and where they'd agreed to meet. She'd given him a smile and a flag and then applauded as the high school marching band passed. Next came several clowns passing out balloons and tossing taffy. He'd managed to snag her several pieces of the candy. She'd kept one and, with the mother's permission, given the rest to the little girl beside her.

"Keepsake," Raven whispered.

He knew exactly what she meant. With her, he treasured each moment. He'd taken a day off to remain in town. Usually, after the parade, he went back to work at the ranch, since he no longer competed in the rodeo. He'd been to only one of the dances. Too many women had designs on him.

Today he was looking forward to all of it and finally seeing and bragging on Raven's peach cobbler. This morning she'd fretted and watched over the cobbler like a mother hen over her chicks. She wouldn't even let him see it after she took it out of the oven. She'd shooed him from the kitchen but allowed Rooster to stay, her coconspirator, who had waited by the front door for a special-delivery package.

"Yeah, Cynthia," Raven yelled, and waved her flag as Cynthia, Miss Elks Ridge, slowly passed in the backseat of the convertible Billy proudly drove.

"I've never seen Billy grin that wide," Duncan commented. "But I can understand the reason."

Raven winked at him, then stared as a man selling hot dogs made his way down the edge of the sidewalk. "I don't see how people are going to be hungry with all the food vendors."

Without thinking, Duncan curved his arm around her shoulder in reassurance. "Don't worry; they'll go though the food tonight like they haven't eaten in days. The parade is winding down. Let's go to the arena and get a good seat for the rodeo."

"Are you going to compete?" she asked as they walked down the congested street.

"I haven't for a couple of years," he said, joining the crowd of people going in the same direction.

"What was your specialty?"

"Calf roping." Stopping, he purchased their tickets at the booth. "Ramon is competing, though. He took top honors last year."

"Hello, Duncan. This must be Raven."

Accepting the tickets and change, Duncan moved out of the way and wanted to groan. Mrs. Ferguson was head of almost every women's organization in the county. Naturally, Duncan had never had too much to say to her. Her husband was a good man, but he could be hard at times. His ranch was so big it straddled two states. His wife had clout and didn't mind using it if displeased. "Good evening, Mrs. Ferguson. I'd like you to meet Raven La Blanc."

"Hello, Mrs. Ferguson," Raven greeted the woman, extending her hand.

The elderly woman, with snow-white hair in a bun she'd worn for as long as Duncan could remember, closed her hand around Raven's. "I've heard a great deal about you."

"Probably too much." Raven laughed and glanced up at Duncan. "I'm going out on a limb here to ask if you're the Mrs. Ferguson who bakes the legendary apple pies."

Mrs. Ferguson blinked, then blushed with pleasure. "I don't know about 'legendary,' but they are popular."

"Extremely so," Raven went on to say. "One of the desserts I considered baking for today was an apple pie. Cynthia Marshall shot the idea down before I could get the words out good. Her exact words were, 'Nobody can bake a pie as good as Mrs. Ferguson.'"

"Well," Mrs. Ferguson said, obviously pleased. "I didn't know people thought that highly of my pies."

Which was a lie, Duncan thought. All the women in the area knew apple pies were Mrs. Ferguson's domain. Taking her on wasn't a good idea. Duncan had to remember to thank Cynthia, who was turning back into the sweet young woman he remembered.

"That's because you're so modest, and I can tell from the way you greeted me you're gracious as well," Raven commented.

Mrs. Ferguson looked at Duncan. "You have a sensible young woman here, Duncan."

"Yes, ma'am," Duncan said, trying not to think of Raven leaving at summer's end. "Would you like for me to get you a ticket so you can sit with us?"

"Thank you. I'm waiting for a few of my friends," Mrs. Ferguson said, glancing at her small diamond watch. "People should be punctual."

"Is your husband here?" Duncan asked, scanning the crowd for the big, rawboned man.

"No, James is tied up at the ranch until later," she told them.

"Would you like for us to wait with you?" Raven suggested.

Mrs. Ferguson shook her head. "It's kind of you to offer, but . . . There they are." She waved two ladies over. They couldn't get their excuses for being late out fast enough. Mrs. Ferguson merely lifted a displeased brow. Silence fell as if someone had flipped a switch.

"Ladies, I'd like you to meet Raven La Blanc. I've been having a nice chat with her and Duncan while we waited," Mrs. Ferguson said pointedly. The women looked nervous, but they shook Raven's hand.

"Pleased to meet you." Raven glanced from Mrs. Ferguson to the women. "I don't know how to do this any way but straight-out. I baked a peach cobbler. If you could bring yourselves to give me your opinion on it before I set it out, I'd appreciate it. Presentation is as important as taste."

"Exactly," Mrs. Ferguson said. "Several of us are going to the community center to set up for this afternoon's celebratory feast. We could always use another pair of willing hands."

"I'd be honored," Raven said. "What time?"

"Around four," Mrs. Ferguson answered. "I like to be punctual and start serving at six." She glanced at Duncan. "Of course, it's a bit of a tradition for the men to come through and point out the dishes prepared by their wives and lady friends."

"I plan on coming by," Duncan said. Out of the corner of his eye he saw Raven smile shyly and momentarily tuck her head. "I'm going to take Black Jack home after the rodeo; then I'm coming back."

"Excellent. Good-bye."

With murmurs of "good-bye," the women moved away.

His arm curving naturally around Raven's shoulders, they started for the entrance. "You did good. Mrs. Ferguson, I hear, can be a bit difficult."

"Cynthia mentioned that to me the day she came to tell me about the desserts." Raven led the way to the first wooden risers. "She's being helpful because I kept her from making a terrible mistake."

"What mistake?"

On tiptoe, Raven grinned and whispered in his ear, "Marrying you."

"What!" Duncan shouted, drawing the attention of the people around him.

Raven chuckled. "That will keep you from getting a big head."

Duncan followed her up the steps, admiring her graceful carriage, the slight sway of her hips. Getting a big head wasn't his problem; getting a big something else that could embarrass both of them was.

"I better get Black Jack and leave while the awards ceremony is going on." Duncan helped Raven to her feet and down the steps in the arena.

Rising, she glanced at her watch. Three forty-five. "And I have to get to the community center. I don't want Mrs. Ferguson giving me that look."

Duncan leaned over and whispered, "I'll protect you."

She grinned up at him for the sheer pleasure of it. "Today has been wonderful. Thank you for taking time off to be with me."

"I enjoyed myself as well." They exited the fairground gates. A few people were leaving, but most were waiting for the mayor to wind down so the top prizes could be given out. "It looks like Ramon will bring home top honors again."

Raven stopped beneath a tree. "The two women in front of me couldn't wait to congratulate him in private."

Duncan's arms loosely circled her waist. "And he would have forgotten them before the night is over. Some women are unforgettable," he said, looking at Raven.

"Just as some men are." She sighed. "I wish I could kiss you."

"I wish it a thousand times more." He leaned closer. "What do you say we leave early tonight?"

"One dance and we're gone." She glanced at her watch again and scooted out of his arms. "I've got ten minutes to reach the community center."

He chuckled as she took off. "I told you I'd protect you."

Raven turned in a circle, lifted her hand to wave. Instead she lowered her hand. The smile slipped from her face. Her gaze was locked behind him.

Duncan whirled, saw Crane staring at him. Crane's face looked gaunt. Usually immaculate, he looked as if he had slept in his suit. Duncan started for him.

"Duncan," Raven called. "Remember what I asked you. It still holds true."

Duncan stopped, clenched his hands. *Does what he says or what I think matter most?* Pleasing her would always come first. Duncan faced Raven instead of the man he wanted to rip apart for trying to belittle her.

"*I'm proud of you*," she mouthed; then she took off again.

You might not be if I see Crane when I turn around. But Crane wasn't there. Pushing the man from his mind, Duncan continued to the empty stable. Everyone connected with the rodeo was at the arena.

He was a few steps inside the stable when he heard the angry whinny of a horse. *Black Jack!* Duncan took off running. He was almost to the stall when Crane rushed out, slamming and closing the door.

"What the hell are you doing to my horse?"

Crane turned, reaching into his pocket. Before Duncan could take another step, he was staring into the deadly barrel of a .38.

Chapter 15

Raven hadn't gone twenty feet before she remembered the ice cream to go with the peach cobbler. Her head fell. She'd wanted it to be a surprise. She'd had Rooster pick up five gallons from the store. When they took Black Jack back to the ranch, she'd planned on picking it up and packing it in dry ice so it would keep.

Only now she wasn't going back. She'd have to tell Duncan at least part of her plan. It couldn't be helped. She reached for her cell phone to call Duncan and came away empty-handed.

It wasn't on her belt loop. She must have forgotten it in her haste to bake the peach cobbler and try to keep her special surprise from Duncan. She glanced at her watch. Eight minutes. She could either go tell Duncan about the ice cream or be on time to help Mrs. Ferguson.

She started back toward the arena. Easy decision. Duncan would always come first.

Increasing her pace, she arrived at the stable. She

had gone no more than five feet when her eyes adjusted to the dimness of the stable. Her blood chilled on seeing Crane with a gun pointed at Duncan.

"Raven, run!"

"If you do, I'll shoot him," Crane threatened.

"Raven, do as I say!"

"Only if you want to go to a funeral."

"The only funeral will be yours, Crane."

"Tough talk, but I have the gun. Now get over here." Crane backed up so he was against the stall door across from Black Jack's.

Raven started walking.

"Raven, no. Please," Duncan said. His eyes pleaded.

"I'm not leaving you. I can't." She kept walking, trying to figure out a way to help them both.

Crane laughed nastily. "So touching. Stop there."

Raven stopped twenty feet from Duncan. "I'm sorry. He's a bigger fool than I imagined."

Crane's head jerked toward her. "I should shoot you."

"No, you won't." Raven casually folded her arms. "If you dare point the gun at me, Duncan will tear you apart. But I wouldn't be too happy about it, either, and I might beat him to it."

"You're all mouth. I bet I could find a better use for it," he sneered.

"Touch me and you'll end up with more than a sore leg," she promised.

"What are you talking about?" Duncan questioned.

"Nothing important," Raven quickly said. She'd been careless in mentioning the incident.

Black Jack whinnied. Duncan whirled toward the stall. "What were you doing inside his stall?"

"Teaching you a lesson. One you didn't learn the other times." Crane swayed the slightest bit. "I'm the one who spooked your herd, who let your mare and that foal out. I thought if you lost some of your herd or had enough problems you might need money and change your mind about leasing. You always came out on top, but you won't this time."

Duncan reached for the stall door. A bullet whizzed by and lodged in the wood inches from his hand. Black Jack reared. "You're a dead man, Crane."

"No, but you'll wish you were before I finish. Because of you two, I was fired. No other real estate company will even give me an interview."

Raven unfolded her arms, holding up her hand for Duncan to be patient. Soon the ceremonies would be over and people would pile into the stable. "Crane, I thought you were a smart man. Looks like you're screwed. Reminds me of a movie—a Western where the bad guy faces certain death either way."

"Shut up," Crane ordered.

"You should get out of here and hire a good lawyer before it's too late," she told him, inching closer. He was too big of a coward to suspect an attack from a woman a second time.

"No, you took everything. None of the ranchers will talk to me." His unsteady hand wiped his mouth. "I'm going to leave you with nothing, just like you left me. A dead horse isn't enough." Crane swung the gun toward Raven.

Duncan pounced, tackling Crane, taking him

down. The gun fired. The bullet lodged in the beam overhead. Wrestling the gun from Crane's hand and tossing it aside, Duncan pounded his fist into Crane's face, again and again.

"Duncan. Black Jack needs us." Opening the stall door, Raven went inside. "Easy, boy."

Duncan joined her, catching the horse's mane, leading him to an empty stall. "Search his pockets. I can't tell if Black Jack is acting up because of the noise and a stranger in his stall or if that scum gave him something."

Raven knelt by an unconscious Crane. From his jacket pocket she pulled out an empty package of rat poisoning. There had been eight cubes. On unsteady legs she came to her feet and reached for Duncan's phone.

"I'm calling the police, and they can get a vet."

Duncan stared at Crane. Blood trickled from his misshapen nose. "I should have killed the bastard when I had the chance."

Raven dialed 911. The blame was hers. She'd kept Duncan from taking care of Crane. "I'm at the stable at the fairgrounds. There's been an attempted murder."

"We found all the cubes of rat poison in the straw in Black Jack's stable," the veterinarian said. "Black Jack is fine."

Duncan happily patted the horse's neck. It could have ended much differently. "Thanks, Doc."

He slapped Duncan on the back. "You're welcome. I'll see you later."

"You're quiet," Duncan said to Raven as the man left, closing the stall door after him. The police had left fifteen minutes earlier with Crane. Now, it was just the two of them.

Her arms folded around her waist, Raven shook her head. "This is my fault. If I had let you take care of Crane, he might have been too afraid to cross you again."

"And he could have gotten drunk enough to set the house on fire or any number of things." Duncan gently took her arms. "I'll blame Crane, blame the booze he's been guzzling lately. You, never. You probably saved my life."

She finally lifted her head. "I was so scared when he fired the gun."

Duncan's mouth flattened into a hard line. "If you hadn't been here, I would have taken him on and probably ended up with a bullet hole." His eyes briefly shut. "I never felt such rage or fear as when he pointed the gun at you."

His thumb brushed across her trembling lips. "We're alive and Black Jack is all right. I want some of that peach cobbler, a dance, and then we're going home."

"There was supposed to be ice cream. I was coming to tell you to bring it back with you," she told him.

"We'll eat it tonight in bed."

The corners of her mouth lifted. "It's five gallons."

"Once Rooster sees it's open, it won't last long. He wanted a piece of Crane as well. All of my men did. If the sheriff hadn't asked them to leave, they'd still be here." He curved his arm around her waist and started from the stable. "Let's get out of here."

Applause erupted the moment Duncan and Raven walked though the community center's door. Rooster and the men from the Double D surrounded them along with other members of the community.

Mrs. Ferguson pushed her way to stand in front of Raven. "We all heard about that nasty man. How you stuck by Duncan, helped with his horse. We decided to wait until you came for the parade of dishes."

Raven was speechless. "I don't know what to say."

Duncan did. "I was hoping there would be some of your peach cobbler left."

"There most certainly is. This way." Mrs. Ferguson led them to the center of the U-shaped display of tables loaded with food. "I think you'll be able to pick out Raven's."

Duncan saw the peach cobbler and was at a loss for words. Cut into the thick cinnamon and sugar–dusted crust was the Double D brand. He stared and then turned to her, finally finding his voice. "How?"

"Brandon sent the specially designed pastry cutter overnight. Do you like it?" she asked.

Duncan spoke to those assembled: "Raven La Blanc can stare down a mountain lion or a man, and still find time to cook and surprise a man." He picked up the cobbler, tilting it slightly so people could see his Double D brand. "She cooks as good as she looks, and that's saying a lot."

Applause erupted again. Raven basked in the

glory, and in the twinkle and promise in Duncan's beautiful eyes.

Immediately after church the next morning, Duncan drove to Alfred Johnson's ranch. Cars and trucks filled the front yard of the modest house. There was already the sound of hammers, electrical saws. Children played in the side yard.

Grabbing his gloves, Duncan opened his door. "Most of the women are probably in the house."

"I can help." Raven got out of the truck and met him at the hood.

He picked up her hand. "No gloves. Please go inside." She hesitated. He brushed his hand across her hair, tugged. "Nothing is going to happen to me. I'm safe."

She swallowed. "I know. It's just . . ."

"I know." Instead of her arm and leg over him, he'd awakened with her entire body on his. "I don't like you being afraid, but I like waking up the way I did this morning."

"So did I."

A door opened and shut. "Raven, we wondered when you'd get here." Mrs. Ferguson waved Raven forward. "Mrs. Johnson wants to meet you."

Raven's sigh was long-suffering. "I hope it has nothing to do with last night."

Mrs. Ferguson came down the steps and took Raven's arm when she didn't move. "Partly. Morning, Duncan. We'll be out shortly to serve lunch."

Raven stopped. "No one mentioned lunch was being served. I didn't bring anything."

"It's being catered," Duncan told her. "See you later."

Mrs. Ferguson paused to watch him walk away. "They don't make them like that anymore."

Raven's mouth gaped.

"Close your mouth, dear." Opening the door, Mrs. Ferguson ushered Raven inside. The room was filled with women and children, and the mouthwatering smell of fried chicken. "Here she is." She stopped in front of a petite woman with salt-and-pepper hair, a kind smile, and a firm hand shake. "Raven La Blanc, Mrs. Molly Johnson."

"I'm pleased to meet you," Raven said.

She patted the empty space on the settee beside her. "You seemed to have livened up Elks Ridge."

"I think people give me more credit out of the kindness of their heart than is due me," Raven said. "I'd much rather talk about you. On the way over, Duncan said you and your husband celebrated sixty years of marriage a couple of months ago. That's an accomplishment few achieve."

"I plan to keep at it," Mrs. Johnson said.

Mrs. Ferguson clapped her hands together. "Ladies, let's get the food set up and get the children and men fed."

The women swept out behind her. Molly Johnson smiled and tried to push to her feet. Raven took her arm. "Thank you. It's easier going down than coming up."

"Would you like to join the ladies and help?" Raven asked.

"Thank you, I would." Mrs. Johnson grasped

Raven's hand and they made their way out the door. On the porch, a smile touched the old woman's lips. "That's my man talking to your man over yonder. He's still a rascal and a flirt. Don't be surprised if he asks for a dance."

The "rascal" looked up and waved. His wife waved back.

"What's the secret of living with and loving a man that long?"

"Marriage is what you make of it. There have been times when I've wanted to pack my bags." She paused and laughed. "Times I'm sure Alfred wanted to pack them for me. But through it all we've stayed, because no matter what, the love is there." She looked across the yard at him again. "The body might get frailer, but the love just gets stronger."

Emotions clogged Raven's throat. She hugged the other woman. "You've found something precious."

Pulling a handkerchief from the pocket of her apron, she dabbed Raven's eyes. "From what I've seen, so have you."

Not wanting to disillusion the older woman, Raven just nodded. Duncan's love was precious. But they might never have the chance to spend the rest of their lives together.

The days had gone by too fast. She wasn't ready to leave Duncan, leave the Double D. But she didn't have a choice. The first faculty meeting at St. John's was on Monday at eight, and she had to be there.

From her earliest college days, Raven had set her sights on teaching at the college level. Her goal, her focus, had been on gaining tenure. Once she'd accomplished that, she'd have job security, and her future and the life she envisioned would be secure.

She'd have the safe life and later the family she wanted. But that was before she'd met and fallen in love with Duncan. Loving Duncan changed everything, changed her. She wanted to remain on this breathtaking, sprawling land and help Duncan build his dream.

It wasn't going to happen. She was leaving in the morning.

Raven put the last piece of equipment from McBride's Lost Cave into the Jeep and looked around. She wouldn't be back. She'd hinted, but there had been no invitation for her to return. She planned to call Blade when she reached Santa Fe and tell him the surveillance equipment could be picked up. She'd waited, hoping, praying, that the call wouldn't be necessary.

Tears pricked her eyes.

"Hush. Don't cry."

Through tears she saw him standing there; then she was in his arms. Her hands clutched his shirt. She opened her mouth to say something, but all that came out was gut-wrenching sobs.

"Babe." His mouth took hers, fusing hot and greedy. His hands unbuckled her belt, his own. Breaking the kiss, he lifted her enough to tug the walking shorts over her boots. Straightening, he picked her up. Instinctively she wrapped her legs around him. He found her, filled her, loved her. Her release came seconds before his. She cried out, holding him tightly to her.

He kissed the side of her neck, leaned against the Jeep, holding her until the little quakes in her body subsided. He placed her on her feet, adjusted their clothes. "I want you to promise to remember something."

"I promise."

His gaze locked with hers. "Remember that you've given me more pleasure, more happiness, in these weeks than I've had in a lifetime. No matter what, being with you will always be my greatest joy."

Tears sparkled in her eyes. She swallowed to keep them at bay. She didn't want Duncan to feel guilty. She wanted him to remember their time together with a smile. "I'll never forget you."

"If I were the right kind of man, I'd tell you to find another man to grow old with," he said, his hold on her fierce.

Telling him he was the only man for her would make things worse for him, not better. But she wanted him to know how deeply she cared for him. "You are the right kind of man. Never forget that." She pushed away. "Don't be concerned if it takes a while for me to reach the ranch."

"You want me to stay with you?"

Forever wouldn't be long enough. "No. You have work to do."

"It can wait." He took her hand. "Let's climb your rock and look at God's handiwork."

She allowed him to lead her up the cliff to the flat rocks high above the cave. Taking her in his arms, he sat down with her in his lap. Her head pressed against his chest. She listened to his heartbeat, trying to find contentment, to commit this moment to memory, but all she felt was a deep growing loneliness that she knew, without Duncan in her life, would always be there.

She was hurting and it was because of him. He'd promised never to hurt her again. It was impossible not to. Their time together was for a short season, not a lifetime.

Duncan swiped his hand over his freshly shaven cheek. He could only pray that he was doing the right thing. Shaking his head, he picked up his shirt and shoved his arms through the sleeves.

Raven deserved a man who didn't come with any baggage—curse or ex-wife. He hadn't known he could love this deeply. With love came responsibility. They were happy now, but what about next month, when they would be snowed in, when she couldn't get to the cave, to town?

He'd failed in his life, but he didn't think he'd get over seeing Raven slowly grow to despise him as Shelley had. He wouldn't recover.

Stuffing his shirt into his pants, he went downstairs to the back door of the kitchen and signaled Ramon and Billy that all was clear. Rooster was out front in case any guests arrived early.

Each man carried in three large food trays from the restaurant. Behind them, Pete wheeled in two large coolers filled with water, soft drinks, and beer. "Raven is going to be surprised."

I hope she'll also be pleased, Duncan thought, taking the huge cake from Harvey. Faith could have told Duncan what to do better. He could have hired a fancy caterer, but he had wanted to do it himself. The last thing he'd ever do for Raven.

"She still doesn't suspect anything, does she?" Ramon asked as he helped Hank slide the white cake decorated with pink and yellow roses out of the box.

"No."

"Cynthia said Raven will probably cry," Billy said.

He and Cynthia were dating. Duncan almost envied the young man. His future was ahead of him. Then Duncan thought of Raven's smile, her laughter. To have been given that, if only for a short while, was worth the void her leaving was going to create.

"Cynthia and her sister said they'd come early in case we needed help." Billy glanced around. "Looks like all we need is the guest of honor."

"I'll go get her. I told her Rooster was cooking something special," Duncan said.

"It's a wonder she didn't leave today," Pete said, laughing. All the men joined in.

Duncan quietly left the kitchen. He didn't want to think of Raven leaving. Soon he'd have no choice.

Everything was packed except the toiletries and clothes she'd need tonight and tomorrow. With her suitcases by the door, the room looked the same as the day she arrived. After she left in the morning there would be nothing to mark her having been there at all.

"Raven." Duncan knocked softly on her door.

Raven smiled despite the ache she felt and opened the door. "I'm ready."

He simply stared at her. She'd always take his breath away, but tonight she had a special beauty in a little black dress, her hair in an intricate knot atop her head. Chic and sophisticated, yet she could herd cattle and handle a rifle with ease.

"Each time I see you, I find a new, beautiful facet." He closed the door, drawing her into his arms, lightly kissing her. "But underneath is the woman a man would give his life to call his own."

She trembled in his arms. "I don't have to go."

His hands clenched. "You don't know how much I wish that was the truth." He took her arm. "Rooster is waiting."

She promised she wouldn't cry tonight. There would be enough lonely nights to cry. "What's he cooking? I didn't look in the kitchen as I promised, but I didn't smell anything."

"You'll see, soon enough."

The moment they could be seen on the railing, a cheer went up. "Raven!" The hands from the Double D stomped and whistled, shaking the walls.

Raven pressed her hands to the bottom of her face when she saw all the people assembled below. Tears sparkled in her eyes.

Rooster thundered up the stairs and took her arm. "You didn't think we'd let you leave without a proper farewell. You're one of us."

"Thank you," she said.

"Here." Rooster placed a large hatbox in her arms. "It's from all of us."

"I'll hold it while you untie the ribbon," Duncan said, sliding his hands underneath.

Raven untied the ribbon, already guessing there was a hat inside. There was. A beautiful white Stetson.

"Read the inscription," Rooster urged.

Raven La Blanc, a courageous and unforgettable woman. She hugged Rooster and all the hands, let her misty-eyed gaze tell Duncan how much the gift meant.

"Hold on," Isaac Marshall said, stepping forward and handing her an envelope. "For making sure Cynthia was safe."

Opening it, Raven found a gift certificate to a spa in Billings. "We can go together when you come back to visit," Cynthia said, holding Billy's arm. "Billy is coming back for Christmas."

"A basket of goodies for the drive from the ladies," Mrs. Ferguson said. "We'll miss you."

Raven swallowed, allowed Duncan to take the basket and set it aside. Her hand was trembling too badly to hold it. "I'll miss all of you. Thank you."

Mrs. Johnson and her husband came next. "You can tuck this into the basket."

"Mama makes the best banana bread in the state," her husband proudly said. "Wins every year at the state fair."

Raven hugged the elderly couple. "Thank you for coming. I know it was a drive for you."

"Duncan sent a car for us," Mr. Johnson said, his eyes sparkling. "Never thought I'd be chauffeured unless it was for my funeral." People laughed at the outspoken man. "It's gonna take us home. I intend to get me a dance with this old woman before we leave." He fondly put his arm around his wife's stooped shoulders.

"You might. Might not." Mrs. Johnson winked at Raven and turned away, her husband close by her side.

"Dancing time," Cynthia said; then she turned on a small CD player. The unmistakable voice of Toni Braxton filled the room with "Unbreak My Heart," a haunting song of a lost love.

"Can I have this dance?" Duncan asked Raven, thinking the song appropriate.

"Always." She went into his arms, felt them close securely around her. "Thank you. This is the nicest thing anyone has ever done for me."

Leaning down, Duncan whispered in her ear, "I beg to differ."

She laughed as he had intended. Leaning back, she simply stared up into his strong face, memorizing every nuance so that she could carry them with her the rest of her life.

"Looks like Old Man Johnson is getting that dance." Duncan inclined his head to the left of them. Raven's gaze followed.

Raven placed her head on Duncan's shoulder and gazed at the older couple. Their steps were slow, but their love shone like a beacon. Time and fate had tested them and they'd withstood the challenge.

"They're blessed and they know it," Raven said softly. "What they have is priceless."

"You won't get an argument from me," Duncan said. "I'd hoped my parents would grow old together."

Another strike against her and Duncan. "A week before I left, your mother got the reservations mixed up and came in a day early while your father was still at Casa de la Serenidad. Your father acted annoyed, but a couple of times I caught him looking at her like a man who wanted a woman."

Duncan nodded. "He's afraid. My father would fight a grizzly with his bare hands to protect his family. Yet he doesn't even want to talk about him and my mother getting back together again," Duncan said just as the music died.

Then he isn't too different from his son, Raven thought, but she left the words unsaid.

"My turn." Rooster caught Raven and bounced and kicked to the fast tempo of the music.

Aware of his host duties, Duncan enlisted Ramon's help to take the tops off two of the trays. They placed the others on top of the refrigerator and served the drinks. Duncan forgot about napkins until one of the women mentioned it. He couldn't find any, so he gave her a paper towel. He figured if the barbeque restaurant in town had paper towels on the table it was all right.

The main thing was that Raven had a night to remember.

Chapter 16

"Good night and thank you for coming." Raven stood with Duncan on the front porch, waving good-bye to the guests.

"Good night."

Billy and Cynthia stood beside her sister's car, obviously reluctant to part.

"Billy," Duncan called.

The young man straightened. "Yes, boss."

"You know where I keep the spare set of keys to my truck. Be back in an hour—if it's all right with Michelle," Duncan said.

Immediately Billy went around to the driver's side, holding Cynthia's hand every step of the way. In a matter of seconds, Michelle's Lincoln roared to life and she pulled off.

"Thanks, boss," Billy called. "I'll have your truck back in the garage in an hour."

Duncan casually glanced at his watch. "Then you're wasting time talking to me."

Laughing, the two young people ran toward the garage.

"That was nice of you."

"I had an ulterior motive. I want to be alone with you, and Billy was taking too long to say good night," Duncan said. "Rooster and the rest of the hands left thirty minutes ago."

"Rooster didn't want to clean up the kitchen."

Duncan's Dodge Ram passed at a sedate 30 miles an hour. Billy honked the horn twice. Cynthia waved.

When the taillights were a faint glow, Duncan picked Raven up and headed for the stairs.

"I need to clean up the kitchen," Raven protested, pushing ineffectively against his chest.

"The kitchen can wait; I can't." He dropped a quick kiss on her lips.

"Since you put it that way." Circling her arms around his neck, she nibbled his earlobe.

Duncan increased his pace up the stairs, elbowed open his bedroom door, then kicked it closed. He didn't stop until he was by the bed. He placed her on her feet. "I want this night to be as special as you are."

"Each time you touch me, hold me, is special."

"I want to show you something." Stepping behind her, he turned her toward the door. "Look over the door."

Emotions clogged her throat. Hieroglyphics. The symbol for a man bent over as if in pain or misery, then, joined by a woman, standing tall, proud.

"I couldn't bring myself to carve him alone again. No matter where you are, you'll be here."

Taking his hand, she placed it over her heart. "And you'll be here."

"Raven." Tonight was for her. He wanted to love her with every breath, every touch. Tonight and in the morning would be all they had left.

He found he was a selfish man after all. He wanted to imprint his body, his taste, on her so that she would want no other man, crave no other man, need no other man.

Stepping behind her, he grasped the zipper and slowly drew it down, letting need and anticipation build for both of them. His hand trembled, his groin thickened, on seeing the elegant curve of her back, the tiny scraps of lace for her black bra and panties.

She wore the decadent perfume again. He leaned in closer, sniffed, and then pressed his lips against the curve of her shoulder.

"Duncan." His name trembled from her lips.

Using both hands, he slid the material off her shoulders. It slithered down, momentarily stopped at her hips, then pooled around her feet. She was perfection. And for the time being, she was his.

One arm slid around her waist, the other across her breasts, bringing her back against him. Her eyes closed, she leaned back against him. His were open and fixed on the mirror across the room.

Would the memory of this moment haunt him or please him as it pleased him now? Only time held the answer.

He was a man used to the harshness of life, the capriciousness of nature, yet here he was, holding a woman who, with her touch, her warmth, the gift of her body, gave him more pleasure than he ever thought possible. It was impossible not to give in return.

His hand moved to cup her breast through the lace of her bra. His other hand slid to cup her woman's softness. His mouth pressed kisses along the curve of her neck, the slope of her shoulder.

Her hips pressed against him, her nipples hardened. Releasing the bra, he placed her on the bed, coming down on top of her, holding himself aloft with his hands. His tongue swirled around one nipple, then the other, alternately teasing and arousing her.

Her hands and arms reached for him to bring him closer, but he evaded her efforts until she moved restlessly beneath him. Hard and aching, he settled himself against her dampness. Her hips lifted, asking for more.

He intended to give it to her. With one sweep her panties were gone and he was there, his mouth hot and insistent.

Shock gave way to pleasure as she cried out. Quickly sheathing himself, he thrust into her again and again until she clamped her legs around him, meeting thrust for incredible thrust. The ride was fast and furious. She went over first. He quickly followed.

Raven slowly opened her eyes, staring up into those of the man she'd die loving. Over his shoulder, she saw the drawings. If tonight and the morning were all the time they had left together, she was going to make the most of it.

She pushed against his chest until he was on his back and she was on top. "My turn."

Her kisses started on his mouth, but as they did, she rubbed her breasts against him; her leg rubbed against his manhood. By the time she swirled her tongue in the dip of his navel, he'd reached his breaking point.

He reached for another condom. She took it from his hand. "Allow me."

"Hurry."

She held the warm, rigid shaft in her hand, then tore the package and rolled the condom on. The instant she completed the task, he pulled her on top, guiding her. Twin sighs of delight mingled. She splayed her hands on his chest, leaned over to kiss him, moving her hips as she did, creating fissions of pleasure.

The need built to move faster. Her back arched. He clamped his hands on her waist and surged into her waiting heat again and again until both were reaching for completion. His shout of pleasure echoed hers.

She curved her arms around his neck, kissed his mouth, and drifted to sleep.

He didn't go to sleep. Duncan's eyes remained on the drawing and accepted what he had not been able to being himself to carve.

Him. Alone. Forever.

Tomorrow night and all those long nights afterward, he would sleep in this bed alone and want a woman he could never have. Her dream and her life were in Santa Fe.

* * *

Raven woke up in Duncan's arms. As usual, she was sprawled atop him with one arm across his chest, her leg thrown across his as if trying to bind him to her. Even in her sleep, she never let herself forget their time was limited.

He felt it, too.

The almost desperate way he held her meant he was awake as well. Holding her, wanting her, but not enough to trust those feelings would last a lifetime no matter what fate threw at them.

He'd fight to leave his mark on the land, but he wouldn't fight for her.

"Raven."

Like her, he could feel the change in her body, from being relaxed in sleep to being tense.

"Honey."

She lifted her head, ready to berate him for not wanting to fight for them and saw the bleakness in his eyes. Emotions swamped her, bringing a quick rush of tears she said she wouldn't shed. He was doing this for her; he didn't want her hurt. Somewhere along the way, he'd switched from trying to protect himself to protecting her.

Hoping against hope he didn't see the sheen of moisture in her eyes, she kissed him, trying to convey the love that she could never confess. He felt bad enough. Her emotions under control, Raven lifted her head, doing her best to give him the smile he needed to see.

"Good morning."

"Good morning," he said, his eyes quietly studying hers, his hand sweeping lazily up and down her back.

"How about we hit the shower together?" she said, hoping to distract him.

"You're the most beautiful thing I've ever seen, the most courageous. No matter what, I'm glad you came, honored you let me love you," he said softly.

Raven's heart thumped in her chest; her breath caught on his last two words—"love you."

Then she realized, as he scooped her up in his arms and headed for the shower, that those two words were all he could give her. He was setting her free.

Duncan checked under Buddy's hood for the second and last time that morning to ensure himself that the Jeep would make the trip back to Santa Fe without incident. Even as he checked the new battery connections, it ran through his mind that if the Jeep had problems, Raven would stay.

He slammed the hood. She was scheduled to report to work on Monday, two weeks before the students were to report. "Everything looks good."

"Thank you, Duncan." She smiled up at him. "I could have made it without the new battery."

"I don't want you stranded someplace," he said. "You stop for gas before it gets to a quarter of a tank. You don't drive at night."

"I won't." Her hand briefly touched his chest, before she turned to the men standing to one side to say good-bye. She gave each man a hug until only Ramon, Rooster, and Billy were left. "I'll never forget you."

"Don't make yourself no stranger," Rooster said, awkwardly patting her. "I'll take good care of your slow cooker and the boss."

She blinked a few times. "I know you will. Good-bye."

Billy stepped forward as Rooster went inside the house and Ramon headed toward the barn. "Without your help, I never would have had a chance with Cynthia."

"If it's to be, it would have happened." She hugged him. "I know you'll do well in law school."

"One more week here, then I go home to spend time with my parents." He grinned. "Cynthia is coming with me for a few days."

"Enjoy life and each other. Good-bye."

"Bye, Raven." Billy ran to catch up with Ramon. They entered the barn together.

She turned to Duncan, remembered the first time she'd seen him, the stoic, unbending stance, the standoffish attitude. They were gone. Misery was in the stiff way he held himself, his beautiful eyes.

"I won't say good-bye."

He jerked her to him, holding her tight. She held him just as tightly. "God, I'm going to miss you."

"I want you to miss me." Her mouth sought his, tasting, savoring, for what might be the last time. She took his face in her hands. "Miss me enough that you'll come to Santa Fe and bring me back home to you."

"Raven—"

Trembling fingers on his lips stopped his words. "Search your heart, Duncan; then trust what you feel.

I'll wait for as long as there are stars in the sky." Briefly replacing her lips with her hand, she got in the Jeep, started the engine, and drove away.

She didn't look back. If she had, she would have seen Duncan fall to one knee, his head bowed, the exact way he had carved the man in his bedroom.

Somehow Raven made the drive back to Santa Fe. Duncan's calls every evening while she was on the road to check on her and make sure she was safe for the night helped. She was safely back and miserable.

Turning into a residential development, Raven slowed down, then eventually stopped. Vehicles—five to be exact—were either in Ruth Grayson's driveway or parked in front.

Raven's hands curled around the steering wheel. Today was Sunday. Ruth and her children always got together for brunch or an early dinner on Sunday.

She shouldn't have come, but she desperately needed to talk to someone. Her mother loved her, but instinctively Raven knew she wouldn't understand. Her philosophy on life was that she had no philosophy. She didn't worry over anything, took each day as it came, with no expectations. That way, she said, she was always pleasantly surprised when something good happened. If it wasn't good, she'd shrug and say that was life.

The honk of a car horn made Raven jump and brought her out of her musing. Waving her hand in apology, she pulled behind a Maserati, Sierra's "off-duty" car. The other truck and cars would belong to Ruth's four sons. Of course, their wives were with them. Raven had heard Faith say that none of the Graysons, their cousins the Falcons, or their extended family of the Taggarts, ever went far without each other or slept apart.

Raven envied them. That was the kind of togetherness she had dreamed of. She wanted to go to sleep in the arms of the man she loved, wake up the same way. If she didn't figure out a way, she was doomed never to fulfill her dream.

Her eyes briefly closed. Loving Duncan had altered her dream. She wanted the stability and permanence she'd always searched for, with him. She might gain tenure, but it wouldn't mean as much. She wanted to establish roots on the Double D, not in Santa Fe.

Duncan called on her cell phone every day while she was on the road, called her each night. He cared, but he didn't trust what they felt for each other to last.

"Raven."

Raven jerked her head up and around. "Hello, Sierra."

Eyes as sharp as her husband's studied Raven; then Sierra opened the door of the Jeep. "Come on inside. Mama will be glad to see you."

Raven shook her head. "This is family time. I forgot."

"You know Mama will be glad to see you, and you can give her and Blade a firsthand report on the caves."

It hit Raven that she hadn't sent Blade a report after their visit, hadn't spoken with Ruth in over two weeks. Raven could offer no excuse that was acceptable: she'd been caught up with Duncan. Ruth might not mind, but Blade was an exacting man. Excuses didn't cut it with him.

"I owe Blade an apology for not keeping him informed." Raven reached for the door. "I'd rather talk to him about it in person."

Sierra sighed. "You're going to disappoint Mama. She's been excited all weekend that you're returning. She's proud of you. I'm almost jealous."

Raven looked at the self-assured, successful woman and couldn't imagine her jealous of anyone. She had a career she excelled in, a close-knit family, and a man who would walk through fire for her.

"Then there's Faith, who'll want to hear all about Duncan," Sierra continued. "His mother will be just as anxious."

That got Raven's attention. "Duncan's mother is here?"

"Arrived unexpectedly yesterday afternoon." Sierra stared at Raven. "Did she know you were going to the Double D to authenticate the caves?"

"I don't know," Raven said, a bit distracted by the knowledge his mother was inside. "Duncan mentioned the caves to his mother; she was the one who told Ruth."

"Hmmm."

Raven frowned up at Sierra. "What?"

"Nothing." Sierra released the door. "If you don't want to come inside and say hello to the people who care about you, helped you in your career, and asked nothing in return, it's your decision."

"You've twisted what I said," Raven said, hurt that Sierra thought she was so shallow.

Sierra folded her arms. "Then perhaps you'll tell me again why you won't go inside."

Because I'm close to tearing up again. She glanced away. When she looked back around, Sierra was headed up the walk. Strange, Raven hadn't thought Sierra was the kind of woman to give up without an answer. She was known to be as tenacious as her mother and her oldest brother, Luke.

The recessed front door in the courtyard opened. Blade, devilishly handsome and casually dressed in light-colored slacks and a beige shirt, stepped out into the enclosed courtyard filled with flowering plants in colorful pots. He glanced at Raven, then back at Sierra.

Raven switched off the engine, sure he'd want to speak with her about her negligence in reporting after he was so generous to fund her research and then go to the extra expense of putting in the surveillance equipment.

Again, she was surprised. Without another glance in her direction, they went back inside the house. The door closed after them.

There was nothing to keep her. She could leave, but inside were people she cared about and respected, who would think less of her if she did.

Grabbing her satchel purse, she got out of the Jeep and went to the door. It opened before she rang the doorbell.

Ruth Grayson, regal and beautiful, in a soft yellow blouse and slim skirt that one of her doting children had probably purchased for her since she didn't like to shop, enveloped Raven in a hug. "Raven, I'm so glad you stopped by. I was coming to hurry you along, but Sierra said you'd be in shortly."

Raven jerked her gaze to Sierra, who was standing in front of Blade, his arm around her waist. It seemed Sierra could be as devious as her billionaire husband.

"Raven, it's so good to see you again," Faith said, coming forward to catch both of Raven's hands in hers. "You certainly made an impression on my big brother. Not an easy task, I can tell you."

"Welcome back, Raven," Duncan's mother, Mrs. Stella McBride, said. "Duncan said there isn't one thing you can't do."

She knew one. *Get him to promise me forever.* She swallowed. Swallowed again.

Faith, as much of a nurturer as her love-smitten husband, Brandon, glanced toward her mother. "You won't believe this. Mother and I just got off the phone with him. He couldn't get you on your cell and wanted me to try. I was just about to call the number he gave me when Sierra said you were outside. He'll be so relieved. I've never heard him sound so worried."

Withdrawing her hands, Raven swallowed again but knew this time she wouldn't be able to keep the tears at bay. "I have to go," she managed, turning blindly toward the door.

"What's the matter?" Faith asked, her pretty, round face creased with a frown.

"Raven, why don't we go out back for a bit?" Not giving Raven a chance to object, Ruth curved her arm around Raven and went through the patio doors.

* * *

Luke Grayson caught Sierra's hand. "They don't need your help."

"I think they do," Sierra said. She looked at Catherine. "Sometimes a man needs a reality check or a swift kick."

"Or a woman, like I did," Catherine said. "Let her go, Luke."

"You know she'll ferret out the information anyway," Pierce, the fourth son and financial planner, said.

"Don't mind him, Sierra," Sabra said, her perfect brows arched at her husband, who had just spoken. "Pierce needed both, as I recall."

Pierce looked abashed. Brandon laughed.

"Brandon," Sierra said. "You needed my help, just as Pierce and Morgan did."

Brandon straightened. His gaze went outside where Raven sat between his mother and his mother-in-law, Mrs. McBride. His wife had pulled up a nearby chair. "You think there's something going on between Raven and Duncan?"

"I know it," Sierra said. "And as usual, men have to make things complicated."

Blade laughed easily. "I, for one, am glad you were there to help me get it right."

"Don't encourage her," Morgan Grayson, the second son and a lawyer, said.

"If Raven and Duncan need help to realize they love each other, I say if Sierra can help she should," Phoenix, Morgan's wife, said quietly. "Who among us isn't happier than we were before we found the one person we'd love through eternity?"

There was silence and shared looks filled with unwavering love and devotion.

"Go on," Luke said.

Brandon agreed. "Cameron couldn't be happier. So are Faith and I. Duncan deserves the same happiness."

Blade kissed Sierra lightly on the forehead. "If there is anything I can do." He didn't have to finish.

"Then we'll do it," Sierra said, stopping to get a glass of iced tea before heading outside.

Raven accepted the glass from Sierra to be polite more than from wanting anything to drink. Her trembling hand caused the ice cubes to clink against the sides of the glass. In the quiet, the noise seemed unnaturally loud.

"You don't have to talk if you don't want to," Ruth said. "We'll just sit here. It's a beautiful day. We haven't been home long."

"Phoenix had an exhibit at the hotel, and we all went," Faith said.

"Faith's idea to incorporate different art forms in the hotel is gaining national recognition," Mrs. McBride said. "She's done wonders at the hotel."

"It's easy to see Faith loves what she does," Sierra said. "Her career is her passion. Just like Mama's is teaching."

Mrs. McBride stared at her daughter. "And she's smart enough not to throw it all away."

"Mother," Faith said, reaching out to take her mother's hand in hers.

"Sometimes you aren't given a choice," Raven said quietly. "You can't have both."

"Have you changed your mind about wanting tenure at St. John's?" Ruth asked.

Raven looked at the glass in her hand, then set it on the marble-topped table in front of her and went to stand by a bed of blooming pink rosebushes. "As long as I can remember, I've wanted security, stability, a place I didn't have to leave, roots. I thought I had found it here." She faced the other women.

"And now?" Sierra asked.

"I'm not so sure." Raven circled her waist with her arms.

"Duncan?" Sierra asked.

Raven blinked. Sierra had lulled her once again into revealing more than she intended. She tried to backtrack. "Sierra, I appreciate all you and Blade have done for me, but my personal life is off-limits."

"Of course," Ruth said, going to Raven. "Sierra, like all of us, just wants to help with whatever is troubling you."

"And I appreciate your concern, but there are more men in the world than just Duncan," Raven said.

Sierra was too sharp not to figure out what was going on between Raven and Duncan. She should have been more cautious.

The last thing Duncan or she needed was a take-charge person like Sierra to become involved. Raven had initially wanted to talk to Ruth because she'd been so successful in marrying off her five children. She'd had a good marriage until her husband was killed in a plane crash. She knew how relationships were built, how they worked.

Too late, Raven realized Ruth had been successful

because she knew her children so well. Ruth and Raven had only known each other a little over a year. No one could help her.

"Faith, don't forget you have to call Duncan and let him know Raven is safe," Sierra said.

Raven's gaze snapped to Faith. She didn't have to look to know Sierra had seen her reaction.

Faith came to her feet. "Is there anything you want me to tell him?"

This time Raven was ready. "Please thank him for allowing me to do the research. It will be immensely helpful on the path to gaining tenure."

"All right." Faith went back inside.

"Then you're staying at St. John's?" Mrs. McBride asked, coming to her feet as well.

"Yes," Raven responded, hoping her smile wasn't as forced as it felt. "What I said earlier was only nerves. I have an appointment with the president of the college on Wednesday to discuss my findings and the paper I plan to write. I guess I was trying to psych myself up in case it doesn't go the way I want."

"Could have fooled me," Sierra said mildly.

Raven glared at Sierra. She might be the daughter of a woman Raven respected and the wife of her benefactor, but Sierra was beginning to irritate Raven. "Since this isn't your concern, it hardly matters."

Sierra's brow shot up. Slowly she came to her feet. "I shouldn't have to remind you that my husband went to considerable expense, then and later, to put security around the cave. It *is* my concern."

"Sierra," Ruth said.

Raven snatched her arms down and stepped toward Sierra. "That's right, *your husband*. Not you."

Sierra met her. "Blade isn't just my husband. He's the other half of me. My heart beats faster when I see him. He's my joy, my everything. Perhaps one day you'll have enough courage to go after what you want and find out what I mean."

Raven gasped.

"Sierra, that's enough," Ruth said.

"Sierra," Blade called. "Let it go."

Sierra kept her gaze on a silently fuming Raven for a long second, then turned toward Blade, stopped, and looked back. "If I didn't like you, I wouldn't care. If you want to talk, you know how to find me."

Raven didn't want to talk; she wanted to throw the glass of tea at Sierra's retreating back. *How dare she!*

"Forgive Sierra," Ruth pacified Raven. "She speaks before she thinks, and isn't shy about interfering in other people's business. She means well."

That's debatable, Raven thought. "I'm leaving."

"I'll walk you to the door," Ruth said.

Good idea. If Sierra said one more word, if she looked at Raven wrong, she would show her what it was to cross her.

"Wait," Mrs. McBride protested when they moved toward the door. "Please. Was she right? I have to know. Are you the woman who is going to break the curse and save my son, save Duncan?"

Chapter 17

Duncan jerked up the phone on the second ring. "Is she all right?"

"Yes, Duncan," Faith said.

He relaxed back in his office chair, then realized Faith, usually talkative and happy, wasn't either. "What's the matter? Is it Mother?"

"No. No," Faith quickly rushed to assure him. "It's . . ."

He straightened abruptly. "You and Cameron are still happy, aren't you?"

"You always worry about us. We worry about you. You deserve a wife and children."

But he'd never have them. "I make a great uncle. Ask Joshua." Cameron hadn't known he had a son until Joshua was over four years old. "Are you and Cameron still happy?"

"We'd be happier if you had what we have," she said.

"Who would have me?" he asked, trying to tease her out of her morose mood.

"Sierra seems to think Raven would."

"What!" He shot up from his seat. "What happened! What did Sierra say? Is Raven upset?"

"Slow down, Duncan, but at least I have my answer."

He tried to think of a plausible explanation for his outburst. "It's just that I remember how tenacious Sierra can be. Raven doesn't deserve to be picked on."

"From what I heard, Raven can take care of herself."

"What happened?" Duncan paced as he waited for an answer.

"Nothing much. Sierra pushed and Raven pushed back. They're both strong-willed women," Faith disclosed. "The thing is, earlier I was watching Sierra. She pushed, but it wasn't malicious. I think it was to get Raven to open up."

About us. "Sierra should mind her own business."

"I got the distinct impression that Blade and her mother will impress that upon her," Faith told him. "The thing is, Sierra has a will of her own."

"She'd better leave Raven alone."

There was a short pause. "Duncan, is Raven special to you?"

She's just my world. "I already told you."

"Yes, you did. Why don't I think you're not being completely honest? What I can't decide is if it is just with me or yourself, too."

"The Double D is the only mistress I'll ever have," he said, gazing out the window to the mountains beyond.

"I don't believe that, Duncan," Faith said fiercely. "Cameron thought he'd never be happy in a relationship after Caitlin walked out on him. Now, he, Caitlin, and Joshua couldn't be happier."

"And Mother and Father are miserable."

Another pause. "I wish we could help them. They were so happy once."

"Forever isn't for everyone." Talking would solve nothing. No matter what he said, his father wasn't taking his mother back irregardless of how much he still loved her. "Thanks for calling."

"You can call Raven yourself. She should be at home by now."

"There's no need. You gave me the information I need."

"All right, be stubborn. Just remember, I love you, and anytime you want to talk, I'm here."

"I'll remember. Good-bye, Faith." Duncan placed the receiver in the holder. The trouble was, he remembered too much.

Raven slammed into her house, paced, and clenched her fists. Who the hell did Sierra think she was? It was a good thing the Maserati was gone or Raven would have been tempted to have Buddy give it a "kiss."

The thought of Sierra's outrage on seeing a dent on her precious luxury car almost made Raven smile. Instead she plopped down on the sofa she'd dragged from California when she accepted the job at St. John's. She might have to move a great deal, but she wanted her surroundings to be constant.

Like her slow cooker.

She leaned her head back. Leaving the slow cooker at the Double D had been her way of helping Rooster take care of Duncan, and she hoped each time he saw it, he'd think of her and miss her and eventually he would come and get her.

Are you the woman who is going to break the curse and save my son, save Duncan?

Her eyes closed. The hope in his mother's eyes tore at Raven's heart. She hadn't been able to answer. Head down, she'd walked away.

Angry, feeling hopeless and helpless, Raven had quickly gone to her Jeep and driven home. How did his mother expect her to break the curse and save Duncan? His mother certainly hadn't figured out how to win back the man she'd loved and divorced.

Life. You never knew what it would throw at you.

Perhaps her mother was right. Have no expectations and you weren't disappointed. Before the thought completely formed in Raven's head, she knew she couldn't live that way. She couldn't drift aimlessly through life. What she didn't know was what to do next. Pushing up from the sofa, Raven went back outside and began to unload her Jeep.

"It didn't work," Stella McBride whispered softly, her voice unsteady. "Raven couldn't save Duncan."

"I wouldn't be sure about that," Ruth answered.

Stella glanced up sharply. "What?"

Ruth sat on the living room sofa beside Stella and placed her hand over Stella's clasped ones. "I believe, like Sierra, that Raven and Duncan were romantically involved. He wouldn't have been so concerned otherwise, and she wouldn't have been so upset."

Stella bit her lip. "But if they can't work through whatever problems they're going through, it will devastate him. Duncan hated that he wasn't able to keep his marriage together. He felt the fault was all his instead of that immoral woman he had the misfortune to marry."

"Failure is a part of life," Ruth told her. "It's what you do afterward that makes the difference."

"Sometimes, no matter what you do, the failure remains," Stella answered, lowering her head.

Aware that Stella referred to her divorce, Ruth gently squeezed the other woman's hand beneath hers. "It won't this time."

Stella's head came up. "What do you mean?"

"We have an unexpected ally." Ruth smiled.

"Who?"

"Sierra," Ruth answered. "You wouldn't know it from looking at her now, but initially in elementary school she didn't have very many friends. She hasn't forgotten those lonely days and is a champion of anyone she thinks could use a friend."

"But Raven and Sierra had words," Stella said with a frown.

"Sierra has a tendency to push people to make them reveal more than they intended." Ruth patted Stella's hands again. "My guess is that Sierra is already working on a plan to help Raven and Duncan realize their hearts' desire and go after what would make them happy."

Hope glimmered in Stella's eyes. "What would make Duncan happy is a woman who loves him."

Ruth nodded. "And just as I first thought, Raven is that woman."

"You're going to help Raven and Duncan, aren't you," Blade said. It was a statement, not a question.

"It's nice when the man you love knows you so well." Nestled on top of Blade in their bed, Sierra smiled; then her expression grew serious. "They need my help."

His warm laughter drifted over her naked length as his hand swept up and down the curve of her back. "I suppose you already have a plan."

"Of course." A smile on her face, she kissed him. "This time Mama needs my help."

Jet-black eyebrows lifted. "Mrs. Grayson set them up?"

"I'm sure of it." A frown darted across Sierra's forehead. "I thought it was strange when she didn't ask Professor Waller, an old friend, a soror, and a professor of archeology at Bozeman University, to authenticate the cave. She lives an hour from Duncan's ranch."

He shook his head. "Your mother does have the talent, and I thank God for it."

Sierra kissed him again, this time longer, deeper. "But unlike all the others, I nabbed you all by myself."

"You still think it wasn't by chance that Mrs. Albright requested Shane's help?"

"Positive. Fate had a hand as well, since Shane

and Paige had met before he went to Atlanta, but it was Mama who brought them back together. Since they're ecstatic, it doesn't matter how it happened, only that it did." Sierra chuckled.

"What?"

"I have a strong suspicion that Rio is on her list, but he seems to have figured it out." Sierra made a face. "He has a habit of disappearing when Mama shows up."

Blade nodded. "I've noticed, and he's not afraid of anything or anyone."

"Shows he's a smart man."

Blade swept his hand through her hair. "He hasn't figured you out. Like tonight when we arrived home and you told him you'd delivered me back safe and sound so he could go to bed."

Her hands palmed Blade's face. "I know that he and Shane used to shadow your every move, that since Shane's marriage Rio is in charge and has to be out in public when he'd rather be in the background. I might tease him, but I'm aware he worries when we're out and he isn't with us. I also know that, if needed, you and he could handle any situation."

"This life isn't what you envisioned, is it?" he asked.

She glanced around the enormous bedroom and saw the fifteen-foot stone fireplace, the elegant English and French antique furnishings, the silk-draped four-poster, then finally the most important thing, the man who held her heart. "There is no way I could have imagined such complete happiness, that I would feel so safe and secure with a man, a man whom I can share my most intimate thoughts with, a man who, with just a look, turns my knees to jelly."

"You're my passion, my life," he said fiercely.

"We're blessed. It would be tragic if Raven and Duncan had a chance at even a fraction of what we have and they didn't take it." Sierra's eyes narrowed. "Duncan's ex did a number on him. She chased men and, when it was over, the entire town of Elks Ridge knew it."

"That kind of betrayal is hard to overcome, but not impossible with the right woman."

"Exactly. Duncan needs a little nudge to realize that Raven is worth the risk. Men have to be shown the way occasionally."

"Since I was a bit slow, I won't take offense for the male population."

As she grinned at him, her hand slid down the warm, muscled length of his body and closed on his erection. "You're not slow any longer." She kissed him, straddled him. "Tomorrow I start on Duncan; tonight is for us."

The next morning, a few minutes past six, Sierra dialed Duncan's phone number. She'd been up since five. A smile curved her lips as she watched her naked husband and the reason she had asked him to wake her up at five enter their bathroom. She wanted to help Raven and Duncan, but she wasn't about to skip the sensual pleasure of slowly waking up in Blade's arms and making love.

"Morning, McBride."

"Good morning, Duncan; it's Sierra." There was a

telling pause on the other end. Duncan, a smart man in most things, probably thought she had called to interfere. She had, but not the way he expected.

"Yes."

"On behalf of Blade and my mother, I just wanted to thank you for allowing Raven to authenticate the caves," she told him, then waited a beat. "Raven is presenting her findings to the interim president at St. John's on Wednesday. She said she's a bit nervous."

"Raven isn't afraid of anything," he said forcibly.

"I'm just repeating what she said," Sierra said innocently. "Perhaps you don't know her that well."

"You don't know what you're talking about. She's the bravest—" He stopped abruptly.

"Mama is certainly in her corner," Sierra commented to get the conversation going again. "I'm thinking of having a get-together Saturday night and inviting some of Blade's single male business associates. A woman can't spend all of her time working."

"You—"

Sierra put her hand over her mouth to smoother her laughter and thought it was a good thing their conversation was on the phone or she might have had to defend herself. "Well, I won't keep you. I wanted to catch you before you left the ranch house. I have things to do myself and a possible party to plan. Bye." Sierra hung up the phone and went to join Blade in the shower. *Let Duncan stew on that!*

Duncan crashed the phone back on the hook. Sierra should mind her own darn business. Raven wasn't afraid of talking to anyone. But what steamed Duncan was Sierra thinking of introducing Raven to other men.

If another man touched her— The kitchen back door opened and Rooster entered the kitchen. Duncan whirled toward the sound.

"Morning. What's the matter?" Frowning, Rooster quickly crossed the room. "Boss?"

"Nothing." Duncan pushed away from the cabinet. Raven wasn't the type of woman to go from one man to the other so soon. But what about six weeks, six months, from now? "Just thinking."

"I bet it was about Raven. I miss her, too." His gaze went unerringly to the slow cooker on the counter near Duncan. "It don't seem right that she's not here, laughing, looking after things."

Duncan's hands clenched and unclenched. He hadn't been able to sleep last night, hadn't tried. The ache, the loneliness, was too deep. Raven had been gone a day and it felt like years.

Rooster picked up the coffeepot. "I'll start breakfast. Raven wanted me to take care of you and that's exactly what I plan to keep doing."

"I'm going to the barn." Duncan was out the back door in seconds, knowing as he did that there was no place on the Double D that he could run that Raven's memory wouldn't haunt him.

Duncan tried, he really did, but he didn't make it past noon before he dialed Faith's cell phone number. Stopping the ATV, he waited for her to pick up.

"Duncan, are you all right?"

"Yes," he quickly assured her. Aware of how busy

they all were, none of the McBride siblings called the others until the evening. He couldn't wait that long. "I just wanted to thank you for the call yesterday."

"Did you call Raven?"

"No." He wasn't that strong.

"You should," Faith told him. "I like her."

He loved her. "This morning Sierra called on behalf of Blade and her mother to thank me for letting Raven authenticate the caves."

"Sierra has been busy today."

Duncan had an uneasy feeling. "What do you mean?"

"She called me as well. She wanted me to keep Saturday night open," Faith told him. "She's thinking about having a party at her home for Raven."

Duncan's hand tightened on the phone. "You said they had words. Maybe Raven won't go."

"She'll go. Blade sponsored her," Faith reminded her brother. "It would be rude and ungrateful for her to refuse. Raven has too much class for that."

"It's short notice for a party," he said, stepping off the ATV.

"Not when Blade Navarone is the host. Only close friends and family have been to their heavily guarded castle estate. Rio has made sure you can't get within ten miles of the place. People are curious," Faith responded.

"Sierra—," he began then clamped his mouth shut.

"Is savvy enough to be aware of the incredible draw of the combination of Blade and their magnificent home. They'll come if they have to walk," Faith said. "It should be fun. Brandon and I are going to dance the night away."

Duncan recalled his last dance with Raven at her going-away party. Saturday night another man would hold her, feel her softness, her warmth. The muscles of his stomach clenched. "Bye, Faith. We'll talk later."

"Bye, Duncan. Take care."

Duncan hung up the phone, his gaze on the cows gathered around the salt lick. He had the ranch, he was living his dream, but it was no longer enough.

He was afraid that without Raven it never would be again.

"This is extraordinary," Dr. Hale said, his silver-rimmed glasses perched on his nose as he studied the panels from the cave laid out on the polished surface of the oak conference room table. "Truly extraordinary."

"I still get chills when I think of the first time I saw the cave drawings." Raven's finger traced over the computer-generated duplicates of the colored paintings. "They're in remarkable condition."

"Did you excavate the floor?" he asked, picking up a magnifying glass.

"No. I didn't have time," she said, recalling that she had planned to before she began the affair with Duncan.

"No matter. It can be done later."

"What?"

He straightened. "You realize that this is the first finding of this magnitude anywhere in North America. This will bring even more distinction and honor to St. John's."

"I had planned to publish a paper."

"A paper?" he laughed. "I see a dedicated Web site, published books—this will rewrite prehistoric history. Scientists will be clamoring to be among the ones to do a thorough study of the cave."

"The owner is a private person, Dr. Hale. That's why he only wanted one person to authenticate the cave."

Professor Hale's white eyebrows drew together. "Surely he realizes the magnitude of what the pictographs in the cave mean."

"He does. That's the reason for his wanting the find authenticated."

"I'll talk to him." Professor Hale pulled out his cell phone. "Give me his phone number and I'll call."

Once word got out, Duncan's ranch would be overrun with scientists and the media. "Dr. Hale, the owner wanted the authentication done quietly."

The president replaced his cell phone. "While I admire you, and you've obviously done a fair job, surely you know that specialists in several fields are needed. You can't do this justice."

"With respect, sir, I will pit my expertise against anyone," she said. "If I hadn't thought I could do the job, I wouldn't have accepted it."

"Perhaps I can speak with the person who contacted you." He took out his phone again. "Give me that person's name and number."

"I'd rather not say."

His head went back. His fingers closed tightly

around the cell phone. "Are you refusing my request?"

Raven could see her tenure slipping away. "Respectfully, sir. Yes."

"We here at St. John's work as a team," he said slowly and distinctly. "If you don't feel you can be a team member, perhaps you would be happier someplace else."

There was nothing left to say. She began rolling up the panels.

"Did you use any of the college's equipment or funds to do your research?" he asked, his hand on the panel with the red drawings.

"No, sir, I did not." She slid the panel from beneath his hand. "I had a private benefactor."

"A benefactor of the college?" he pressed.

Her hand paused.

"I want the name," he demanded. "If you used your connection to the college to obtain funding, the college deserves the right to these."

She finished rolling the three panels and placed them back in their tubes. "Good day, Dr. Hale."

"You'll be hearing from me," he warned.

Raven kept walking. She'd not only lost her position; she'd just lost her chance at tenure as well.

All the way home, Raven tried to think if any of Ruth's or her associates might connect them. Since Duncan had wanted the studies done quietly, once Ruth had contacted her she hadn't shared the information with anyone.

But what if she hadn't been Ruth's first choice? Her job might be in jeopardy as well.

Raven could only think of one person who could find all the answers. Leaving the Jeep in the drive, she rushed inside and picked up the phone and dialed a private phone number known to few people.

"Navarone."

"An unexpected problem has emerged that might cause difficulties for Ruth. We need to talk in private."

"Where are you?"

"Home."

"A car will be there in ten minutes to bring you to me."

Raven had heard about the impregnable castle Blade and Sierra called home outside of Santa Fe, but she'd never seen it or been inside. She barely glanced at the elegant interior as Rio led her down a wide hallway, then opened the door.

Raven stepped inside to see all five of Ruth's children. None of them looked happy. Aware that she needed to explain quickly to do damage control, Raven told them what had happened.

"Son of a—," Pierce bit off. "Davis, the past president, never would have done this."

"I'm resigned to losing my job, but Ruth shouldn't have to go down with me."

"Mama isn't losing her job," Sierra said. "Let him try."

"You need to find out if she asked anyone else to

authenticate the caves," Raven said. "There are some people in academia who don't mind stepping over people to get higher on the ladder."

"We're glad you're not one of them," Blade said.

"Never," Raven said. "Ruth went out of her way to make me feel welcome. I respect and love her."

"She feels the same way about you," Luke said. "She'll be spitting mad once she finds out about this."

"You're going to tell her?" Raven asked, amazed.

"You can't keep a secret from Mama," Brandon said.

"And in this case, it wouldn't be fair," Pierce added.

Raven bit her lower lip. "Maybe you should rethink this. Your mother isn't one to fake it. He'll know something is up and he might become suspicious."

"You let me take care of Hale," Blade said, his eyes cold as he looked at Rio, then Luke.

Raven nodded. She wished she would be around to see it. "Please tell Ruth good-bye for me."

"You're leaving?" Luke asked.

"For a few days. I don't have any meetings that I'm require to attend until Monday," she said, her face resigned. "With me gone it will divert Hale's attention away from Ruth."

Sierra walked to her. "You could have told him what he wanted and kept your dream."

"The price was too high." And her dream had changed. Raven looked at Blade. "I'd hoped to publish a paper; that's impossible now. I'm sorry."

"Your find is important. I'm glad I could help."

"Thank you. I'm going home to pack," Raven said. "I'd like to leave this evening."

"Rio will take you back." Blade went to her. "If you need anything, you have my phone number."

"That goes for all of us," Luke said.

"Thank you," Raven said, touched. She had friends here, but once again she'd have to leave. If Hale learned Ruth was the one who had referred Raven to Duncan, it might jeopardize her job. Ruth loved teaching. Raven would do whatever was necessary to protect her. She turned and walked from the room.

"Let's go tell Mama," Luke said, moving toward the door. "Hale made a huge mistake. Mama will have him for breakfast."

"He won't know what hit him," Brandon said. "Wish I could."

"When Mama gets through with him he'll probably wish you had," Pierce said.

"If there is anything left once I'm finished with him," Blade said.

"Mama gets first dibs," Morgan told him. "She fights her own battles."

Blade's gaze moved to Sierra as she rounded his desk. "Like mother, like daughter."

"It's the only way we know." Sierra picked up the phone and dialed. "I need to make a phone call and then we can go tell Mama."

"Duncan," Blade said.

"Yes," Sierra replied. "Time just got shorter."

Duncan answered on the fourth ring. "McBride."

"A brave woman like Raven deserves a man to match her courage; I'm betting you're that man."

"Sierra, this is none of your concern."

"That's where you're wrong. Raven needs you."

"What happened? Is she all right?" he asked sharply, the words almost tripping over one another.

"That will depend on you."

"Answer me: is she all right?"

"Depends on your definition of 'all right.' "

"You're pushing me, Sierra."

"Someone needs to. Raven is willing to give up her dream for you. Are you willing to let go of the past for her?" Sierra parried. "Make up your mind now or I'm hanging up this phone and I won't be calling again. If that happens, you'll regret it until your dying day."

"Is she all right? Just tell me that much."

"Are you all right without her?"

There was a long pause, then, "I'm listening."

Raven placed her suitcase and overnight case by the front door. She looked around the front room she'd enjoyed decorating. She'd thought she'd moved for the final time. She'd been wrong, but it couldn't be helped.

Picking up the largest suitcase, she opened the front door. She usually liked driving, but she wasn't looking forward to it this time. Returning, she picked up her overnight case and went to place it in the backseat with the suitcase. Her suitcase was gone.

She glanced around and gasped. *Duncan*. Her body trembled. "What are you doing here?"

"Why didn't you call and tell me about Hale threatening you?"

"I know Blade didn't call you, so it must have been Sierra."

He moved to within inches of her. "Why?" he repeated.

"I didn't want you to become involved," she said, drinking in the sight of him. How she missed him, loved him.

His hands closed around her arms. "Do you think I'd want you to lose your dream because of me?"

You are my dream. "Do you think I'd trade my dream for yours?"

"Baby." He pulled her fiercely to him. "I could tear him apart for hurting you."

"Let Blade take care of him."

"That's what Sierra said."

She lifted her head. "Since I get to hold you again, I guess I'll forgive her for interfering."

He dropped a kiss on her forehead. "Same thought crossed my mind. Let's go inside." Picking up the luggage, he urged her inside the house, then placed the suitcases in the bedroom. Raven followed.

"When did she call?"

"Apparently just after you left her house." Removing his hat, he ran his hand over his head. "She said some other things, too."

"Such as?" she asked; she'd never seen Duncan nervous.

"She said you had more courage than I had." He gently pulled her into his arms. "I started to tell her to keep her opinion to herself; then I looked beyond my anger. I thought about what you were willing to give up for me, for Mrs. Grayson, how you never backed away from a challenge no matter what. A woman that courageous would stick when the going got rough."

"It's about time you figured that out," she said, her voice tremulous.

"So I accepted Sierra's offer of a jet to pick me up on the ranch. It can take us back in the morning, or you can stay and show Hale he can't boss Raven La Blanc around."

She didn't understand. "You want me to stay?"

"I want you to leave of your own accord. I don't want you to look back on this when we're old and gray and wish you had stayed and called his hand."

Her heart thumped. "Old and gray."

"I love you, Raven. Will you marry me?"

"Yes! Yes! You're my dream, my life."

He kissed her. "Now, do we take the jet back in the morning or do I stay and watch you show Hale he threatened the wrong woman?"

"You're staying?"

"For a few days. Ramon and Rooster can take care of things," he said. "Without you the ranch didn't bring me the satisfaction it once did. When I first saw you, I thought you were trouble. I was wrong. You're my salvation."

"Duncan." Her voice trembled.

"Your choice."

"Hale might figure out the caves are on your ranch if he sees us together or hears about you being here," she said, worried.

"He's welcome to try and prove it, but I have a feeling Hale is going to be too busy watching his back," Duncan said with satisfaction. "Sierra said they were going to tell Mrs. Grayson what Hale did. According to Sierra, once her mother gets through with him there won't be much left for them or Blade."

"She's right. I'd forgotten Mrs. Grayson is not to be crossed. Even the college board of regents have a healthy fear of her, and it's not because of her famous in-laws." Raven grinned. "I guess I'll forgive Sierra, since it brought us together. Now we have to call your mother. She was worried about you."

Duncan pulled his cell phone from his belt and pulled Raven to him, staring down into her happy face. The phone was answered on the second ring.

"Hello."

Duncan's hold tightened at the sound of his mother's teary voice. "Hi, Mama. Looks like there's going to be another McBride wedding. Raven just said yes."

"Duncan. Oh, Duncan."

He shifted restlessly and looked to Raven for help. "Don't cry, Mama."

Raven took the phone from him. "Mrs. McBride, you asked me if I was going to break the curse and save Duncan. I didn't answer then. It seems we're going to save each other."

"I'm so happy for you both," Mrs. McBride said, her voice unsteady.

"Thank you." Raven gave the phone back to Duncan.

"Good night, Mama," Duncan said. "How about we meet for lunch tomorrow?"

"I'd like that. Good night, Duncan. You've made a wise choice for a wife," Mrs. McBride said.

"I think so. I'll call Dad in the morning. Good night."

"Good night."

He replaced his phone and kissed Raven on the lips. "Is it all right if we call your family in the morning?"

"Yes." She stared up at him and began unbuttoning his shirt. "You're right. I'd regret walking away, but I'd regret more being apart from you. So as soon as a replacement for my teaching position can be found, I'm coming home to you."

"And I'll be waiting." He drew her knit shirt over her head. "In the meantime, let's go to bed."

"The first night of many to come." Her hands went to his belt buckle.

Off came her bra. "Because one night with you could never be enough."

"I couldn't agree more." His shirt hit the floor.

Picking her up, he headed for the bedroom. "Life with you is going to be such a pleasure, and I can't wait," he said as he placed her on the bed, his lips finding hers.

"Neither can I. Neither can I."

Epilogue

Duncan and Raven had two marriage ceremonies. One in Santa Fe with all of his parents' friends and then another a week later in Elks Ridge at Duncan's church. Reverend Radford officiated at the standing-room-only affair. Afterward the guests had a lavish sit-down dinner in the community center transformed into an elegant dining room with ice-sculptured centerpieces, exotic flowers, and scrumptious food.

At the head table, Cameron, the best man, tapped his flute of champagne with a knife and stood, raising up his glass. "A toast to my big brother and his beautiful wife. May the happiness of this night continue a lifetime."

Raven, beautiful in an off-white wedding gown, leaned into Duncan, who wore a black tuxedo. "Thank you," they said in unison.

Duncan kissed Raven's waiting lips, held her closer. Thank goodness she wasn't crying again. Although she said they were tears of joy, he felt helpless and a little bit panicky seeing the tears glide down her cheeks during their wedding ceremonies.

He had everything he wanted and he hadn't a doubt he'd keep it. Hale had done a complete turnaround on his position once Ruth and Raven confronted him. It hadn't done him any good. A week after his threat to Raven, the board of regents asked him to resign.

It had taken five very long weeks for a replacement to be found for Raven. Every weekend she'd come home to the Double D, to Duncan. It hadn't been lost on him, his family, his friends, or the townspeople that Raven, unlike his ex, wanted to spend as much time with him as possible.

Like him, she and Sierra had settled their differences. Together with Faith and Ruth, they'd planned the wedding.

Raven had decided she wanted to take time off and study the cave instead of teaching. Her dream, like his, had shifted, evolved. In the winter, she'd work on writing a book on her findings. If she ever decided she wanted to teach at the nearby university she had a standing offer.

Duncan had his dream and Raven had hers. They were both extremely blessed. Looking at his parents, each trying to covertly look at the other when they thought the other wasn't looking, he could almost believe that, somehow, they'd find their happiness, too.

He couldn't help but notice that Mrs. Grayson, Sierra, and Faith watched his parents as well. Perhaps they planned on giving them a little nudge. He hoped so. Living without the one you loved was hell on earth.

He could only pray that, like him, his parents would get a second chance. Each time he looked at Raven he fell in love with her all over again and counted his blessings. One day he hoped to carve the symbol for a child over their bedroom door.

Smiling, happier than he ever believed possible, he held his bride, his life, his salvation, closer.

Life was good.

William H. Ray

FRANCIS RAY (1944–2013) is the *New York Times* bestselling author of the Grayson novels, the Falcon books, the Taggart Brothers, and *Twice the Temptation,* among many other books. Her novel *Incognito* was made into a movie that aired on BET. A native Texan, she was a graduate of Texas Woman's University and had a degree in nursing. Besides being a writer, she was a school nurse practitioner with the Dallas Independent School District. She lived in Dallas.

"Francis Ray is, without a doubt, one of the Queens of Romance."

—*A Romance Review*

DON'T MISS THESE OTHER NOVELS
BY BESTSELLING AUTHOR

FRANCIS RAY

THE GRAYSONS OF NEW MEXICO SERIES

Only You

Irresistible You

Dreaming of You

You and No Other

Until There Was You

THE GRAYSON FRIENDS SERIES

All of My Love (e-original)

All That I Desire

All That I Need

All I Ever Wanted

A Dangerous Kiss

With Just One Kiss

A Seductive Kiss

It Had to Be You

One Night With You

Nobody But You

The Way You Love Me

AGAINST THE ODDS SERIES

Trouble Don't Last Always

Somebody's Knocking at My Door

THE FALCON SERIES

Break Every Rule

Heart of the Falcon

A FAMILY AFFAIR SERIES

After the Dawn

When Morning Comes

I Know Who Holds Tomorrow

THE TAGGART BROTHERS SERIES

Only Hers

Forever Yours

INVINCIBLE WOMEN SERIES

If You Were My Man

And Mistress Makes Three

Not Even If You Begged

In Another Man's Bed

Any Rich Man Will Do

Like the First Time

STANDALONES

Someone to Love Me

The Turning Point

ANTHOLOGIES

Twice the Temptation

Let's Get It On

Going to the Chapel

Welcome to Leo's

Della's House of Style

AVAILABLE WHEREVER BOOKS ARE SOLD

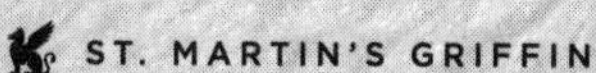